THE SURGEON'S MATE:
A DISMEMOIR

Alan M. Clark

IFD Publishing
P.O. Box 40776, Eugene, Oregon 97404 U.S.A.
www.ifdpublishing.com

Acknowledgments

Thanks to Bunyan Webb, Brian Keene, Dave Conover, Allie Conover, Troy Guinn, Beth Gwinn, John Davis, Randy and Zoe Fox, Joan Clark, Dr. William M. Clark, William M. Clark Jr., Carol Clark Evans, Keith Evans, Ethan Evans, Cynthia Clark, Melody Kees Clark, Dr. Frank Freemon, Cameron Pierce, Eric M. Witchey, Elizabeth Engstrom, Charles Atkins, John McNichols, Laurie Ewing-McNichols, Paul Groendes, Matt Hayward, Melissa Hayward, Turtle, Ann Green, Jill Bauman, Ross E. Lockhart, Stephen T. Vessels, Bob Garcia, and Frederick Bledsoe.

Dedication

To my mother and father, Joan and William Clark, and my wife, Melody Kees Clark, who did their best for me even as I strove to be undeserving. Because of you, I survived my worst behavior, learned a thing or two, and have had a good life. I love you all.

THE SURGEON'S MATE: A DISMEMOIR

Alan M. Clark

IFD
Publishing

Eugene, Oregon

Foreword

My wife, Melody, believes I'm working on a novel. In fact, I make a record of my actual experience in an effort to pin down the truth of my life, even though actions I've recently taken in the distant past have changed history.

The name I wear now is uncomfortable since it's not the one I remember having for most of my life. For the telling of the tale, I'll use my original name, Aiden. Although some who read this manuscript will know me, they don't know me by that name. Some may recognize parts of the tale I'll tell, yet I'm certain that not all of my story will appear as fact, based on the world they know.

If not for an attempt to mitigate regrets from my young adulthood, I'd have my original existence, one I'd prefer to have. In my mind, I do have that life, as memory persists, despite the current reality. That should be enough, I suppose, but the desire for others to know my history as I do isn't going away. Like the phantom pain and stirring of an amputated limb, that missing part of me remains insistent. I hope that what I reveal in the writing may in some small way return to life what has been lost.

—Alan M. Clark
Eugene, Oregon

Aiden:1

"*Ten* weeks in the hospital?" I spoke with outrage, hoping to disguise my fear.

"Mr. Clark," Dr. Frank Reed said, "may I call you Aiden?" He did a good job projecting calm.

I nodded as I chewed my dry lower lip, and I tried to think of a way out of my predicament.

"Yes, ten weeks of intravenous antibiotics, here in the hospital. The doses of penicillin are so numerous because we have to get past the blood/brain barrier. You'll have to be pickled with the stuff if we want it to reach the infection in your right temporal lobe."

I lay in a bed that had been inclined so I could talk more easily with the doctor. Looking around the bland, grey-green/white-green secondary care unit, with its tan curtains, chrome and plastic fixtures and fittings, and the cold faces of machinery arrayed on two sides, the pit of fear that had already opened in my gut, yawned wider. I knew I wouldn't be allowed to drink alcohol while in the hospital. Ten weeks in that sterile, uninspiring environment without a drink seemed like a prison term.

"I can't do that," I said.

"If you want to get better, you don't have a choice." His dark, deep-set eyes held steady, his heavy brow deadly serious.

"I have to get out. I have work to do." I needed a drink. "I'll do the antibiotics at home."

The hospital staff had given me a narcotic for the head pain. The painkiller felt good and warm in my system, entirely mitigating the need for a drink, but old habits die hard, and I assumed the desire for alcohol would come back with a vengeance.

"The risk of infection is too great. You must stay in the hospital. You may not have to be here for the full course of the medication, yet you should remain for now, at least."

"I don't think I can do that," I said, though with the warmth of the drug in me, I'd already begun to see reason, or maybe I merely saw the narcotic. I'd also already talked to my father, a neurologist, about what I should do, and he'd told me I needed to be in the hospital.

"Aiden, brain abscesses are *very* rare. If you'd gotten them twenty years ago, you would not have survived because medicine wasn't what it is today. You're lucky."

Perhaps a few more days of the narcotic wouldn't be so bad. I'd be able to get the hospital to release me soon enough, and then I'd do the rest of the antibiotics at home.

Dr. Reed seemed to notice I'd begun to relax, and he nodded as if the matter were settled.

I didn't feel at all well, having stitches in my tongue, an upset stomach from ingesting my own blood, raw tissues from the tubes the doctors had stuck in me, and a severe headache, among other things. A surly bastard, I wouldn't show any appreciation for the care I'd received. "Lucky," I said, "is not getting brain abscesses at all."

Later I would decide I'd been wrong about that.

~ ~ ~

A couple of weeks before that conversation with Dr. Reed in the hospital, I began to have persistent, dull headaches. I had returned home from the 1989 World Science Fiction Convention in Boston, Massachusetts, where I'd participated in the art show and been a discussion panelist. A cold or mild flu had come home with me. I thought the head pain a symptom of the virus. Since I had used such viruses as a cover story for hangovers when dealing with Melody, the illness wasn't altogether unwelcome. Usually, I returned from conventions wrung out from hangovers.

At age 32, I'd been an active alcoholic for sixteen years. I had been seeking freelance illustration work for about six years. Good at maintaining myself and my responsibilities, I'd just begun to realize some success despite my addiction. The art director at Ace Books, a woman I had met at the convention, called me on the phone, and gave me an assignment to produce cover art for the science fiction novel, *Redshift Rendezvous* by John E. Stith. Although the headaches—progressively becoming one continuous pain—distracted me terribly, I set about to produce a color comp—a painted color sketch—for the book cover image.

Our little clapboard house, built in the 1930s, had settled awkwardly over the years so that its small rooms were rather crooked. Normally I saw that as giving the place character. Yet, as I worked in my studio, the smallest room in the house, I felt claustrophobic, even though I could look out the tall, old-fashioned windows. One of them gave a view of the driveway, overhanging hackberry trees, and the side of the neighboring brick house, a structure I thought was way too close to our own. The window facing the street had the roof of the porch over it, blocking some of the natural light. The bright artificial lights I used at my drafting table couldn't dispel the gloom that seemed to collect in the shadows of the studio.

I knocked off work frequently as I progressed. I drank to kill the pain in my head. Perhaps because of that, I couldn't see that I became more delirious with each passing day.

Melody came home from work several times during those two weeks to find me sprawled on the couch with the curtains closed over the windows that looked out of the front of the house. No doubt she thought I'd been drinking. That, of course, was only part of my problem.

"You haven't fixed dinner for several days," she said at one point. Since I cooked our meals and had been shirking the duty, she wasn't pleased.

"I caught a flu in Boston," I'd said, "not just a cold. I can taste it."

She didn't buy the old, threadbare excuse entirely. Still, she didn't like conflict, so she let the matter go.

Our marriage suffered great stress because of my drinking. At first, because she also drank, I'd been okay with being a drunk. The more she saw of how I consumed alcohol, the less interested she became in drinking. Her disapproval was merely implicit at first. Even then, because I loved her, Melody's attitude made me think about my habit differently. I'd lost my ally in overindulgence, and I didn't like hanging out with other drunks. Trapped within the confines of my addiction, I grew lonely and defensive.

Toward the end of the second week of my persistent headaches, Melody found me in the bathtub when she came home from work. She put her hand in the water. "It's gone cold," she said, looking concerned rather than disgusted. "You've taken a lot of baths lately. You were making a monotonous humming sound."

The baths I took during that time were so long, I'd periodically drain the cold water and refill the tub with warm. The humming—a rhythm really—helped distract me from a pain that had changed slowly, but steadily, from dull to sharp. Surely, I appeared to be losing my mind.

"The water helps."

"I'm gonna get you out of the house tonight," she said.

"No, I don't feel up to going anywhere."

"Yes, we're going to the State Fair."

I'm certain an argument ensued, yet somehow we did end up going to the fair.

The outing became an island of memory in what was a great and growing sea of delirium. I wasn't getting around well. Even so, pride made me stand up straight and pretend. I'd learned to do that during many hangovers. What I experienced felt different from a hangover. All the same, if I'd been honest, I would have said that my problem came from too much alcohol.

An elongated circuit, the midway at the Tennessee State Fair ran perhaps three quarters of a mile around, with vendors and attractions on either side, and forming an island in the middle. The vendors sold tickets to the attractions, souvenirs, or various substances that might have once been nutritious food before they were boiled in hot grease or drowned in fake butter. Sideshows offered freaks, pickled punks, or girlie shows. Then there were games of skill and chance, and scary rides flashing multi-colored lights and whirling dangerously close to the walkway itself. Hay covered the graveled surface of the fairgrounds, soggy from intermittent rains, spilled drinks, and no telling what else, littered with food containers, cigarette butts, lost or broken State Fair souvenirs, and whatever managed to fall out of the pockets of the people on the rides. Barkers shouted at passersby, challenging them to play games that were no doubt rigged, or to step into sideshows and see highly unlikely things. Teen girls and young women strutted in the heat and humidity, showing as much skin as they dared, while their male counterparts seemed to favor polyester with large perspirations stains at crotch and pits.

I caught Melody smiling as we walked. "The fair is cool," she said, "but it's also frightening. I like that it's fake and thrown together. I like the flashy colored-light-glamour mixed with the creepy dirty edges of everything. The guys running the place are the scariest, though."

I understood. Although squeamish about such things as rough, unwashed carnie-types, she was also a horror fan, and had an attraction to the dark and disturbing. As a child, she'd played with the usual skinny adult-shaped dolls. To terrorize them, she brought her brother's monster models into her playtime. Melody had always been emotionally complex. That's part of why I liked her. Like me, she preferred her entertainment to be weird and disturbing. She had a good sense of humor and we laughed together a lot.

Melody came from the small Kentucky town of Russellville, a rural community surrounded by a lot of tobacco farms. She had been my sister, Carol's, roommate at college at Western Kentucky University. Unassuming and light-hearted, despite real trauma in her childhood, she'd been attractive to me from the moment we met. We married in 1981 after dating for about a year, and we lived in Nashville Tennessee, the town where I grew up. In 1989, she'd reached the age of twenty-seven.

Melody was rather gullible. While that might not sound good, I'd have to say that if one loves an alcoholic or a drug addict and stays with that person the way she stayed with me, one has to be generous with the benefit of the doubt and hoping for the best. I'd much rather be the gullible person she was than the liar I'd become.

As I stumbled a couple of times, Melody tried to support me. "You'll feel better soon," she said. "You just need to get out like this and move around more." Her prescription would not turn out to be a good one, yet her heart was in the right place. I think she treated me with sympathy because she believed I suffered something new, something I had not brought upon myself.

"The fair is scarier than I remembered," I said. "Do people here seem weirder than usual?"

She looked around. "No. What do you mean?"

"Unhappy, angry, or something." I shrugged, unwilling to work hard at putting my feelings into words.

"I don't notice anything different."

Perhaps because I walked the midway with an infection in my head, the place had a malevolence I hadn't known before. The eyes in the crowd gleamed strangely and seemed to move in unusual ways. Mouths strained wide, and shouted to be heard over the screams of those on the rides above. My mind fixed more readily on the laughter, shouts, and occasional altercations, including one that became a fist-fight, among the throng. To be heard over the music that cat-erwauled from the rides and warped in the humid air, some of the barkers used small portable amplifiers that turned their words into the moaning of ghostly wooly mammoths, totally incomprehensible. With people of all sorts giving the muddy track life, the midway became a snake eating its own tail; the flashing lights its gaudy scales, and the blaring music providing a sense of its restless writhing. As a boy, I'd spent hours each year with my brother and friends exploring the greasy attractions of its raw and tarnished hide, but I'd never found the atmosphere oppressive. With the abscesses in my head, the experience was nearly more than I could bear.

Still, as a horror fan, the fair's dubious charms held my interest, and restored my energy incrementally. Melody allowed me time to rest here and there as we progressed. She left me only to go buy tickets.

"I bought the smallest, a packet of twelve," she said, showing me the dull-red tickets "They're good for any of the rides, side shows, games. The rides are all five tickets each." She looked around, and pointed out a giant red and yellow flashing cylindrical monster. "Let's ride The Rotor."

Melody had always liked that one. We got on with at least twen-ty others and the big machine spun us around so fast that we be-came glued to its walls. Then the one-armed guy running the thing dropped the floor to prove it. The motion made me *worse* than dizzy.

As I stumbled off the ride, Melody steadied me again. "You okay?"

"My head feels like one of those ocean-in-a-bottle things."

"What color?"

I frowned at her, then realized what she meant. "It's a red one. Red for the blood in my head."

Again Melody smiled and showed me a brave face. She attempt-ed to enjoy herself, even as she tried to draw me back to the land of the living. I didn't respond well, I suppose.

After The Rotor, if my head got tipped to one side, I tended to lean and move in that direction. Not until later did I understand why.

"There are two tickets left," she said. "You use them."

I looked around. Everything I saw called for either three or five tickets. "I'm tired. I'll wait for you while you ride something."

"No, I've had enough. I used to love these rides, but that last one made me sick to my stomach."

"I'd need to buy more tickets to do anything. We could just throw them away and go home."

"We paid good money for those!" Her eyes held a stern warning.

As slow in the head as I felt that night, I thought the fair was clever to sell tickets in even numbers, and require odd numbers of them for everything. Like Melody, most folks would look at the tickets they had left over, and, not wanting them to go to waste, consider buying more. Since the tickets only came in even numbers, though, there would always be at least one left unused.

We had little money back then, and Melody had always kept a close eye on our finances. The more successful bread-winner in our home at the time, she worked at a bank as a teller supervisor, and took charge of our funds. Although she earned more, her pay didn't amount to much, yet she had pride in the position she'd achieved back when she'd been just twenty-one. She was a worrier, and pre-ferred not to take risks, which made her choice of marrying me a strange one, since I've always been a risk-taker, often foolishly reck-less when drunk. Despite her cautious nature, she'd been quite will-ing for me to quit the low wage job I worked until late 1984, and go freelance as an illustrator at the beginning of 1985.

I was always grateful to her for that.

We had little money in large part because my income as a free-lancer had not grown into much, and remained sporadic. I spent a lot of money on travel and supplies for the business, and even more on beer. We'd bought our home in the mid-1980s. The house stood in a bad Nashville neighborhood referred to as The Nations. People said that many of the folks who lived in the area had friends or family locked up in the state prison on that side of town. The place was all we could afford.

Next to our home, sat a smaller, neglected brick house, painted a boring light brown. During the time we'd lived in the neighborhood, that little place had housed prostitutes and drug addicts.

The bad neighborhood aside, we'd bought the house because Melody thought ahead, well beyond my next beer, to what having an investment would do for us, rather than just paying rent. She stayed on top of our money, even though she didn't really nag me much about what I spent on drinking.

From the look in Melody's eyes, I knew we weren't going to be getting rid of those two remaining State Fair tickets without using them.

I looked around again and decided perhaps I'd been wrong about the State Fair's sales strategy. Above the entrance to a tent in the distance, I saw a hand-painted sideshow banner that asked for two tickets to see a giant rat weighing fifty or sixty pounds. "Drinks gallons of water every day!" the sign bragged. The painter had included an image of a wild-eyed, rabid-looking creature with fangs instead of incisors and wiry hair jutting out at odd angles. In my half-delirious state, the sideshow intrigued me.

"I'll go see that," I said, pointing.

Melody followed me to the tent and waited as I handed over the two red tickets and went in. Inside, I found a pen containing a capybara, a South American animal known, I believe, as the largest rodent in the world. The creature wasn't a rat. While inside the tent, I didn't see it drink any water at all. The interior smelled of alien doo-doo, so I turned around and left. I'd seen capybaras before.

When I emerged so soon after entering, Melody decided I hadn't spent sufficient time with the rodent to get my money's worth. "You get back in there and look at that rat!" she said in all seriousness.

We didn't laugh at that until nearly a month later.

"Just take me home," I said. "I feel like shit."

At that point, I think she understood better than I did that something had gone terribly wrong inside me. My headache wasn't getting better. She wanted to call my father for advice. Dr. William M. Clark, could not be reached, though. In 1989, few people had cell phones. My parents—I referred to them as "Mama" and "Daddy"—vacationed in England at the time, and were due home the next day.

I spent one more delirious twenty-four hours. Melody came home from work to find me in much worse shape. She called and spoke to my father in the early evening and told him what she could. He suffered from jet lag and no doubt wasn't in a mood to deal with his alcoholic son. "Try not to worry. I'll talk to you about it again tomorrow."

I learned later that Daddy called Melody about 2:00AM that night. "I couldn't sleep," he said. "Please take Aiden to the emergency room at St. Thomas, and I'll meet you there."

I had a grand mall seizure in the emergency room and bit my tongue almost completely off. The doctors hurried to sew me back together before I bled to death. I had no awareness of any of that.

Frederick: 1
St. Pancras Station, London, 1873

Frederick took the piece of luggage from the man in the brown bowler, a tradesman of some sort. "The MR to Leeds," the man said.

Nodding his head, Frederick placed the bag on the trolley for the appropriate Midland Railway train. The tradesman tossed him a penny. Frederick snatched the spinning bronze coin from the air. Numerous coins had been tossed to him over the last few years by those of the upper classes, the few who handled their own money. He'd decided they did so to avoid touching one of a lower station. More and more frequently, the practice had become popular among some within the upper middle class and even the middle class. No matter who tossed a coin, though, Frederick saw the seemingly light-hearted way of delivering gratuity as a sign of disrespect. As far as he was concerned, the tradesman put on airs.

Still, a man like that wanted an open smile and a nod with his service. Without that, he'd offer a mere farthing or nothing at all to the porter handling his luggage. Knowing he could not see himself well, Frederick had practiced various expressions. Most of the time he knew what they felt like when he wore them.

"Thank you sir," he said with what he hoped was a pleasant beaming.

The tradesman merely turned away.

Frederick had tried to learn to read others clearly enough to know what they wanted, and he believed he was getting better at it. He wanted to be able to look at a man on the platform and, without much in the way of clues, perhaps seeing only the top of the fellow's head among the crowd, know whether he was coming or going, if he'd had pleasant travels or not, what sort of services he might need, and how best to approach him with conversation. With a woman, especially a lady, he would want to know whether she was married or not, and how many children she'd had, if any. If she were a tart, he'd want to divine how much she charged and what she'd be willing to do for it. If a girl, or young woman, he'd want an intuition as to the state of her virtue, and what sort of kind word must be applied to gain a smile from her. He knew the ability to discern such things must be hard won over the course of several years. His employment at the station had afforded him valuable experience. Such insights were needed in a trade that depended on gratuity, and an increase in his earnings had demonstrated his steady improvement. The intuitions would be useful in other pursuits, as well.

As the tradesman walked down the platform, he left a gap in the crowd that afforded Frederick a view of a young woman stepping off the MR from York into his work station, Platform number 2. She wore a blue velveteen bodice and skirt, both slightly worn, and a matching bonnet. She gazed at the crowd for a moment, then up at the great iron arch overhead. With the harsh echo of a signal whistle within the confines of St. Pancras Station, she cringed as if fearing the metal structure might come crashing down.

Frederick found her interesting. Obviously those she expected to meet her had been delayed. Not a worldly creature, at an age between fifteen and twenty years, she had an innocence he liked. Her clothing suggested that no one of means would miss her.

He marveled at how things had changed. Not so long ago, young women hadn't been allowed to travel alone. Where were her people, her family?

Yes—she was a good prospect. Frederick would cut her, if he could just get her alone. He'd believed the desire to cut young women had become a thing of the past, set aside ten years earlier when he'd returned to London after his service in the Royal Navy. At first, he hadn't indulged the notions that arose unbidden in his mind. Lately, though, he'd found himself planning to get away with murder.

Two things had reawakened the dark urge. Noting the growing trend of women traveling alone had given him the idea of snatching one. Then finding a mongrel bitch and amputating her infected leg had sharpened his desire to cut flesh.

Offering help would be an easy way to get the young woman away from the crowd. He'd worked out just how to talk to a prospect. "You shouldn't be alone here, miss. Too many dippers and mug-hunters hereabouts. I'll stay with you until your people come, but perhaps we should wait away from the crowd." He'd lead her toward the hotel entrance, then pause, and appear to think for a moment before saying, "When those who come to collect people are late, they don't expect the traveler to remain on the busy platform. Most often the traveler is collected in front of the Midland Grand Hotel, just here." He'd point to the back entrance to the hotel, the one that connected to the station platforms. "That's where your people wait for you now, I have no doubt. May I guide you through the hotel to the front?"

Mr. Temes, the Stationmaster, wouldn't miss Frederick for the ten minutes of effort required to tuck the young woman away until later. Once he got her into the hotel, he'd lead her through to one of the back stairwells, where the staff stored the rolling laundry carts. He'd "tap" her into one of those, throw laundry over her, and wheel her into the basement to the unfinished stone vault he'd discovered there. With the outer bolts shot on the heavy steel door of the chamber, no one would hear her, even should she awaken and begin to cry for help.

Frederick hadn't worked out exactly how to get her back to the cellar room he rented in Midhope Street, but he'd take one step at a time. He had at least a partial plan.

His expression needed to be just right. He reached up to trace his facial features with his fingers. After several mistakes, he'd learned to do that, and to disguise the effort as scratching an itch. Satisfied with the expression he found, Frederick moved toward the young woman.

Finally, he might have his satisfaction!

Almost upon her, he saw her head bob up a couple of times. Then she stood on tiptoes, trying to look over the crowd. She smiled.

Her people had arrived.

Frederick turned away disappointed.

He pictured the bitch back in the cellar room, and thought about how she looked at him with adoring eyes during his visits. The poor creature no doubt wondered what had become of Frederick, and when he'd return. He hoped she hadn't made too much of a mess in the two days since he'd looked in on her. A young woman the dog was not, yet he might take small satisfaction from the mutt that night, all the same.

As Frederick thought about what he'd do to the dog, a gentleman handed him a piece of luggage. "The MR to Leeds," the man said.

Frederick's head filled with *the smell of the grave*, the odor that had always been a sure sign of an imminent fit.

Simon's ghost comes to punish me again.

19

His balance shifted oddly back and forth, reminding him of sea legs on land after a long voyage. Then his left leg began to jerk, and he saw the platforms tilt like the deck of a ship. The shuddering limb slipped out from under him and he sat down hard on the deck, losing awareness of the train station. Thinking the piece of luggage would keep him afloat if the ship went down, he gripped it tightly. His body quaked.

Frederick temporarily left the station, and found himself in an environment so unusual, he would find few words to describe it. An apparition—a man much like Frederick, although he could not say how he knew that—lay on his back, strapped to a bed in a room with curtained walls. Cables ran into his mouth and down his throat. The fellow's features flowed and shifted. Frederick thought he recognized the elusive face several times.

"Are you Simon?" he asked. "Are you punished, tortured?" The words weren't any more recognizable than the man on the bed. Not since shortly after Frederick betrayed Simon had the boyhood friends seen each other.

The supine figure gave no response. Strangely, he breathed easily, rested with eyes closed. The room itself seemed somehow unkind, having the same undecorated feel of the one at the St. Marylebone Workhouse infirmary where Frederick had sat for two days many years earlier, watching his poor mother die of typhoid fever. Light shone too brightly in the room, illuminating objects harshly. The furnishings, many indescribable objects, were unpleasant to look upon.

Though the man appeared to sleep, somehow he awakened in Frederick's head. Briefly, they knew each others' thoughts.

The scrutiny hurt.

The man had a morbid bent, something Frederick didn't remember in Simon. Despite the fellow's inclination, he clearly saw Frederick as vile and dishonorable. The apparition was a damned hypocrite.

Moments later, Frederick returned to himself in the station, still clutching the piece of luggage. The visitation of *Simon's curse* had ended. Even though Frederick tried to remember what he'd seen in the vision, the environment to which he'd been transported had been so unfamiliar, the details fled like those of a dream too bizarre to comprehend with a waking mind.

Aiden: 2

I came to, strapped to a bed, stitches in my tongue, and tubes coming out of me. The one that emerged from my nose probably provided extra oxygen. The one I could see between my legs was a Foley catheter so I could relieve myself without having to get up. I didn't know what purpose the one running down my throat served. Machinery stood around me on all sides. The dull, green room had curtain partitions, presumably to create a pocket of privacy. I had small, scabbed-over holes in my forehead.

I didn't panic, even though I had a severe claustrophobic reaction to finding myself bound with straps to the bed and threaded into machinery. I had an intense icy dread of finding out what I might have done to myself, to others, or what I had lost while unconscious and out of control, perhaps during an alcoholic blackout. Alone at first, I could only wonder about how my world might have irrevocably changed. With all that, although I was awake and had a sharper awareness than I'd had for some time, I had a separation from my emotional reaction and remained strangely calm.

That separation reminded me of an experience from early childhood. My family and I were at a family reunion. I was perhaps six years old. The event took place outdoors, during a hot, humid Tennessee summer at a home with several acres and a swimming pool. Fifty to one hundred people attended. By the way I was treated—folks reacted as if they were familiar with me—I had the impression I should know them, but I didn't. Uncomfortable with that, I distracted myself with all the various foods available. My brother and I kept our eyes on the galvanized wash tub full of ice and sodas because we craved sweets. I'd already had one soda.

"That's enough for now," Daddy said when I'd asked if I could have another. "You can't have any more until later. There will be home-made ice cream in a while. Go put on your bathing suit and play in the swimming pool."

Daddy was tall—taller than most people—confident, and loving, an absolute authority for me at the time. While my brother, Bill, wandered off, I did as I was told, yet I'm certain what happened

Alan M. Clark

wasn't what Daddy had expected or wanted. I don't think my parents ever knew what occurred next.

Shy and not familiar with most of my "cousins" playing at one end of the blue pool, I jumped into the water at the other end. I sank to the bottom. The fact that swimming pools had deep ends wasn't part of my experience until that moment. Although I couldn't swim, I didn't think I was in trouble yet. I kicked off the flickering bottom and rose to the surface, took a breath, and reached for the tiled edge of the pool, but I immediately sank back under the water.

With no time on the surface to cry for help, no one knew I'd run into trouble. I was on my own.

Emotion insisted that I should scream. Despite that, I knew I would need the air I'd expel, and I kept my mouth shut. Something inside me preferred to think the problem through. I knew I could kick off the bottom, rise and get a fresh breath, so I did. Just before I went back under, I noticed I'd gotten slightly closer to grabbing the edge of the pool. Still, my head wanted to panic. I held the feelings down and kept kicking off the bottom, going for the air and the edge of the pool. Finally, after what seemed an age, I caught the edge, climbed out exhausted, and lay on the sun-heated concrete.

Shame kept me from telling anyone what happened, when I should have been proud for having controlled feelings that might have gotten me killed. I had indeed panicked—I'd felt full terror, a total loss of control, and feared eminent doom. Even with all that, I'd separated myself sufficiently from my feelings that I functioned well enough to survive.

Since then, the ability to create a separation from my most extreme emotions had become an asset that helped me survive numerous misadventures in life, including the horror of awakening in the secondary care unit of the hospital after the grand mall seizure.

Lying in the hospital bed alone, still waiting for someone to notice I'd awakened, I recalled a nightmare I must have had while unconscious. In the dream I'd seen an apparition, a dark-haired man with a thin face clutching an old-fashioned, brown leather suitcase. For a moment, I had the impression he'd fallen from a ship that had gone down in the sea.

He had a desire to cut a woman's arms off. Somehow, I knew the arms were compensation for something taken from him and that

22

disgusted me. He seemed to think he might know me. Even as I experienced the dream, I wondered how I knew those things. I asked myself if he'd already taken the woman's limbs and held them in the piece of luggage. Now that I'd awakened, I had to wonder why I knew one thing and not the other. But how does one know anything in dreams?

Still reflecting upon what increasingly felt like a nightmare, I had other intuitions. I knew the dark-haired man remained unaware that his cruelty came from a desire to seek compensation. His urge became associated in my mind with my psychological abuse of my youngest sister, Cynthia (the family called her Cindy). When we were children, I used to tell her I'd put her in a garbage can and the garbage collectors would haul her off to the dump. Watching her cringe as I described her fate had felt good for some reason.

How could I know that the apparition sought compensation through his vile desire if he didn't know that? How did I know he didn't know? And why would I find all that so troubling once awake? Perhaps because, as a child, I hadn't known why I'd treated Cindy that way. What had been taken from me that I needed to do that to her? Strange, the things that come in dreams.

My thoughts had become as horrible and twisted as my physical situation. All I could do was to keep kicking off the bottom of the current deep end and reaching for the edge.

Eventually, someone noticed I'd awakened. Daddy came in. I wanted to speak to him, yet the tube running down my throat prevented that. As I tried anyway, I began to choke on phlegm produced by the virus I caught in Boston. *I really did have a virus.* A nurse appeared and sucked the mucous out of my throat with a large rubber dropper-like tool. Presumably, she'd done that for me while I was unconscious as well.

With a question in my eyes, I looked at Daddy and pointed at the tube running down my throat.

He shook his head, produced a pad of paper and pencil, and gave them to me.

Deadline, I wrote. *Need to finish sketch, send to New York.*

Strange—I didn't want to face my medical situation. I could deal with the art, though, the deadline.

He told me about my condition anyway, and gave me information about the seizure I'd had in the emergency room. I don't recall his emotional state. Dr. William M. Clark could be anything from stoic and coldly business-like to warm and playful, even becoming silly and acting foolish to get a laugh. His words on that day must have been delivered with all seriousness.

"You have two brain abscesses, each perhaps the size of a marble, in the right temporal lobe of your brain. At least one of the abscesses has ruptured through the ventricle."

Am I in danger? I wrote.

"Yes," he said, "but you're where you need to be for help."

Did he mean that I might die? I didn't want to ask that question. He remained calm, and that helped to keep me from becoming more upset.

I trusted and loved him. Although in my teen years, we had been at terrible emotional odds, as I reached adulthood, we became good friends and remained so despite my alcoholism. He was honest and thoughtful, a man with widely varied interests. He loved trees, gourmet food, camping, Japanese culture, archeology, sports, gardening—I cannot begin to make the list long enough to cover all the subjects and activities that delighted him. My mother, Joan Clark, shared many of those interests. As children, my brother, two sisters, and I had benefitted from our parents' various enthusiasms. We traveled, visited many museums, went spelunking, hiking, camping, scuba diving—again, I can't make the list long enough. Daddy's hobbies at home included painting, sculpture, wine and beer making, photography, raising bonsai, playing classical guitar, turning vessels on a potter's wheel, building a model railroad with full scenery, creating dollhouse miniatures—again the list problem. He read voraciously, not just science fiction and fantasy, but all kinds of fiction as well as nonfiction. His toilet-time reading alone, the medical journals, science magazines, numerous novels, and hobbyist's publications cluttered the bathroom of his home as they slid in disarray from the loose stacks he made of them on the windowsill, the back of the toilet, and floor. Hell, everything in life fascinated my father, as far as I could tell. His mind was sharp and inquisitive, and he had always been willing to share his font of knowledge. I could ask him anything and often did.

Again, I pointed at the tube running down my throat.

"Orogastric tube," he said, "to pump out the blood you swallowed."

What are the holes in my forehead? I wrote.

I'm not certain I understood properly his response to the question. Here's what I thought I heard: "Oh, that's where they bolted your head to the CT scan to steady it so they could look inside your brain. While they had you hooked up like that, they made a small hole in your skull and drew some of the abscess material out to analyze. They found streptococcus bacteria."

I don't know if he told the truth, kidded me, or if I misunderstood. Daddy had a dark, mischievous sense of humor. That's where I got mine. Being bolted to the machinery seems an odd, extreme measure, but perhaps I still shook from the seizure and the doctors wanted to make sure I stayed motionless. Kidding about that and expecting me to get the joke wouldn't have been unusual for Daddy.

I would have laughed with him in that moment if I'd been capable. If he wasn't serious about their origin, I'm certain I didn't give him any further reason to chuckle about the red, crusty holes in my forehead. I had suffered a trauma and was fearful about what the future held. No doubt he could see how troubled I'd become.

"There's nothing that you can do at this time," he said, touching me affectionately on the shoulder. "I'll see what I can do about your sketch." He got up and left.

Knowing I'd have his help with the medical matter as well as the deadline came as a relief. Both art lovers, my parents had always rooted for my success as an artist. They never discouraged me from considering painting as a career, and had supported my decision to go to a fine arts college. When I turned to illustration several years after college, they approved of that too.

A technician came into the secondary care unit and put an intravenous port into my hand. "We're starting you on doses of penicillin," she said. She connected the tube running from my hand to an IV pump from which hung a bag of liquid that seemed like a lot of fluid for me to take in. "This may burn a little."

Yes—the medicine did hurt going in.

~ ~ ~

Daddy went to my home and got my color comp, some brushes, and the paints I had mixed for the project, mostly shades of blue and red, as I recall. He brought them into the secondary care area at the hospital and helped me finish the work. I don't know what sort of strings he had to pull, but I don't think the hospital would have let just anyone do all that there. Having painted and drawn on and off throughout his life, he had skills much needed since I'd become unsteady. When done, the image looked good. I felt grateful for Daddy's help. That afternoon he shipped the color comp via next-day service to the art director at Ace Books.

I met Dr. Frank Reed, my neurologist, for the first time when he came to the secondary care unit to check on me. After our conversation about whether or not I should stay in the hospital, two doctors who specialized in infectious diseases came in and introduced themselves as Dr. Danforth and Dr. Faulkner.

"We've spoken to Melody," Dr. Danforth said. "She's told us a lot about what has happened. We're hoping you might know something to help explain how your abscesses occurred."

I shrugged.

"Please tell us about what's happened in your life in the last few months," he said.

I told them what I could, including things as unremarkable as my visit to the dental hygienist two months earlier. That got their interest.

"Was there anything unusual or different about that visit to the dentist?" Dr. Faulkner asked.

"The hygienist tested the depth of my gums with a graduated probe. She stuck it up under my gums."

Dr. Danforth smiled tightly and glanced knowingly at his colleague. Dr. Faulkner nodded. I got the impression these intensely serious men considered me a fascinating puzzle-lock to be opened. In that moment, I felt more like an object than a person.

"There's no way to know for certain," Dr. Faulkner said, "but the hygienist might have pushed streptococcus bacteria from your mouth into the soft bony tissue of your upper jaw. From there, bacteria can sometimes find a route past the blood/brain barrier and cause the kind of infection you have."

Seemingly satisfied that they'd found the key to the puzzle, the infectious diseases doctors conferred with Dr. Reed quietly for a moment, then exited.

"The abscess material might have ruptured through the ventricle while you rode The Rotor at the fair," Dr. Freeman said. "Melody told me about your reaction after the ride."

I nodded, remembering the odd feeling. "Let's talk about when I'll get to go home. What will we have to do to make that possible?"

"Try to relax," he said. "We'll get you into a room soon."

I refrained from pointing out that he hadn't answered my question.

Frederick: 2

Mr. Temes, the Stationmaster, sent Frederick home early after the spell. On his way, Frederick saw the cat's meat man, Walter Stewart, on Argyle Street. Wearing a bright red a white spotted neckerchief and crying, "Beep, beep," the man stood out amidst the many people in the street as he made his rounds with his small barrow.

Frederick caught up with him. "Two, please," he said.

"Yes, sir," Mr. Stewart said, handing Frederick two short skewers that held green horse meat. "Tuppence, then."

"Why is it green?"

"Not fit for man to eat." Mr. Stewart said. "It's the meat what can't be used for nothing else; some is too old, others is diseased. Don't hurt cat nor dog, but a man…"

Frederick still didn't understand. "*Because* it's green?"

"No, I add the color. So many unfortunates in need would eat it if I didn't color it. I sell to you since I see you have employment. Don't leave the meat where the mucksnipe might find it." He opened an oilcloth parcel toward the back of his barrow, took out several skewers with meat on them. They looked slightly bluer than those Frederick had purchased. Mr. Stewart placed the skewers of meat in the jar of brine at the center of his cart. "And don't you take a fancy to that meat, either." He winked at Frederick. "I've enough hungry ghosts following me."

"Do you mean that some have eaten your meat and died, or do you mean them?" Frederick gestured toward the numerous mewling felines and whining canines pacing and begging from a distance.

Mr. Stewart shrugged with a mischievous glint in his eye, then he glanced at the animals. "Those poor beasts are lovely enough," he said, "yet dangers abound. They follow me wherever I go. Some are abandoned pets, others feral. While the cats give me no fear, one aggressive dog among the canine can excite the others to violence. Hunger is hunger. Had a colleague what were badly mauled by a pack. Lost a leg."

Frederick smiled.

"You don't believe me?" Mr. Stewart asked.

"Yes, indeed I do."

"And that's cause to smile, is it?"

"Gave some deserving surgeon work to do, I suppose."

"You're right about that," Mr. Stewart said with a grin. "Good day to you, then."

Frederick decided he liked the man. "Good day."

Mr. Stewart took up his barrow, and moved forward. "Beep, beep!"

Frederick put the skewers into his jacket pocket. He made his way to Midhope Street to the cellar room he rented. He'd taken the place a month ago after deciding to snatch a young woman. The ancient house above the cellar had rotted, become dangerous, and had been abandoned. Finally, the structure collapsed about a year earlier. The landlord cleared off most of the debris, and rented what remained: Two cellar rooms partially below ground level. The floor above, currently forming a solid roof, would eventually rot away. Then the landlord would have nothing left but an exposed cellar.

For now, the room was secure. The thick stonework of the foundation rose three feet above the ground. The floor, supported with heavy wooden beams, formed a stout ceiling for the cellar. Stairs led downward to the entrance to Frederick's half of the lower ground floor. The thick wooden door stood half below ground level, half above. Outside, one had to listen with an ear to the door to hear the sound of the dog barking within. The room on the other side of the cellar had its own entrance, and two small windows. A man named Door kept a couple dozen chickens there. They created a constant muted chuckling sound. Occasionally one crowed.

Two days earlier, when Frederick had visited the cellar, he caught a stranger, an unfortunate, trying to break in to Mr. Door's side of the lower ground floor through one of the windows, no doubt to grab a chicken or some eggs. Concerned the fellow might try to break into the other side, Frederick snuck up, and tapped him on the shoulder. The man stood and spun around. Frederick shoved him, and the fellow fell onto his backside. He scrambled to his feet and ran away.

Frederick descended four stairs to the entrance, turned a key in a padlock, removed it, and opened the door a crack. The small, brown dog with short fur appeared in the opening immediately. She whined and pawed at him with her left front leg, while the stump of her upper right one waved uselessly. He put his right leg in the gap to keep her from getting out.

"Sit," he said.

She ignored Frederick's command. All fifteen pounds of her went for the skewers of meat in his right hand jacket pocket. He'd remember to put the skewers in the other pocket next time.

"Sit," he said again.

The bitch backed off hesitantly and sat, her snout twitching and her brown eyes glancing from his jacket pocket to his face. Frederick had had a relatively easy time managing her because, apparently, someone had loved and trained the dog earlier in her life. She'd been sick with infection when he found her.

As an Assistant Surgeon in the Royal Navy, Frederick had learned to recognize wet gangrene by its smell. He'd served under a surgeon named Wistwater. The man had taught Frederick more than what the average Assistant Surgeon was required to know, and entrusted him with duties well above his position. In one case, that had been the amputation of a woman's leg.

Frederick had gained the dog's trust, or he would not have been able to remove the limb. The infection had smelled strongly of corruption. If he hadn't removed the infected segment, she would have died. He'd given her food, calmed her with petting, then using a cleaver, he'd cut off the lower leg so quickly, she didn't have time to consider what he was doing. With time, the leg seemed to get better.

In the Royal Navy, Frederick had seen pus pour from the stump of a man's hand for weeks. The fellow appeared to get better, only to have to lose the forearm later. Sometimes, a surgeon had the opportunity to keep taking parts off a man as the infection in a limb, arm or leg, spread upward. If not stopped before reaching the torso at the shoulder or hip, the corruption would kill.

He pulled the skewers out of his pocket and tossed them into the cellar. As the dog left him to go after the meat, he quickly shut the door. He headed for his room in Chalton Street too eat his supper.

Removing the limb while the creature looked upon him as a trusted friend had been pleasurable. He'd found regaining the creature's trust afterward more delightful still. Frederick knew from experience that putting a young woman through that process brought much more satisfaction. Currently, he planned to start with one who wouldn't be missed.

The young woman who stepped off the MR from York had looked good. He'd been unhappy to miss his chance with her, but being honest with himself, he had to admit that he wasn't quite ready.

Keeping the dog provided him with practice, which helped him organize his thoughts and plans.

What would bring him the greatest satisfaction would be to take apart the innocent daughter of a man of means, a rich industrialist if possible. Yet that project required a strategy that would take time to develop.

For now, he'd find satisfaction where he could. Frederick would return to the cellar with a lamp, a sharp knife, and his cleaver after dark. The dog's upper right leg had looked red and swollen. If the infection had moved upward, he'd get to remove that part of the bitch as well.

Aiden: 3

The next day Dr. Reed released me from secondary care into a room of my own on the fourth floor of the hospital. Some machinery went with me. Not allowed to walk, I rode in a wheelchair. I didn't know at the time that I would not leave that fourth-floor neurological ward, except for a few surgical and test procedures, for the next seven weeks.

Melody, Mama, and Daddy came to see me shortly after I arrived. I settled in while they talked quietly.

The room had a whitish vinyl floor, a window with uninteresting, neutral blinds and curtains, and walls covered with some sort of nondescript plastic wallpaper. The furnishings consisted of a bland table and chairs, a black wall-mounted TV, an adjustable bed with controls on a paddle at the end of a long cable, and dull cabinets containing things as interesting as alcohol wipes and a blood pressure cuff. The wall at the head of the bed held mysterious chrome and plastic fittings and fixtures. The bathroom had lots of extra handles and railings. I hated everything about the place. For relief, I looked out the room's window, hoping for a view of something interesting, but saw only the weathered roof of a nearby building, possibly another part of the hospital, with its pigeon dung-bespattered air conditioning units, water tank, and various other equipment.

A male nurse appeared in the room with a small animal. He crouched on the floor and did something horrible to the creature.

Outraged, I cried out. Daddy restrained me as I tried to get out of bed to stop the guy.

The nurse seemed to notice me for the first time, and I froze in abject terror as he spoke to me. Even though I don't think I heard what he said, I knew the intense dread I felt came from his attempt to communicate. The guy had a malignant aspect I couldn't pin down. Despite being vivid, the bizarre episode with the male nurse was like a dream too strange to be understood. To this day, I remain unable to describe the experience with anything more than these few words. Even as the scene unfolded, I couldn't have explained to anyone what the nurse looked like, what the creature was, or what cruelty the animal suffered.

Then the nurse was gone and I heard Daddy calling out for Dr. Reed. He seemed to be on hand, which surprised me. He'd known my father for many years, and had a lot of respect for him. Since Dr. Reed didn't know me well, he may have stuck around the hospital that day to make himself available to Dr. William M. Clark.

"I think Aiden has had a temporal lobe seizure," Daddy said. "Perhaps he should be on Trillepetol."

"What happened?" Dr. Reed asked.

I struggled to describe what I could about the male nurse and animal.

"A hallucination that comes with the seizure," my father told me.

Dr. Reed nodded his head.

"All we saw," Daddy said, "was a look of childish terror on your face as you reached for something."

Although shaken by the hallucination, I found the event intensely interesting.

Dr. Reed added Trillepetol, an anti-seizure medication, to the cornucopia of pharmaceuticals I took. I was already on one such medicine, pheno-something or other. "Trillepetol is especially good for the temporal lobe seizures," Daddy told me. "You may have a few more hallucinations before the drug does away with them."

~ ~ ~

That afternoon, a surgeon put a set of ports, called a triple lumen, into my left shoulder so the hospital staff could more effectively continue my ten week course of intravenous antibiotics. When I woke up after the procedure, my shoulder hurt like hell. The surgeon had accidentally nicked the clavicle bone, and the tiny cut ached terribly. The first time the hospital staff tried to use the port, that hurt like hell too. The medication infiltrated the muscular tissue instead of going into the blood vessel. The port had been installed improperly. I was scheduled for another surgery.

I got the "okay" for my color comp from the Art Director at Ace. The hospital allowed me to have my painting supplies, drafting table, et cetera, brought into my room so I could do the book cover painting. My family hauled all of that from my home to the hospital. Although I found the task mentally and physically difficult, I started the work. At least I had something to do.

I needed a drink, but the hospital, my doctors, the nurses, my family, and my wife had no intention of letting me have that. "Just some beer?" I asked. My pleading did no good. While I'm sure that for some time they had all wanted to tell me not to drink, they'd had enough respect for me as an adult to restrain themselves. For the first time, they had a legitimate reason to deny me the stuff.

~ ~ ~

On the morning of the second day, I went into surgery to have a Hickman catheter installed instead of another triple lumen. Because the port would put the antibiotic into the superior vena cava, the vessel returning blood to my heart, the medicine would spread throughout my system at the fastest possible rate and prevent the burning feeling in the tissues. This one, put in the right side of my chest, worked fine until I stepped on my IV line and jerked the catheter right out of my flesh. They scheduled me for another surgery.

I also had an MRI, one of those X-ray-like tests that creates images that are thin slices of the tissues under examination. The technicians in charge of the procedure used me as filling for the hole in a throbbing, high-tech metal donut. Dr. Reed brought an MRI film to my hospital room to show me the brain abscesses. The film looked much like an X-ray of my brain. He pointed out two white spots next to each other in the right temporal lobe of the image, one the size of a marble, one the size of a pea.

I found the image unaccountably disturbing. I'm not talking about just the white smudges of the abscesses. No—something about seeing the organ itself deeply unsettled me, whereas images of brains had never upset me before. In fact, I had done several paintings of brains. Finally, I turned away from the image. I had the strangest feeling that a Pandora's box—*my skull?*—had been opened and that I would suffer the consequences.

Repulsed, yet intrigued, I asked, "May I have the film?"

"No," Dr. Reed said, "you're not supposed to keep it."

That seemed an odd way to put that. Later, he would give me the film or a similar one to keep.

~ ~ ~

The afternoon of the same day, as I lay in the bed among the scratchy, starched bedclothes, I looked for a specific description in the manuscript I'd already been through once for my illustration assignment. While I read, a male nurse entered the room. I didn't pay much attention to him. He seemed to fiddle with my IV pump or perhaps one of the mysterious fittings on the wall behind my head. Smelling a peculiar odor, something like rotten meat, I put the manuscript down, and looked up. Instead of a nurse, I found the ineffable figure that appeared in the earlier hallucination.

Although he made no menacing move toward me, I recoiled, pulling the blanket with me as I got off the bed, and spilling the loose, dog-eared pages of the manuscript onto the floor. Somehow, I knew he had malicious and depraved intentions. He disgusted me. The apparition said something that brought on a more potent, heart-withering dread than the time before. As with his appearance, and earlier that of the animal, I found his message indescribable. I could not have repeated his words or described their meaning in any way. Even so, my emotional response suggested that I did understand him on some level. That deepened my curiosity about what he might have said.

Despite the vivid quality of the hallucination, which led me to take the event so seriously, I knew I experienced another temporal lobe seizure, and assumed the episode would pass quickly as the previous one had. That gave me courage. Instead of being crushed by the dreadful feelings, I became curious and interested in what happened. I stared at him, though I made little sense of what I saw. Again, the ability to separate myself from the emotions had become a benefit.

Sure enough, the hallucination ended quickly, having lasted, at most, a minute. When I found myself suddenly alone in the room, my fascination with the seizure intensified.

Nothing about the experience had been truly harmful as far as I could see. Nor would the episodes become dangerous, I decided, as long as I understood that what went on in them had no basis in reality. I recognized the pattern now. I hoped that the medicine didn't take the hallucinations away too quickly, before I'd had a chance to really experience them fully.

That evening I picked up the manuscript again. Since the pages had been dumped on the floor, I put them back in their proper order. To find my place, I reread the section I'd been going over when my brain had so rudely interrupted. Reading the words I'd seen the moment the seizure occurred, I had another one. Somehow, that sequence of words had become a code to unlock the epileptic fit and hallucinatory response. The cruel apparition, that I'd erroneously thought of as a nurse, put in a weak appearance in the hallucination. I could see a mouth moving among the phantasmagoria of his face, but I couldn't hear anything. Still, the sense of dread came over me, slightly diminished from what I got during the earlier seizures. That gave me the impression the Trillepetol had begun to take effect. Despite my interest in the episodes, I wasn't sad to see the apparition's presence diminish. His persona screamed "creep" in every way imaginable.

~ ~ ~

The second Hickman catheter went into the left side of my chest. I succeeded in keeping that one. Several times a day I had to take in penicillin through the port. This process involved cleaning the area around the catheter, swabbing the exposed and adjacent tissues with alcohol and an iodine-like solution to kill whatever bacteria might be lurking nearby, hooking the IV line from the IV pump to the plastic sack of antibiotic at one end and the sharp, pointy end of the line going into the Hickman catheter at the other. After the fluid had all disappeared into my chest, the line was disconnected, and a fresh four by six inch plastic adhesive dressing went over the catheter to keep bacteria out until the device was used again. Unable to breathe over extended periods of time, the skin tissue at the site of the plastic dressings died. The area became a raw and oozing mess. The brown/yellow iodine-like solution worked its way into the tissue, and I sported a big golden rectangle tattoo that took at least a year to fade away.

~ ~ ~

Mama spent a chunk of every day in my hospital room. She brought me tasty foods she'd prepared as well as other things.

Short, dark-haired, and with a billion freckles, Joan Clark contrasted dramatically with her tall husband. She came from New York. Her parents had been jazz people back before the musicians' strike of 1941. They'd lost everything during the strike and ended up in a rural area of Long Island. By the late 1940s they'd risen out of poverty again, but my mother wanted to get away from Long Island. "I didn't want to grow up and marry a potato farmer," she once told me.

She went into nurses training, and eventually got a job in the psychiatric hospital at the Columbia Presbyterian complex in New York City in the 1950s. While working as a nurse at the facility, she met my father.

In the 1980s, as a family, we'd watched a video tape of the film version of Ken Kesey's *One Flew Over the Cuckoo's Nest.* Mama kept rooting for Nurse Ratched. When we'd asked her why, she'd said simply, "Because I know what those other assholes are up to."

My mother enjoyed taking care of me in the hospital because that gave her the chance to be a nurse again. I loved her and was grateful for her help and companionship. She sat and read or watched her soap opera, General Hospital, while I worked or slept.

The difficulty in concentrating on my work persisted as my headache continued, yet I had lots of time and I suffered boredom, so I had an incentive to fill my time with something constructive.

With the level of the Trillepetol rising in my blood, the temporal lobe seizures changed oddly, even as they diminished in power. The third day in my hospital room I'd had maybe five of the seizures. Sadly, the hallucinations no longer had a visual aspect. I say that because, as a horror fan, I remained fascinated, yet I did truly want to get better. Since the apparition had always been at the center of the visuals, I didn't entirely mind the loss. I continued to have the feeling of dread, and I began to lose my sense of personal identity. Those things that made me an individual seemed to slip away. I remember looking at a portfolio of my paintings Melody had brought to show to curious hospital staff and wondering how the pieces of art might have been accomplished. Starting on the fourth or fifth day in the hospital, and running for about a week, I had twenty or thirty seizures within each twenty-four hour period. They were much lighter, had the accompanying sense of dread, and something new: A feeling that I was becoming someone else.

"I think I might be one of the characters on General Hospital," I said to Mama, trying to be funny. She was absorbed in watching the soap opera on the television in my room at the time, and probably didn't find my statement humorous.

"I hope you're one of the good guys," she said. "Most of the male characters are a bunch of jerks."

During the third week in the hospital, I had hundreds of the seizures within each day.

"I remember doing things in places I've never been," I told Melody during one of her night visits.

"What does that mean?" she asked.

"It's weird. I have these memories, like…" Frustrated, I wanted to take back my words. Hoping for inspiration to explain my experience, I looked out the window. The moon, though beautiful as it rode a long, dark cirrus cloud in the deep blue sky, offered me nothing. "…I don't know!"

"Tell me."

I took a deep breath, recalled things that weren't my recollections. "Okay, so I remember moving around in a Victorian-era train station, and walking along cobblestone streets through an old world slum. The women on the street are dressed in floor-length skirts, and the men all wear hats and old fashion suits."

"Yeah, that *is* weird."

"I think it's just another symptom of the seizures, but I get this haunted feeling."

"You mean the fear?"

"No, not the dread. It's like I should know about something that's going to happen because I was there when it started, yet it's unclear what that is."

"You're not making any sense."

"I know."

I watched a new batch of clouds swallow the moon, its glow becoming as fuzzy as my experience with the hallucinations.

"The seizures are going away, though—you said."

"Yeah."

Within two weeks the seizures had begun to bleed together, and only that sense of dread remained as a constant buzz. Then that slowly diminished in intensity and went away.

~ ~ ~

The hospital room felt increasingly like a cell. Adding to the penal atmosphere, moans and cries of pain came from other patients in the ward, especially at night. I wanted out in the worst way. I persuaded

38

the nursing staff to allow me to walk the halls of the ward at night. Since saline solution was being pushed through my catheter at a constant, slow rate, I remained connected to my IV pump, and had to take it with me where ever I went. My "blue buddy," Melody had dubbed it. Wheeling the thing along with me, I moved quietly about the ward in the wee hours. When no one was looking, I took small excitement from raiding the snacks cabinet and a little freezer that held cups of ice cream in the nurses' station.

"When can I leave the hospital?" I asked Dr. Reed every time I saw him.

At first he'd say, "Let's not decide that today." When I became more insistent, he changed to a delaying tactic. "In two days," he'd say.

He gave me that answer for at least three weeks. I survived without drinking because I had regular intramuscular injections of narcotic for the pain in my head.

The high from the drug is infinitely more delicious than that of alcohol. The staff gave me an injection every four hours. The trouble with the narcotic is that tolerance to the drug develops quickly. What at first would knock me down and take away much of my coordination, soon wasn't nearly enough. The staff at the hospital and my doctor wouldn't increase the dosage. I watched the clock and didn't let them miss a dose.

The tissue at my regular injection site, my shoulder, got a crunchy, crystalline feel after several doses, as if the muscle held small gravel. When time for the narcotic came, if the tissue of my shoulder was too crunchy, a new site, like a butt cheek, would be used. Apparently a body can't take the drug just anywhere, though.

"You've got too many rocks," a nurse complained playfully one day, referring to my shoulder. She was a nice one, a black-haired, pale woman from Georgia, named Trudy Jenkins.

"Give it to me somewhere else," I said.

She checked my other sites. "You're all full-up with rocks. It's not good for you."

Immediately, I became concerned. I needed the drug, and admitted as much. Trudy looked at me squarely. "You don't need all this. I'll give it to you this time, but if the rocks don't clear up, we'll have to lay off the injections."

Her words frightened me into looking for a solution. I found that if I rubbed the tissues, the gravel slowly softened and disappeared. Results took hours of massage. At the time, the effort seemed well worth the trouble.

~ ~ ~

Melody came nearly every day. She brought me better foods than the hospital offered. She brought me books and games for us to play. She brought the mail and my phone messages. I kept in touch with folks by phone and told them what I could about what happened to me.

I got the painting done for Ace books. More illustration work came in, and I got all that done. Being a pre-digital age, the actual artwork had to be shipped to the publishers. Melody helped me get the work packed up and she'd ship it.

The days she couldn't come, she expressed a lot of regret and apologized unnecessarily. She had precious little time at home.

"I can imagine how difficult coming to the hospital so often and getting to work each day has to be," I told her. "You have nothing to apologize for." Still, she persisted in expressing her regret, and I truly didn't understand why she had such strong feelings.

We got along well, perhaps because we weren't living together, yet she had become increasingly emotional the longer I remained in the hospital.

One day in tears, she made an admission to me. "I'd hoped you would die when you first went into the hospital. Your drinking, the way you were, was too much. I just wanted it to end so I could start over." She held me and cried.

I understood, and I didn't hold her feelings against her. How could I? I knew what I'd become. I'd selfishly married her, put up a shoddy front, and gone on with my self-indulgence. Unlike me, she didn't know that I'd gotten no better, that the narcotic merely forestalled my need to drink. I remained too selfish to tell her. I did love her, and I wanted to be with her. Despite my addiction, I had hope for better times, a better me, and I tried not to look at the present too closely.

"I can't forgive myself," she said. "I do love you. Can you forgive me?"

"Yes," I said, trying to comfort her. "I don't blame you for feeling that way."

I felt like a real shit for deceiving her.

Frederick: 3

Simon's curse had brought Frederick another fit while he worked on the bitch's leg. He came to on the planking he'd put down as a floor of sorts in his rented cellar.

The dog lay quietly beside him, her infection-ravaged upper right leg missing. She gnawed weakly at the tourniquet he'd placed around the leg, just under her shoulder. The partial limb, along with the cleaver and a smaller knife, rested in the dirt a few feet away.

At the age of twenty-seven, Frederick had suffered spells for more than ten years. They began while he served aboard the corvette, HMS Challenger, during the vessel's operations with the French and Spanish in Mexico in 1862. A block in the rigging of the vessel had swung loose, and struck him in the right side of the head. He'd remained insensible for eight hours. The spells started a few days thereafter.

Because of Frederick's epilepsy, the Royal Navy had deemed him unfit for service and turned him out before he'd won a certificate of service that would have made him eligible for a pension.

Frederick believed the ghost of his boyhood friend, Simon, had thrown the block as a form of vengeance. When they were young men, living on the streets with other boys, Frederick had challenged Simon and his authority, coercing him into taking a dangerous risk. If not for that, the young man might have still been alive.

Until recently, Frederick had merely blacked out during his spells. The visions accompanying the recent seizure episodes were new and troubling. Moments ago, during his fit, he'd again seen the apparition in the unkind room. Even with the constant shuffling of the fellow's features, Frederick knew the man was not Simon. The chamber appeared different this time, more open. The man wasn't strapped down. He didn't appear to be tortured. He'd cried out and reached for Frederick, but something unseen stood in his way.

Dream stuff, of no consequence, he decided, although he didn't find the thought entirely persuasive.

Frederick sat up, and tried to release the tourniquet. The dog snapped at him when he got too close. Yes—he'd have to regain her trust. He looked forward to that.

As he considered the bloody stump, Frederick's heart beat faster, and he gained a partial erection. Removing a portion of the dog gave him an odd satisfaction, accompanied by a feeling of power over a merciless, mean, and arbitrary world. Frederick's action had irrevocably diminished the creature's prospects in life, and thinking of that felt good. The first amputation, the one that had destroyed the functionality of the limb, had been the most satisfying. The act would have been more satisfying still if the limb had not needed to come off. With all that, he'd also felt glad for having saved the dog's life again. And, of course, she needn't suffer unnecessarily.

Frederick retrieved his jacket from a peg beside the cellar door, and took the bottle of gin from one of the pockets. He'd given the dog some before the amputation. She'd need more if he was to finish the job. He pulled the cork, and poured some of the gin into the crockery bowl of water he kept for her. He set the bowl beside the animal. Again, she responded immediately, hungrily lapping at the clear liquid.

With time, the dog relaxed and eventually she slept. While she remained subdued, Frederick tied off the blood vessels with suture. Before cutting through the muscle and bone of the upper leg, he'd peeled back the skin to give him flaps to overlap at the end of the stump. As he worked, placing stitches to close the wound, he thought again about the apparition in his vision.

The scorn evident in the man's eyes deeply troubled Frederick. The apparition clearly hated him for traits they both shared, yet Frederick couldn't have explained exactly what that meant, nor how he knew those things. *If he isn't Simon, if he is mere phantasm, why do I care?* Frederick didn't have an answer, but he couldn't shake the feeling that the apparition's opinion somehow mattered.

Finished with his mending, he released the tourniquet and removed it. The dog lay undisturbed, asleep. He noted that she'd responded differently than he expected. Rarely did a man consume enough liquor to allow him to sleep through the pain of applying stitches.

Frederick ran his hand through the dog's soft, oily fur. He knew he and the dog should like that. She was asleep, though, and he gained nothing from the experience.

Gathering up his jacket, the bottle, cleaver, knife, and the partial limb, he let himself out into the night and put the padlock on the door. As he walked back to his room in Chalton Street, a figured appeared out of the shadows at the entrance to a derelict shop. Frederick recognized the unfortunate he'd seen trying to break into Mr. Door's side of the cellar.

"Your purse," the man said. He brandished a small knife.

Frederick slowly reached into his jacket as if for his purse, and pulled out the cleaver instead.

The mug-hunter's eyes grew wide.

Frederick swung the cleaver toward the hand with the knife.

The stranger withdrew the knife, backed off, and fled.

As Frederick continued toward home, he remembered speaking to the other stranger he'd seen that night; the apparition from his vision. Not knowing the man's identity or station, he spoke to him as an equal. What had Frederick said? His anger and meaning were clear enough, yet the words he used to express himself seemed to belong to a language he'd never heard. "The flawed organ in your head will turn you, just as mine has done me." But why would he say that? He had no evidence that Simon's curse had changed him.

For the first time, he considered the idea that the spells might not come from Simon, but were instead a curse of a different sort. No—Frederick preferred the known-unknown to the completely-unknown. The fits had to remain Simon's curse.

And the visions that recently accompanied them? *The visions are mere dream stuff!* Frederick thought. He did so with all the authority he could muster, as if the statement alone might diminish the apparition enough that the fellow would leave him alone.

He seemed to get his wish, as the visions that came with Simon's curse dimmed over the ensuing months. The apparition appeared in the spells as if seen through the bottom of a brown bottle. With each passing fit, the view of the fellow became murkier, and he seemed to lose interest in Frederick. The man's thoughts and feelings became less evident each time. Then the visions ceased entirely.

Frederick experienced relief—he hadn't liked seeing himself as through the fellow's hypocritical eyes.

Although Simon's curse didn't go away entirely, Frederick felt better than he had in years, quite well enough to pursue his goal of taking a young woman apart. His planning continued.

Aiden: 4

The fevers started slowly and quietly. Within a few days, the alternating bouts of chills and hot sweats had become severe.

"You're allergic to one of the medications," Dr. Reed told me. "The question is, which one? It's probably the antibiotic."

"I'm not allergic to penicillin."

I lay in my bed, miserable from lack of sleep, as the chills and sweats had given me no respite at night.

"With the massive doses you're receiving, you might have become allergic to it."

"So, take me off the penicillin."

"That might not be what's causing the fevers, and we don't want to lose any ground already gained in fighting off the infection. We'll start with the other drugs."

One at a time, the hospital staff switched my medications with new and different ones. Between each switch, time was allowed to pass so the results could be observed. If no change in my fevers occurred, then the next medication was switched, and so on for five or six medications. I remained in bed, becoming steadily sicker during the process, as the fevers increased in severity. Sure enough, the culprit turned out to be the penicillin, but by the time they had that pinned down, I'd grown deliriously ill. They took me off the antibiotic, and put me on one so molecularly similar to it that my body continued to see penicillin and I got even worse.

One night I had temperatures of over one hundred and five degrees. A couple of nurses got me up out of bed and wrapped me in a rubbery, grey quilt-like thing filled with Freon coils hooked up to a compressor; a sort of flexible freezer called a cold blanket. I lay back down, and they put bags of ice in my crotch, in my armpits, and on my forehead. None of that felt good with my ongoing, now fever-pitched headache. For all the cold, my agony reached a point of white-hot intensity and stayed that way for an indeterminate amount of time before suddenly backing off so that I hardly noticed the pain. Gratefully, I closed my eyes and relaxed.

I believe I reached some sort of limit for pain that night. For whatever the reason—an inherent limit to physical pain or the blessed gesture of an angel of mercy—the agony had done its work and gone.

"Are you alright, sweetie?" one of the nurses asked, touching my cheeks and turning me to face her. I recognized Trudy's Georgia accent. I realized she'd been with me throughout that high fever event, although I hadn't been particularly aware of much beyond what went on inside me.

I opened my eyes. "Yes."

She looked concerned. "I stopped hearing you, honey."

I'd been moaning in misery for what seemed like hours.

Normally, if a woman I hardly knew referred to me as "honey" or "sweetie," I'd become suspicious of her motives. That happened in the South from time to time, usually from someone offering a service and hoping for a good gratuity. When Trudy said it, though, the words felt good, like she cared what happened to me. I needed that then, and I think she knew it. Many of the nurses I encountered during my hospital stay were embittered from years of serving unhappy people. Not Trudy. She was one of the good ones.

"The pain stopped. Why is that?"

"I don't know, but it's good."

She stayed with me as I dipped in and out of sleep. Within an hour or so my fever had dropped enough that I was no longer in danger, though the staff, mostly Trudy I suppose, closely monitored my temperature for the rest of the night. Doctor Reed put me on a third antibiotic, and within a day or two the fevers ceased entirely.

~ ~ ~

One day I got a phone call from my friend, Jack Daves. He was laughing. "I just heard from a friend, that a friend of his said he'd heard you had died while flossing your teeth."

"Somehow, I suppose the story about my dental hygienist testing my gums got into the rumor mill," I said.

Later, during a visit from my father, I told him what Jack had said, and then laughed. I was sitting up in my hospital bed while he sat in a chair, looking rather uncomfortable as he looked around the characterless room. I don't think he liked the hospital any more than I did.

"I've watched you laugh and joke about your condition throughout your stay at the hospital," he said. "This is serious stuff, and I'd think you'd be more frightened."

Even though he sounded a bit upset, his expression told me he was curious.

"How can you have a sense of humor about it?"

The question surprised me. He'd always enjoyed gallows humor before.

Daddy had introduced me at a young age to lots of the weird. We saw an exhibit of paintings by Salvador Dali in New York City when I was about five years old. He loved the droll lyrics of Tom Lehrer's music, and played an LP record of his songs periodically during my childhood. Daddy's favorite piece from the record was "The Irish Ballad," a darkly humorous song about killing family members. He read to his children from dreadful texts. I remember particularly *Ruthless Rhymes for Heartless Homes* by Harry Graham, and the illustrated extreme cautionary tales of *Der Struwwelpeter* by Dr. Heinrich Hoffman, a book he'd picked up while in Germany, one he had to translate as he read aloud. As a family, my parents, siblings, and I watched *The Twilight Zone, The Outer Limits*, and other weird, dark TV shows. Daddy enjoyed the films of Alfred Hitchcock. He was a reader of science fiction and fantasy. As an adult, I'd watched many horror movies with him. When I'd shown him *Return of the Living Dead* in the 1980s, he'd said the film was his new favorite. He'd laughed so hard watching the movie, especially during the split dog scene, I'd thought he'd hurt himself.

Daddy had perhaps gotten his appreciation for dark humor from his father, Dr. Sam Lillard Clark, a neuroanatomist and one time head of the Anatomy Department at Vanderbilt University. Grandaddy, as we grandchildren called him, died in 1960, and I was too young to really get to know him. I wished I'd had more of an opportunity to do so. I've heard several tales of mischief he got up to, including one that my father told me when I was a teen.

"One day before a demonstration for his students involving a cadaver," Daddy said, "your grandfather had a rather rare steak at lunch. Looking at the pink meat gave him an idea. He shredded pieces of steak and put them in a paper cup. Before his students came in, he put the cup into a cavity in the abdomen of the cadaver. Periodically during his demonstration, he peeled off his glove, reach into the cadaver for a piece of the meat, and ate it."

I don't know if that story is true, and, if so, how the students had reacted, but I was delighted with the tale.

Grandaddy had been on the Tennessee Anatomical Board, which was charged with the task of making sure the medical schools of the state had sufficient cadavers. He called the group "The Board Stiff." Back in the 1930s, when medical schools experienced a shortage of dead bodies to carve up, Grandaddy employed a body snatcher to get them illegally. The authorities turned a blind eye to body snatching as long as nothing but the naked corpse was taken from the burial. They understood the value of cadavers in medical education. In the 1940s, Grandaddy wrote a paper about the history of body snatching titled "Medical Education from the Ground Up." He made a recording on his wax cylinder recorder of the body snatcher he employed talking about his resurrectionist exploits in the Nashville area. Grandaddy included the man's words at the end of the manuscript. He delivered "Medical Education from the Ground Up" to his gentlemen's club, reading the paper aloud.

My interest in the disturbing is therefore third generation. My father gave to me what his father had given to him. Of all Dr. William M. Clark's children, I seemed to be the only one who consistently connected with him in that way.

Even with all that, I couldn't help thinking that during the time I was in the hospital, his concern for my well-being might have frightened his humor away. Watching him as he sat in a chair talking to me, I realized that when he came to my hospital room, he was all business. Had he seen my condition as much more deadly than I realized? Had he protected me from that knowledge? Maybe so. As I got better, and there was finally *real* talk about releasing me from the hospital, perhaps he'd let his guard down. I didn't ask because I didn't want to know if I'd been in worse danger. What good would that do?

He'd asked, "How can you have a sense of humor about it?"

"I haven't had much choice," I said. "I have been frightened. Laughing at it helps."

With a grim smile, he nodded, and I knew he understood.

~ ~ ~

After seven weeks in the hospital, I went home to the little clapboard house in The Nations. Fall had come and gone while I lay in the hospital, and the neighborhood had turned gray. The perennially overcast winter sky pressed down on the house from above, and the leafless hackberry trees surrounding the property seemed to lean in, adding to the gloom. The sound of the rain-soaked gravel passing under the tires of our car was strangely unfamiliar as we pulled into the driveway.

My IV pump had to go home with me since I wouldn't be finished with the antibiotic treatments for another three weeks. Entering the house with my equipment felt uncomfortable. Oddly, I wanted to return to the hospital.

"You may have scar tissue in your brain that will cause more seizures," Dr. Reed had said to me before I left the hospital. "Because you had the grand mall seizure, you are not allowed to drive for one year."

"But I'm on Trillepetol to prevent the seizures."

"It's a state law requirement because the medication may not work absolutely."

I couldn't imagine how I would get along in the world for a year without driving. As selfish as I was, I had no intention of following the rule. I didn't admit that to my doctor.

The home nursing service that brought my medications got the instructions for the narcotic wrong. Instead of coming to my home every four hours to administer the drug, they dropped off a box of one hundred syringes and a box of twenty-five, fifty-milligram ampules of the stuff. After Melody went to bed at night, or to work in the day, I'd hole up in my tiny studio in a small, antique reclining chair, and abuse myself with the narcotic. As stoned as I got on the stuff, I was careful to hide all the evidence behind books on a shelf within arm's reach. One morning I saw that I'd done eight hundred milligrams of the drug within an eight hour period the night before. That scared me.

I called Dr. Reed and told him what I'd done. "You've got to take it away from me," I said.

"We can't do that, *now*," he said, the implication being that I'd obviously become addicted and couldn't get along without the drug. "I'll place your prescription in a pharmacy a half hour away from your house. You'll have to appear in person to have it filled. The pharmacy closes at six pm. Your wife gets off work at five, right?"

"Yes."

"Since you can't drive, you'll have a small window of opportunity to get it."

Melody and I went to get the narcotic once. Not convenient enough for me, I went back to drinking. I wasn't supposed to drink while on the Trillepetol because the combination could cause seizures as well as complications in the liver, but alcohol was the easiest route to intoxication. Three liquor stores existed within a mile of my house.

The Trillepetol doubled the intoxicating effect of alcohol. I'd get drunk, then have hangovers twice as powerful as any I'd ever known. I closed the curtains of the house and stayed indoors as much as possible. I missed the spring of 1990.

People who saw me during that time, both family and friends, did little to disguise their loathing, and that frightened me. Melody threatened to leave. I couldn't get my work done. I hurt, both physically and emotionally. I wanted out of my predicament.

With the end of my course of antibiotics, I saw my chance. The brain abscesses and all the medical crap would become a thing of the past. I cleaned myself up and stopped drinking. Melody and I cleaned house. We got rid of everything having to do with the hospital and the illness. I cleaned my studio out and prepared to take on new work. Melody's smile came out of hiding. Hope returned to the gazes of friends and family. My head cleared, I became rational, confident, happy—I was in love with my wife!

Still, I didn't truly believe the good stuff could last, that I could remain sober. I did not like who I'd become. I went maybe a month without drinking.

When work came in, I wondered why the publisher wanted to hire someone as broken down as me. Of course, I merely felt sorry for myself. Few but family and close friends knew what went on with me emotionally or physically.

I drank in celebration of the new work. At least that's what I told myself. In truth I felt unworthy of the trust that went with receiving the illustration assignment, and I drank to quiet my dark thoughts about how I would fail to do the job well. After bingeing heavily for a couple of days, I headed into a two week long hangover that took me dangerously close to the edges of delirium tremens.

"I'm sick," I told Melody, although clearly she'd known I'd been drinking. She'd heard the excuse so often she no longer responded. Once she'd gone off to work each day, I lay on the bathroom floor so I could be near the sink and toilet. I'd stay there all day, taking in the smallest amount of alcohol I could, just enough to dull the headaches and abdominal cramps a little bit. The peeling, tan lino-leum floor tiles and the blistered self-adhesive wallpaper, with its pink and blue flowers, were poor company as I tried unsuccessfully to sleep time away.

When Melody came home in the evening, I'd scrape myself up off the floor and spend a few more hours pretending to be sick.

At night I'd lie in bed next to her, unable to sleep, sweating, my head full of emotional weirdness. The streetlights shone too brightly through the thin slots in the closed window blinds in cold and unfriendly colors. The cars going by on the road out front were sneaky, moving too slowly and making too little noise on the rain-soaked asphalt. What were their drivers up to? I imagined that the water heater, which brooded in a closet in the corner of the bed-room, considered doing something destructive with scalding-hot water. I heard burglars moving through the brush just outside the windows, looking for a way in. Since I didn't hear the sump pump coming on, I feared that the basement filled up with water from recent rains. Recognizing that my ridiculous thoughts/feelings/concerns were imaginary, a product of an overwrought mind, I re-mained in bed. I tried to hold on and wait out the weird-storm.

Like jumping off the bottom of the deep end and reaching for the edge, day by day I slowly reduce the amount of alcohol I took in until I had weaned myself off drinking.

And once again, my work got done, Melody's hope peeked out again—perhaps a bit more cautiously. We got along beautifully, life became wonderful. That second dry spell occurred in the summer of 1990, and lasted about a month and a half. I, too, had begun to have hope.

Then I got another good job and the cycle started all over. During the next epic hangover, I saw double for nearly twenty-four hours, and could do little during that time but sit and hope I didn't go completely blind. Even the horror of that experience didn't move me to quit drinking. I told no one about the vision problem because I feared the help that others, particularly family, might force upon me.

Even as I emerged from that second epic hangover, Melody had little to do with me, coming and going from the house without co-ordinating with me for meals or anything else. She seemed to be giving up.

One night while she was out, I felt particularly pitiful, and thought of something to pump me up. I drove down to a bar that a lot of Vanderbilt students frequented. Carrying a portfolio containing photo samples of my best artwork with me, I entered and stood around for a moment as if looking for someone. As usual, the place was full, with few unoccupied seats. I approached a booth that held two couples and asked. "May I sit with you for a moment? I'm wait-ing to meet with an art director and I'm getting tired of standing."

"Sure," they said.

"You're an artist?" one of the fellows asked.

"Yes, an illustrator. I do book cover paintings for publishers of science fiction, fantasy, and horror. Want to see?"

I offered my portfolio and they went through the pages in the dim light. That bothered me. I wanted them to get a good look at the images. I wanted to *wow* them. Sure enough, they seemed to like the artwork. They offered some oohs and ahhs.

I felt stupid trying to derive pleasure from the deception.

"Doesn't look like the art director is going to show up," I said after a time. "Thanks for looking at my work."

I got up and left, feeling smaller than I had when I'd set out from the house to pump myself up. *God Damn*, I was an idiot!

~ ~ ~

All my efforts to build up my illustration business would go to shit if I didn't do better. Even though I lived in a state of constant fear and self pity, I sobered up just enough to organize my participation in the 1990 World Fantasy Convention art show.

I had produced some good artwork during the recent dry peri-ods, including a painting that would be the first in my Deadwood Series, one titled "Half Scairt." The piece depicted what at first glance appeared to be a partial corpse—head, shoulders, arms, and torso—hung on a post in a cow pond in a chilly fall scene at dusk or dawn. Upon closer inspection, the viewer would discover that the corpse was merely sticks, leaves, and other natural detritus caught in the barbed wire on the post.

At the World Fantasy Convention in Chicago, Illinois, that painting won the art show award for Best Horror. That meant a lot to me, yet again, I didn't feel worthy. Somehow, those running the convention would find out the painting wasn't really any good. Someone knowledgeable about illustration would enter the art show, see the award plaque hanging beside the painting, and tell the staff that the artwork wasn't worthy of the honor. The award would be taken away from me in as public a fashion as it had been given. The shame would be devastating, my budding career ruined. Everyone would know I was a fraud.

I needed to pack up my work and leave as quickly as possible. I found my traveling companion, a good friend named Carl. "We need to go as soon as possible," I said.

He looked at me strangely, since the convention wasn't quite over. "Is something wrong?"

"No, just need to get home."

I saw my thinking on the matter as ridiculous. Rationally, I could not take such a fantasy scenario of shaming seriously. Even so, the feeling side of me *did* believe in such things. Seemingly, all creative individuals, even the truly accomplished, have some fear of being exposed as a fraud—witness Sally Field's response to winning the Oscar in 1985. "You like me," she'd said with surprise. In my weakened emotional state, I had the fear in spades.

Dragging Carl with me, I beat a hasty retreat. Hurrying across the hotel parking lot, I dropped the walnut award plaque on the asphalt and dinged one of its corners badly. Once home, I hung the plaque on the wall, hoping to enjoy the honor, but all I could see was the damaged corner, which made me think about what a scared little man I'd become.

Under the guise of celebrating the win, I drank. The binge involved, and the two-week-long hangover that followed, left my alcoholism fully exposed to anyone paying attention. Again, I hid away the best I could, going out of the house as little as possible and not answering the phone. The "I'm sick" excuse did me no good as my slurred words told Melody the truth.

"I found the bottles in the closet of your studio," she said in passing on her way to work one day. "I know how much you drink." Yet she didn't throw the stuff away.

I'd begun again the process of lying on the bathroom floor all day, lying awake sweating in bed at night, and trying to wean myself from the alcohol.

During one of those nights, while Melody lay asleep in bed beside me, I felt the presence of the apparition from my hallucinatory episodes. Perhaps I'd missed a dose of the Trillepetol, I thought, and suffered another seizure. Despite believing I hallucinated the presence, I became alarmed as he seemed to reach for Melody. I stood and turned toward him in the darkness. Although unable to see anyone, I felt his mind in our bedroom. Something told me I could touch his brain. I imagined reaching into him, even as he reached for the woman—not Melody, I realized, but a woman on the platform of that Victorian era railway station I'd imagined. The vision ended when the fellow—I still thought of him as a nurse—seemed to convulse and fall away.

Melody had not stirred. I lay back down, continued worrying at the unraveling edges of my mind. The event didn't seem significantly different from the emotional hallucinations I'd had during that time, like seriously wondering what medical procedure would be necessary to excise from my chest the rotted tissue that was a product of all my dishonesty, or the scenarios that rolled through my thoughts in which family and friends shunned and even hated me. As time passed I thought little of any of the visions that came with my night-sweats.

~ ~ ~

On a Saturday a couple weeks after the convention, Melody said, "I'm leaving."

I'd gotten far enough in my weaning process that I didn't have to spend my waking hours in the bathroom. I lay on the couch watching television in the living room. "When do you expect to get home?" I asked.

Tears slid from her eyes. "I'm not coming back. I'm going to stay with your parents for a few days, then I'll decide where to go."

My love for her had been pushed away into a dark corner of my mind while I pursued my annihilation. Now, the prospect of actually losing her brought me fully awake and sober. I sat up and looked at her. More than anything else, she seemed to be mourning.

I begged and pleaded. I couldn't get along on my own. The look in her eyes appeared to be one of grim resolve, and I feared she'd already fully accepted the loss.

Melody had packed a few things in a travel bag that she'd set down beside the front door. She was ready to go, yet she shifted from foot to foot on the worn and stained brown berber carpet. I couldn't let her walk out the door. She lingered, I knew, because she didn't want strangers on the street out front to see her crying.

"I'll get better," I said, pitifully. "Ever since the hospital, I haven't felt good about myself. The Trillepetol takes a toll on me, leaves me feeling run down all the time."

"Excuses," she said bitterly.

Finally, she'd wised up and would receive no more excuses. In defense of her own well-being, she'd set her mind to lock me and all my bullshit out. She wouldn't look at me.

I'd have to do a lot better than that.

"I don't want to drink anymore," I said.

She shook her head, and I knew that wasn't the key to the lock.

I would have told her I'd quit if I thought she'd believe me, but over the years I'd consistently broken all my promises of cutting back, drinking only beer, drinking only on weekends, and quitting all together.

"I'm miserable and I don't know how to stop," I admitted.

She took a deep breath, wiped her eyes, and looked at me.

Somehow I'd found the key. At the same time, I'd expressed the truth! As simple as that may seem, I felt lucky to have stumbled upon using honesty to hold onto her. She remained my lifeline and I wouldn't let go willingly.

Just because she hadn't walked out the door, though, didn't mean I wouldn't screw up in the next few minutes. Yes—I'd found the key, and I knew I'd better use it.

"I don't trust myself either. Once I start drinking, I can't stop. I know I can't go on as I have. I'm killing myself."

Mute and watching me closely, Melody sat at the other end of the couch.

"Over the summer, I went as long as a month and a half without drinking. Everything worked then. Life was good."

She nodded with a guarded smile.

I thought about how I'd felt going without drink, and some of my fear fell away.

"I found out about a substance abuse program," Melody said. "Insurance will pay for almost all of it."

Another hospital. Another prison term! Immediately, I wanted to say no, but knew I couldn't if I wanted to be with Melody.

She told me more about the place and the program, and I realized the experience couldn't be more miserable than what I went through at home.

I had nothing left to lose.

"Yes, I'm willing to do it."

Frederick: 4

Frederick had spotted a new prospect. She stepped off the MR from Leeds and appeared to be traveling alone.

He considered waiting for his present state of ill temper to subside before approaching her, yet he didn't want to miss his opportunity. The hostility he felt had grown as glances toward platform number 3 had revealed a gathering of top-hatted gentleman. One or two swells amidst the crowds meant nothing, but at least twenty of the gentleman now stood together. No doubt they awaited the arrival of a traveling colleague.

The sight had brought intense resentment and memories of a similarly large group of the well-to-do who arrived in the neighborhood of Frederick's childhood home for a ground-breaking ceremony, one to which the residents of the district weren't invited. Shortly thereafter, he and his family, among hundreds of others, were turned out of their homes so the heartless industrialists could tear up the streets and raze the tenements to make way for railway lines. Within the decade, many more would be turned out of their homes to make room for St. Pancras Station.

Frederick's beloved mother suffered with typhoid fever during the time of the eviction. His father, the cruel bastard, had died the year before. Good riddance, Frederick had thought. Then he'd been too young to help his mother once they became homeless. She hadn't lasted out the month. After her death, family in Manchester had taken in Frederick's older sister, Abigail. They did not take him. Until he went to sea two years later at the age of fifteen, Frederick had survived as a beggar, scavenger, and small-time criminal on the streets with other homeless boys, including Simon.

Bitter memories are like wounds that show in the eyes, he thought. His new prospect wouldn't likely respond well to a man with a scowl. Not wanting to lose her as he had the last one, he struggled to quickly adjust his face to hide his pique. He reached up to check his features with his hands. Satisfied with what his fingers found, yet still out of sorts with animosity toward the gentlemen on platform 3, he moved toward the young woman.

Loud conversation and laughter rose up from the group of self-satisfied swells. Frederick glanced in their direction, saw one of the toffs use his cane to tip the cap off a porter's head. When the young man, a porter still in training, bent to pick up his hat, the swell rapped him on the backside with the cane.

They have no decency, Frederick thought. They *want everyone to know their gloating happiness.* Resentment had turned to hatred by the time he got close to the young woman.

She turned to him with an open and welcoming expression, then seemed to see his anger. Her eyes widened and her mouth opened in fear.

The smell of the grave that often warned Frederick of an oncoming spell, arrived suddenly.

The young woman backed away toward the edge of the platform, and let out a short cry, lost in the hubbub of the station.

Frederick wanted to turn away, and leave her. Instead, as his left leg quaked under him, he blundered into his prospect, knocking her off the platform. Her head struck one of the rails and split open, killing her instantly. Of course, he was unaware of that until a constable spoke about the event later at the Platt Street Police Station. Frederick had gone over the edge of the platform as well, but had not been harmed.

~ ~ ~

As he awaited trial at Newgate Prison, he presumed he had no chance of being found innocent of the charge of manslaughter. He tried to think of a way to end his life. Although he believed his spirit might stay in the prison, at least suicide would end the control others had over his person. Since the guards had taken away from him everything sharp or hard, and anything he might use to make a rope, he had precious little with which to work. The methods of suicide that remained—forms of self-strangulation, self-bludgeoning, or somehow wearing through his flesh with a dull object to open a blood vessel—he found too daunting to seriously consider.

Frederick wished he had died alongside the woman he'd killed. She'd been beautiful, and he would have gladly been wed to her through all eternity in that manner. Haunting St. Pancras Station with her would be preferable to being trapped, along with the rats and the ghosts of angry felons, within the damp stone and brick of

Newgate Prison.

Frederick paid a guard, named Dunmore, to take his cellar key and free the dog. When the man returned, he said he'd decided to take the dog in. "She's healing up well. Three legs or no, my boys love 'er. What do you call the dog?"

"I found her."

"Did you not give the dog a name, man?"

"No."

Mr. Dunmore frowned and turned away. He didn't engage Frederick in conversation after that.

~ ~ ~

At trial, Frederick pleaded not guilty. St. Pancras Station's Station Master, Mr. Temes, lied as he testified that Frederick had withheld the fact that he had epilepsy. The man had treated Frederick well, which somehow made the betrayal much worse. If ever the opportunity arose to kill Mr. Temes, Frederick thought he might do so with less feeling than he experienced when stepping on a cockroach.

When pronounced guilty, Frederick's throat tightened as if the hangman's rope were already cinched around his neck, but then sentencing didn't go as imagined.

"Would that the jury had found a verdict of Chance Medley," the judge said. "Sadly that has fallen out of favor."

Surprised with the man's tone, Frederick realized the judge thought him innocent and had nearly said as much.

"I've had it brought to my attention that you were a Surgeon's Mate aboard the HMS Challenger." The judge had used the old, obsolete term for Assistant Surgeon.

Frederick preferred the newer appellation because the title had a more official ring. He refrained from correcting the judge. "Yes, sir."

"That is a skill useful to Her Majesty's service. I'll offer you a choice. You may serve a prison term at Newgate of five years, or the same aboard the HMS Quicksilver, which has recently been hulked in the River Medway. She's a receiving vessel for criminals going into military service. If you choose the HMS Quicksilver, you'll perform the function of a Surgeon's Mate in her infirmary, but without rank."

Turned out as unfit notwithstanding, Frederick's time in the Royal Navy had been the period in his life of which he was most proud. He nodded vigorously. "Yes sir, I would gladly become the

Assistant Surgeon." There, he'd given the judge the proper term without seeming to correct. "I choose the HMS Quicksilver, sir."

Aiden: 5

Substance abuse treatment worked for me. I became an inpatient at a facility on several acres in the country, just outside of Nashville, Tennessee. The twenty-eight day treatment was based around the twelve-step program of Alcoholics Anonymous. I feared AA and its sister program, NA, because I thought I'd find myself involved with religious zealots. Even so, I entered the facility willing to do almost anything to get sober.

As a life-long agnostic, I had difficulty with the concept of a higher power at first. Admitting to the other patients that I had no religious beliefs didn't go over well. Many of them tried to persuade me to believe as they did. I got the impression that most had been godless until they'd seen the need to quit drugs or alcohol, then they'd grabbed up the faith they'd been introduced to as children. I didn't have that, since my parents weren't believers.

Troubled with the idea that the program wouldn't work for me unless I believed in a god, I spoke to the facility's pastoral counselor—a tall Methodist fellow named John Isaacson who had giant, false front teeth. We sat in his office that had a large window looking out over grassy fields that led down to the Harpeth River. The place had once been a farm, and the acreage was broken up into rectangles bordered by wind-break trees. I saw a couple of Indian burial mounds out in one of the fields.

"I've tried to believe," I told him, "I've meditated, prayed, and listened, searching for some sort of mystical presence, and I got nothing."

"Belief in a higher power," he said, "as called for in the twelve step-program, can be anything you have faith in that's greater than yourself. What have you got to work with?"

"I have the love of family and friends," I said apologetically with a shrug.

He nodded, gave me an expectant look. That gave me the impression he waited patiently for me to think the matter through. I felt comfortable in his presence.

I looked out the window for inspiration, saw again the Indian burial mounds. Whoever had owned the farm before the place became a substance abuse treatment center, had left the mounds alone, farming around them. I knew that the Indians of middle-Tennessee—Cherokee, Chickasaw, Choctaw, Creek, and Shawnee—buried their dead in the area because nearby salt springs attracted animals and so the hunting was good. Those Native American communities looked after their own, even in death.

"I have the society that raised me," I said.

His eyebrows arched. Perhaps he wasn't used to patients trusting human beings as a group.

"Sure," I said, "lots of people in the world are up to no good, but so many more try to keep the best interests of human kind in mind. I've had people I don't know, at risk to their own safety, save me from danger. How could they have known if I was worth the risk? They didn't."

He nodded. "Love of fellow man."

"Yes," I agreed. "I suppose those acts of kindness are an unconditional love I can look up to."

"That's important."

I feared in that moment that he might begin to evangelize, yet he didn't.

I knew that many people had the opinion that the goodwill I spoke of wouldn't exist without religious faith. With such compassion common among religions that were at odds with one another, I was of the opinion that goodwill arose from human society, as did the religions themselves. The community of man was a lot bigger than me, and had supported and safeguarded my existence. While as a higher power, human society didn't represent the level of perfection some sought in a deity, I'd never needed perfection. I was a gray-area sort of guy.

"I believe in human beings," I said simply.

"Sounds like you've got some good stuff," John said.

That hardly settled the matter for me. Still, some of what weighed me down had lifted.

"Try not to be troubled by the idea of failure," John said. He paused, smiled crookedly, and said, "One guy who came to us, chose the campus dog as his higher power because dog spelled backwards is God. He'd talk to her. My impression is that he told the dog about what troubled him. He left us years ago and comes back regularly, at first to visit the dog, and eventually to visit her grave. He's still sober as far as I know."

I liked John and his goofy teeth. He had a sense of humor. I could see it in his smile. I left his office feeling a lot lighter.

Since religion wasn't required, I remained agnostic.

I couldn't have concisely explained my higher power. Suffice it to say that I had one, and therefore not only got sober with the twelve-step program, but was also relieved of the desire to drink. With the help of substance abuse treatment and AA, I gained some understanding and acceptance of myself. Terribly flawed and won-derfully capable, I found myself to be particularly human. I could accept that. I could drink, and chose not to. I was an alcoholic and always would be. With that knowledge came an awareness that I was a danger to myself when I drank, and to others as well.

Finding so many sober alcoholics surprised me. If I'd known how many survived their disease, I might not have waited so long to get sober. Figuring that knowledge of my struggle and sobriety might help others, I became vocal about being an alcoholic instead of staying anonymous.

~ ~ ~

I came home from substance abuse treatment and started a new life, one in which all the things that addiction made difficult had suddenly become a lot easier. A layer of complexity had fallen away. No longer did I have to worry about keeping lies straight.

"I don't have to take beer with me everywhere I go," I told Mel-ody. "Waking up in the morning is painless. I don't have next-day embarrassment from the thoughtless and foolish things I said the night before."

"Do you mean that you don't care anymore what you say and do?" she asked sarcastically.

"You know what I mean."

With sobriety, everything seemed possible. Melody and I became close again. She seemed much happier and more sociable with friends and family. We found endless projects, especially around the house, to work on together. We traveled more, some for business, some for pleasure. She became more involved in my illustration work.

When Melody wasn't traveling with me, often Mama did. Since

her other children lived in various places outside of Nashville, and Daddy went to work each week-day, she had a lot of free time and wanted to travel. She'd ask me, "What cities are you going to this year?" I'd tell her, and she'd pick some. "We can take my car and I'll pay for the gasoline," she'd say, and I'd jump at the chance.

Joan Clark and I went to a lot of science fiction, fantasy, and horror conventions together. She'd go to galleries, museums, gardens, or sit in the hotel room and read as I attended the event. The authors, illustrators, and fans I hung out with enjoyed her company when she joined us for dinners and lunches.

We also went to New York so I could meet with art directors. Since Mama was from New York and we still had family and friends there, I always had a place to stay in Manhattan. Looking for illustration work, I'd been making that particular run since 1985.

~ ~ ~

In 1980, right after college, while still living with my parents, I'd had a show of paintings at the Vanderbilt University Club. The art gallery at the club was spacious, with lots of well-lit wall space for large paintings. The show and reception were well-attended. I'd included in the exhibit of twenty or thirty pieces several surreal planetscapes; odd alien worlds seen from space with surrounding scenery, like nebula and other stellar events. The Nashville Science Fiction Club president, Ken Moore, bought a painting from the show and spoke to me at the artist's reception. He was a tall lanky fellow who cussed a lot.

"If you could paint space ships," he said, "well, shit, you could make it as a science fiction illustrator."

So far, I hadn't done well at getting my artwork into galleries. I got the show at the University Club because my parents knew the art director well. Gallery owners frequently told me that my surreal artwork wasn't appropriate for their clients. One actually said, "Surrealism is a dead art form."

Since I'd always enjoyed reading science fiction and frequently liked the cover art, I listened to Ken Moore carefully. "You should enter your stuff in the fucking art show of the science fiction convention here in Nashville, Kubla Khan."

I would later find out that Ken had a large collection of science fiction and aviation art. He'd been a big influence in making art shows a staple of science fiction conventions across the United States.

I went to Kubla Khan and met several artists. Long before I got sober, I spent most of my time there drunk. I saw that science fiction illustration seemed a promising route for me. The seasoned illustrators I met eagerly helped the younger artists, even the drunkard newbies, like me. My artwork was well-received, and I sold several pieces.

"I know most of the editors in New York," Ken told me. "You build a goddamn portfolio to present to paperback art directors, and I'll help you connect with folks in New York." I'd been to Ken's house and had been wowed by his collection of illustration. Every wall in his home held a great piece of art, professionally framed and under non-glare glass. He had work by a couple of my favorites, Richard Powers and Paul Lerh, both surrealists as far as I was concerned, and an inspiration to me as I considered how my work might fit into the field.

The effort to build a portfolio took me a while because I had to learn how to paint science fiction hardware. I also had a lot of drinking to do between bouts of painting.

Ken commented on some of my early efforts. "Hell, Aiden, those spaceships look more like pieces of fruit,"

Yeah, well, I was a surrealist. I kept trying.

By late 1984, I was ready. I went to Ken's house and we made phone calls. Sure enough, he had connections and I ended up making appointments with art directors for many of the major mass-market paperback houses.

I was grateful to Ken for that.

My first trip in 1985, I got no work, yet I learned a lot. I got around the city in cabs, did a lot of walking, and paid way too much to keep myself fed and watered. I had been going to New York once or twice a year ever since then. I made appointments with art directors, met with them, left samples of my artwork, and hoped they'd call me with book cover assignments. Slowly but surely I'd gotten work.

Before one of my trips, my friend, Jack Daves, gave me a buckeye. "Take this with you to your appointments," he said. "Rub it and it'll bring you luck."

I don't automatically believe in such things, so I showed skepticism.

"Just carry it with you in your pocket," Jack said. "Do it for me."

Jack had always given me lots of emotional support for my efforts to get work. He was a horror writer, a good one. He and Melody got me to produce paintings for my portfolio that explored horror subject matter. Back then, horror books didn't usually have much more than a skull on them, so I didn't think creepy illustrations would fly far. I was wrong. Publishers didn't pay much attention to me until I started creating the darker subject matter.

I needed all the help I could get with art directors in New York, so I did as Jack suggested and put the buckeye in my pocket.

At a science fiction convention, I'd worked up the courage to speak to the senior editor for the Doubleday Science Fiction Book Club. Although she was a small, unassuming middle-aged woman, quite friendly, I was particularly uneasy and overawed by her presence.

"Call me Ruth," she said.

She looked at my work with me in the convention art show, then asked me to come see her at the book club offices when next I came to New York so she could introduce me to the company's art director.

When I arrived for my appointment, Ruth was busy working on a large jigsaw puzzle of a popular soda pop logo. She told me the art director would be in shortly, and that while I waited I should feel free to help her with the puzzle. Uncertain what to make of that, I stood about nervously, rubbing the buckeye in my pocket. If the office were in a film, there would have been a large window to look out on the city. Instead, a small window gave a gloomy view of the back sides of other buildings. Ruth graciously allowed me to fidget until I relaxed. Eventually, I put a couple pieces into the puzzle.

The art director, a young man named John with a head full of curly red hair and a scraggily beard, arrived and I showed my work there in Ruth's office. They both seemed pleased with what I'd done. I left samples of my artwork, and then moved on to my next appointment.

Not long after I got home to Nashville, John called from the Doubleday Science Fiction Book Club to offer me a book cover assignment. "The job has a short deadline of two weeks," he said.

"You'll receive the manuscript tomorrow."

I accepted the assignment, wrote down the particulars, and hung up.

Excited, I called Jack.

"What's the job?" he asked.

"Manly Wade Wellman's *John the Balladeer*."

"Oh man," he said. "Manly Wade Wellman is just about my favorite writer."

"So you know the stories?"

"Know them? John is known as Silver John. Wellman's stories about that character are his best work. John fights evil in the Appalachian Mountains with hoodoo; folk magic, charms, and wildcrafting. The stories appeared in old pulp magazines, but now I guess they'll all be collected in one place—that's great."

The next day, the manuscript arrived at my home—a lot of pages—and I realized I had some intense work ahead of me. I had to get a feel for the material, come up with a sketch, get that approved, and do the cover painting. At that time, we didn't have the ability to view work remotely with computer or cell phone technology. Without the means to receive a scan of an image, publishers had to have the original artwork in hand. Actual sketches and paintings were shipped for approval. Once they had a finished cover painting, they'd have a large format transparency made of the image from which color separations were made for offset printing. Even fax technology wouldn't work well enough to get the point of my sketch across to the art director. No—he'd have to hold the original in his hand.

"I'm a slow reader, and have little time," I told Jack over the phone. "I've been asked to do a depiction of Silver John. Can you give me advice?"

"I can point out three or four of the stories that will give you the feel for what you're doing. Oh, and for John, you could use Troy Guinn for a photo shoot. Dress him in a floppy hat, jeans, and combat boots, put a guitar in his hands, and he'll be perfect."

I read the stories. Our friend, Troy, agreed to help and we did the photo shoot in my back yard. I did a sketch which was approved. I produced the cover images and shipped the painting to New York. Everyone seemed pleased, especially Jack. I got paid.

Nearly a year passed before I received my contributor's copy. I sat down to read the stories I had not yet read. In one of them, Silver John mentioned carrying a buckeye for good luck.

Astounded, I called Jack to tell him.

His reaction: "Yeah, I know. That's where I got the idea."

Mysteriously, delightfully, he would not respond to questions about his lack of surprise.

~ ~ ~

All of that was before I had brain abscesses, before substance abuse treatment. With sobriety, I had a new confidence and my work had improved. I was finally getting assignments on a consistent basis. Many were for magazines that didn't pay all that well, but I filled my days with whatever work I could get.

Not all was rosy. The James family—brothers, sisters, and a mom—moved into the little place next door, where prostitutes and drug addicts once lived. Melody and I had thought they would be an improvement. Instead, they turned out to be a surly bunch. Okay, so they were much worse than that. I tried to be friendly. The James family didn't want that. They had keggers that resulted in fist fights out front of their house that rolled on over into our yard. The folks who showed up for their parties used our front lawn as a place to park their giant trucks. We had numerous items stolen from our property such as a porch swing, bonsai, and a bicycle. Intuitively, I knew I shouldn't piss those people off, so I tried to live and let live. We installed a security system, and felt marginally better about our safety.

The Trillepetol was an uncomfortable part of daily life, hampering my memory and sapping my energy. I had to make lists of the things I hoped to get done each day. I took naps in the afternoon to recover energy so I could go on with the day.

With Mama's help in traveling, and Melody's assistance with my work at home, I got more done than I might have on my own and my illustration business did well.

All the good that had come from becoming sober didn't prevent my anxieties about the possibility of relapse—going back out, as they say in AA. Perhaps all the good actually made me fear relapse more because the contrast with my old life was so obvious. I knew the first drink would take me right back to the hell of where I'd been.

One day while Melody and I painted the house a pale lavender with gray-purple trim, I made the mistake of talking to her about my fear. "Because I haven't had any desire for alcohol, I'm afraid it's going to sneak up on me."

She got a pained look as she listened, and had no words to reassure me. I knew that was because she shared the fear and didn't want to face it.

"I lied, cheated, and broke promises for so long, there's no wonder we're both afraid," I said, not knowing when to quit. "All I can do is to stay away from the stuff long enough that I demonstrate to both of us that I'm capable of being a different sort of person."

Melody had nothing to say about my drinking, and clearly didn't want to talk to me about it. She cursed as she got trim color where it didn't belong several times. My words had shaken her. Stupidly, I'd been unaware that she remained tormented by my addiction. From then on, I would only talk about the fear of relapse in AA meetings.

Melody remained on edge for a long time, waiting for my next binge, but she didn't allow the discomfort she felt to make things more difficult for me. She didn't watch me closely. If she had any suspicions about what I got up to when out of her presence—and after the way I'd been, I have no doubt Melody had them—she never expressed any to me.

I felt lucky to have no desire for alcohol. I went to AA meetings and moved forward with my life.

With time, I felt a lot more emotionally stable. Looking back on what I'd been through, I saw the suffering as part of a transition necessary for a good life. Without the abscesses and then the Trillepetol making the drinking so much more miserable, I might not have been willing to try abstinence. Although I remembered telling Dr. Reed, "Lucky is not getting brain abscesses at all," I decided that they'd been the best thing that ever happened to me.

Much later, I would change my mind again.

Frederick: 5

The monotony of life on the hulk of an old ship wore on Frederick for the first year as he had time to endlessly review the events that led to his incarceration. Forced to look at himself, an uncomfortable process that never worked well, he decided he wasn't as smart as he'd previously believed himself to be. Even if he hadn't had the fit which resulted in the young woman's death, he knew his plan had been too complicated. If at the moment he'd put his scheme into motion, a random circumstance had rendered all his careful planning useless, how many other ways might the effort have failed, given the hours necessary for him to take the desired satisfaction from the young woman's body, piece by piece? He tried to put his notions about young women to rest. With time, he seemed to succeed.

An overseer named Milner, a crew of guards, and a cook—landsmen all—manned the hulk. The surgeon, Mr. Swoon, was the only one among them who had gone to sea. The middle-aged man had a pink, cheerful face, a head of curly gray locks, and a plump, pear-shaped body. He kept a room in Chatham, and occasionally spent nights on the hulk, sleeping on a folding army cot.

The overseer had the captain's cabin, the cook slept and worked in the galley, and the mess deck had been converted into quarters for the guards. The hold of the ship was broken up into small cells with no doors, each with a bunk and a shelf. The prisoners ate in their cells. They worked by day, keeping the vessel clean, and spent nights arguing, singing, and telling tall tales.

Frederick settled into his roll on the hulk, and kept to himself when not on duty. He read anything he could find. Each morning except Sunday, he rose at six o'clock and ate a simple meal of porridge, then reported to the infirmary where he was at the beck and call of the surgeon for twelve hours, even during the fifteen minutes provided for luncheon at noon.

At night, Frederick returned to his cell among those occupied by the criminals waiting to ship out.

"You needn't fear the prisoners," Mr. Swoon told him early on. "They know they may well have to depend on your physics. They will treat you with respect, begrudgingly perhaps, but respect none-theless. If I were you, I'd keep my distance from the guards. They'll turn on you."

"I'll keep it in mind, sir," Frederick said. He would have felt safer with a knife in his belt. If one of the prisoners got the blade away from him, though, there would be hell to pay. "I would think they'd lock us in at night."

"Few of these men can swim. The odd one who can, if he were to leap overboard and try for the shore, a guard on the upper deck would put shot in his back. If that guard failed, those on either shore would be alerted. By the time the felon got to one or the other bank, he'd be spotted and captured."

Frederick could swim. He considered making an escape. If he got into the water unnoticed and floated far enough downstream before climbing ashore, he could get away. If the work he was given to do hadn't been interesting, he might have made the attempt.

"You have a good way with those suffering," Mr. Swoon said one day while watching Frederick treat a man who writhed in pain from ulcers of the feet.

"Thank you, sir. I have only one strength when it comes to pro-viding care to the sick and wounded. I am able to remain calm no matter how they carry on, wailing their pain and misery."

The older man looked the younger squarely in the eyes. "It is that calm manner to which I refer."

The surgeon had a wealth of medical knowledge Frederick hoped to mine. He proved his willingness to perform for Mr. Swoon at every opportunity. With a few well-placed compliments of his own, earnest conversations about techniques and treatments, he drew the surgeon out over time. Frederick held Mr. Swoon in high regard. The man wasn't ambitious. Bordering on guileless, he preferred to trust his fel-low human being, and wanted nothing so much as to do good.

Frederick's efforts paid off after eighteen months.

"If you're willing," the surgeon said, "I'll teach you what I know."

"I am more than willing, sir," Frederick said.

More than interesting, his term on the prison ship became a use-ful one as well. He enlarged his knowledge of treatments for all man-ner of illnesses and injuries, especially those to which hard men who'd led desperate lives were susceptible. Only occasionally did he see a man in a condition he hadn't seen before, but the surgeon introduced Frederick to new methods in the preparation of medicinal powders, poultices, salves, and injections. His techniques in lancing, bleeding, cupping, blistering, as well as minor surgeries improved as well.

Frederick became excited when he heard fist fights break out among the prisoners. Mr. Milner, a strict disciplinarian, had given the guards orders to mercilessly put down such conflicts with truncheon, bayonet, or pistol shot. If Frederick were lucky, one of the combatants ended up on a table in the infirmary, needing stitches or, better still, the amputation of a severely damaged limb.

Mr. Swoon performed the first amputation Frederick saw on the hulk. The second, the removal of a left foot, he performed under the surgeon's guidance. As he did so, he felt himself gain an erection. The act of cutting into human flesh brought to mind sexual penetration, and Frederick's past daydreams of taking a young woman apart presented themselves again.

What harm if it is mere fancy? No, I would be in London but for those notions. He angrily pushed them aside, and concentrated on his work. Still, his erection persisted.

"You have some experience, I see," Mr. Swoon said after the procedure had been completed.

Frederick chewed his lip and looked toward the exit of the infirmary. He feared that his flimsy uniform left his erection obvious. "I must go to the head," he said.

Mr. Swoon looked at him sympathetically. "Even those of us with a strong constitution become queasy when it comes to removing a limb. Off you go, then."

Thankfully, night had fallen and the upper deck watch avoided the head because of the smell. Stroking his erection, Frederick quickly brought himself to release as he stood before one of the rectangular chutes that emptied into the river below. Having felt little need to find sexual release since before his charge of murder, he'd presumed that the cooks at Newgate Prison and on the hulk put salt peter in his food. If that were true, his need after the amputation had been powerful indeed.

~ ~ ~

The insect population from the marshes around the River Medway, particularly the mosquitoes that bred in profusion, vexed

Frederick through much of the year, most of all during the summer months. The rats on the Quicksilver and their turds, the weevils and maggots in the food, the fleas, and the infestations of lice brought aboard whenever the hulk received new prisoners, remained intermittent irritations year-round. When the tide was up and the river ran sluggishly, the stink of fecal material in the river below the head became powerful, especially during warm weather. The waterway also carried to the sea the waste from Chatham and Rochester, among other towns. Riddled as the structure was with worms and other aquatic life, the reek of the slowly rotting hulk added to the horrid fetor. All of the wretched smells got into Frederick's nose as one great stench he feared might give him a terrible disease. He brought up his concern with Mr. Swoon.

"Yes," the surgeon said, "the miasma rises from the water and at times becomes trapped within the hulk. It preys upon those of a weak constitution. Many of the illnesses the prisoners suffer are brought on by the smell, but they are men with weak minds. A weak mind leaves the body vulnerable to certain diseases. You and I are made of sterner stuff."

Mr. Swoon had never asked Frederick what he'd done to be sent to the prison ship. Whatever the surgeon might have believed about his assistant's crime, he didn't seem to hold that against him.

The most pleasant times on the Quicksilver occurred when the breeze from the sea picked up speed and cleansed the vessel and surroundings. Holes in the immobilized ship's structure sang hollowly in the wind. Drying laundry, dangling from lines running from what spars the hulk had remaining, snapped and flapped rhythmically.

On a Saturday evening, Frederick had returned to the infirmary for a purgative to help his constipation, when he discovered Mr. Swoon in the locked cell where the medicines were kept. The man lay insensible on the cot within. Beside him, on a small table rested a bottle of chloroform. A handkerchief, still smelling of the drug, dangled from the fingers of his left hand. Frederick decided to mind his own business and left the infirmary.

Frederick found the surgeon in the same condition numerous times and with increasing frequency. Each time, Mr. Swoon had spent the night on the cot, and a bottle of chloroform stood nearby. With time, the surgeon gave up his room in Chatham, and spent all his nights on the hulk.

One morning, Frederick discovered the surgeon just as the man awoke on the cot. "If you please," Mr. Swoon said, "don't tell anyone about this."

"Who would I tell, sir?" Frederick asked. "What would I say? No one should concern themselves with your nightly needs."

"Yes, it has become a nightly habit." Mr. Swoon looked troubled as he said the words, but then he smiled. "Let me take you ashore to the Friend or Foe for a meal."

"I can't leave the hulk, sir."

"We'll see about that."

Mr. Swoon took Frederick before Mr. Milner. "I'd like my assistant to accompany me to Chatham to help in retrieving supplies."

Frederick had attended Mr. Milner a month earlier for nearly a week while the man suffered an anal fistula. Frederick made incisions into the infected tissues twice, returned every hour to express pus from the fistula for two days, and provided warm compresses throughout the overseer's recovery. Frederick worried that he might experience sexual excitement during the surgery, yet the grotesque nature of the malady, especially the reek of the corrupted tissue so close to the bowel, had been anything but stimulating. Although Mr. Milner suffered embarrassment upon being examined in such an indelicate manner, Frederick attended him with a professional air that restored the overseer's dignity. Mr. Milner had shown his gratitude with praise and a gift of dried fruit.

"Of course, he may go," the overseer said. "He is the Assistant Surgeon."

Frederick smiled to hear the title.

That night, they had a fine fish dinner at the Friend or Foe tavern in Chatham.

"And what shall you have to drink?" Mr. Swoon asked as they sat down for their meal. "They have a good stout."

"I'll make do with water, sir," Frederick said.

"Oh, but a bit of drink will do you good. I would have all the prisoners on the hulk take mild drink regularly if it didn't excite some to violence. Susceptibility to diseases carried by the miasma of the river settles first in the bowel. The alcohol in mild drink helps one purge such illnesses through the stool. And, of course, it'll put you at ease."

Frederick didn't like becoming intoxicated. He had difficulty enough seeing himself as others did. When intoxicated, he found his words and actions somehow unexpected and therefore frightening. "I don't like the feeling drink gives me."

"Takes getting used to for some." Mr. Swoon nodded. The surgeon's face took on a bright smile and his blue eyes seemed to focus on something far away, beyond the confining walls of the tavern. Then he looked at Frederick and spoke low as if he feared someone might overhear. "A better intoxication can be had. The visions I get with chloroform! I joined the Royal Navy in the hopes of seeing the beautiful islands of tropical climes. All I got was the Baltic Sea. I had begun to think that life had passed me by until I discovered chloroform. I doubt the West Indies has anything to compare with the gardens I visit with but a few inhalations."

Visions—Frederick had had enough of those!

"You have always seemed on the edge of yourself," the surgeon continued, "so serious and guarded. Intoxication in small doses does us a world of good, restoring good humor, and fortifying us against the hardships of life. My use of the chloroform truly serves that purpose. You would do well to try it sometime. I could recommend that you stay the night in the infirmary or come to your cell at lights-out and administer a dose, if you'd like."

Frederick assumed that the quality of visions, like noses, varied with the individual. He would not willingly return to his visions, and the judging presence that seemed to inhabit them.

"You are generous to offer, yet I must decline."

"As you please."

And Frederick *was* pleased with the surgeon. The man had taken him under his wing, and seemed to want him as a friend as well as a colleague. After that first outing, Mr. Swoon found other reasons to take his assistant with him when he left the hulk. Frederick was grateful for the short tastes of freedom.

~ ~ ~

As the end of Frederick's five year term neared, Mr. Swoon sat him down with an offer. "I work well with you," he said. "You've kept my secret, and I'm most grateful. If you would stay on after your term has ended, say another five years, I will see that you are reinstated with proper rank and that you receive your certificate of service. That will provide you with a pension. Since we are not truly afloat, your pay will be that of an Ordinary Seaman."

Although the pay was next to nothing, Frederick felt himself grin. He so rarely smiled, he had to feel his face with the fingers of both hands to verify the feeling.

"Don't stand there pulling on your face," Mr. Swoon said, also smiling. "Give me an answer."

Frederick had put aside the dangerous urges of his past. He rarely thought of women at all, except on the few occasions that he'd divided human flesh with a surgeon's knife. When that happened, he found a moment to seek release and thought little of the act or the need. His anger seemed to have seeped away over the years. He enjoyed his work, the security of his position, and the level of respect he received.

"Well, yes, sir," he said. "That would be a fine thing."

Aiden: 6

After the self-imposed isolation of my heavy drinking, I craved social interaction. I wanted that with creative people who had a sense of humor, because I definitely needed to laugh, especially at myself.

"Start meeting with friends once a week here at the house," Melody suggested. "You can sit around and get silly with them."

I was lucky to have kept my pals. Most weren't heavy drinkers—I'd never enjoyed the company of drunks, even when that happened to be me—so I had no problem hanging out with old friends while sober.

I started a creative group, a mix of artists of different sorts; musicians, visual artists, writers. We met around the dining room table at my house. The room had been painted pink by the previous owner of the home, and Melody and I hadn't gotten around to changing the color yet. The oak table, which we'd bought at a naked furniture store and finished with tung oil, seated eight, and took up most of the tiny room's floor space. The back of the room had a door that led into the kitchen and a broad passthrough in the wall, good for serving snacks and drinks.

The members included Randy Fox, and my cousin, Stephen C. Merritt. Those two got me writing again. I hadn't done much since college. Having grown up in rural Kentucky, Randy had a strong southern accent. He loved rockabilly and country music. A funny guy, he got really goofy at times to make folks laugh. Stephen was one of my tall relations, a first cousin on my father's side. Having grown up in Nashville in the same weird family, we had a lot in common.

We also had Beth Gwinn, a photographer, Troy Guinn, a musician and writer, Jon Davis and Jim Goad, both writers, and several more who came and went over time, like Dave Conover from Louisville, Kentucky. Dave was a great story-teller and funny as hell, yet he remained shy for the first couple of hours of any visit before opening up. His creative territories included film, special-effects makeup, sculpture, screen-writing, and short fiction.

We had one member, Mark Edwards, just along for the ride. He said he had no artistic aspirations. We kept him because of his contagious enthusiasm and his sense of humor.

At the first meeting, I showed the group a sketch for a painting that I would eventually title "Mr. Hands." I passed the drawing around the table. The artwork depicted an ugly, fifteen-foot-tall monster walking through an icy landscape on giant, over-sized hands. As the beast stood on hoofed finger-tips, the short, atrophied stumps of its legs dangled uselessly above the ground. A basket strapped to the creature's back held several dead human beings, their blood, frozen in icicles or bloodcicles as I called them, hanging from the bottom of the basket.

"Why is he carrying the dead people?" Jim Goad asked.

"That's up to you," I said.

"I think he eats them," Randy said, holding the sketch up. "He's got some saved for later. They keep well in the frozen air."

More questions and possible answers followed. The group had a lot of fun with the image.

Finally, Jim asked, "Why'd you say it's up to me?"

"It's up to each of you. Make up your own minds about what's going on in the piece. I've been eavesdropping on conversations around my artwork at art shows and noticed that the images that pose lots of questions are the ones audiences find the most interesting."

"Don't you have something specific in mind, though?" Randy asked.

"I suppose I do, but I've decided there's real value in allowing viewers to make up their own minds. I want the image to be suggestive in a way that pushes viewers toward their own story-telling. Many book covers are frozen action scenes with the conclusion of the action inevitable and predictable, often something we've seen before. We, the audience, have little or no work to do while viewing the art. We aren't invited in and asked to contribute. In my illustrations, I want to suggest possible stories, yet not pin them down too tightly. The axiom used in teaching writing, 'Show, don't tell,' is a good way to think about how I want to set up the narrative quality in my illustrations. If my audience has work to do when viewing my images, as they do in reading a good story, I think the artwork will be more memorable."

That set the tone for future meetings. After that, everyone brought in works in progress, and talked about how they pursued their goals and why. Critique wasn't welcome unless asked for. Even then, the members weren't heavy-handed. Intuitively, they all knew that works in progress, incomplete projects that remained highly flawed, could be torn apart easily, and no one wanted to receive a bashing when their time came to share. Trusting one another to show that kind of respect fostered a willingness among the members to reveal the often tender and vulnerable early stages of creative process.

Each member could invite guests to the meeting. Guests weren't members until invited to a second meeting. Trust in the members being paramount, any of us could veto a guest being invited back.

At the beginnings or endings of meetings, while we sat around in the pink dining room talking about whatever came to mind, we had a tendency to tell stories. Randy arrived one night all worked up over something that happened at the bank where he worked.

"A fellow came in wearing a hoodie pulled down low over his face. By the time I noticed him, Sharon was handing over the cash from her drawer."

Since she also worked at a bank, Melody got interested in the story, and sat at the table to join us.

"Instead of leaping into action," Randy said, "I heard myself say 'uh-oh' loud enough for everyone to hear, including the robber. As he neared the exit, I snapped out of it and turned to trigger the alarm. Then I hesitated. Maybe I was about to make a terrible mistake. What if the guy had just made a large withdrawal?"

We all laughed at him. Randy invited that, as he laughed too.

"But, no—I was on top of the situation, heroic in fact, as I assessed the hoodie, the furtive look in his eyes, the pillow case full of loot, the speed of the guy as he hurried to the exit. Finally, I triggered the alarm.

"He got out the door and halfway across the street before the dye bomb went off, dousing him in purple paint. The police must have been in the neighborhood because they rode up at that moment. The bank robber just got into the police car and they drove away."

Randy's giggling kept us all laughing. Like me, he preferred to laugh at the scary things in life. He and Melody then competed to see who could tell the most ridiculous bank-robber-dye-bomb stories. They'd both been involved in more than one robbery and had seen several stupid criminals become purple.

Early on, we decided we needed a name for our group. We liked the formality of calling ourselves a society, yet it had to be something ridiculous: the (ridiculous name) Society. Before one of the meetings began, we sat around trying different ideas. Nothing seemed to stick, so we quit, and I told a story Daddy had told me, one that had always left me skeptical.

"My father was a boy when his family moved into the house where I grew up. Across the creek, a farmer had cows in a field. One had grown a huge gut over a couple of days. Then, one afternoon, even as my father watched, the cow grew bigger, and bigger, it's stomach stretching out like a balloon and becoming translucent. Finally, the cow exploded!"

They all stared at me dumbly for a moment, with big goofy smiles.

"Yes, it literally exploded, or so he told me. He said he later found out that sometimes cows get a disorder in which they can't fart properly. The gas builds up, and, well…"

They broke from their surprise into scoffing. Nobody believed the story any more than I did, but the tale was good for a laugh, an important part of the story-telling we did.

When the meeting began, and my turn to present came along, I appropriately delivered a cow. I'd tried to make a poem out of visual elements from my Deadwood Series. Since producing the painting, "Half Scairt," I'd done at least three more pieces that depicted sticks and dry leaves, dead tree roots, trunks, and broken limbs in the shapes of corpses or skeletal demons. The poem had a dumb line: "Bovine smoke in the distance," inspired by vapor rising from the nostrils of cattle seen in the background of "Half Scairt."

Everyone laughed, and I cringed. Yeah, I was insecure about my writing. I've never been much of a poet. Even as I read the words, I knew the line sounded dumb. I meant the poem to be creepy and disturbing, not funny.

John saw me cringe. "No, it's amazing."

"*Amazingly* bad," I said.

"Yeah, not the poem. That's shit. I mean the image in my

head!"

"Yes, bovine smoke," Mark Edwards hooted. "Exploding cows! You wrote that thinking about your father's story, right?"

I pictured what he meant and laughed. "No, just a coincidence," I said, "a pretty funny one." I still felt small and embarrassed, even though I knew I shouldn't—not with those friends.

Randy had become lost in thought for a moment. He emerged with an idea. "That's our name, The Bovine Smoke Society! We could have a logo of an exploding cow."

When we'd stopped giggling, we agreed that would be the name of our group.

The next week, Randy brought in a catalog of farm supplies and equipment that he'd picked up while visiting family in Kentucky. One of the products for sale looked something like a giant syringe as big as my arm, with a needle the size of a railroad spike. The text description for the item didn't quite say the thing deflated cows, but that seemed obvious enough.

The sharing continued over the next few years. A member who presented the start of a project one week might bring the finished work in the next or show progress over the course of several weeks before the work was completed. I got to witness a lot of creative process, which I've always found more educational than instruction from professors. The Bovine Smoke Society got weird together, unabashed and with no regrets. We honed our various crafts and found publishers for some of our projects. My writing improved and I began to make professional sales of my short fiction to anthologies and magazines.

~ ~ ~

Melody had always wanted to work in the travel industry, to do something involving hotels, air travel, and vacation planning. She took a course to gain skills in that field, then got a job with a company that ran a travel club. They started her on the night shift. She wouldn't have taken the job, though, if they hadn't promised she'd be moved to a day shift as soon as possible.

"All they want me to do is man the phone," she said after the first few days of work. She lay on our bed while I tickled her back. That was the best way to help her relax. "They listen in on my conversations with clients. I never know when. They scrutinize and criticize constantly. Although I try to do a good job, I can't seem to do a thing right."

I assumed she'd eventually settle in and be okay with the job, yet things kept getting worse for her.

After a week, she came home wrung out from stress. "I hate that job," she said. "The management's policies are invasive and oppressive. I'm trying to get along, but it's difficult."

I fed her dinner, then said, "You should get some bourbon and have a drink."

"I wouldn't want it to tempt you."

"It won't."

She looked at me like she knew better.

"I never get tempted when I'm around people who drink. I use wine and beer in some of my recipes."

"We're not having it around the house," she said. "No, just let me complain."

I listened and tried to be supportive, to tell her she was smart and capable. Melody already knew I loved her, though, so she didn't really hear me.

Her experience on the job got worse.

"I feel horrible all the time, and dread each day." She looked bad, with dark circles under her eyes, a creased brow, and a wary look about her. When not at work, she slept most of the time, and her waking life became almost exclusively about that stinking job.

"Come home and work with me," I said.

"We won't earn enough."

"We'll cut back on what we spend. Your happiness is more important than the money."

By the time she gave up the job, she'd become a nervous wreck.

Melody worked with me for the next two and a half years, her help with my illustration business invaluable.

~ ~ ~

About the time Melody quit that crappy job, the James family next door took up a new profession. They ran a chop shop on the property, with customers coming and going in front, while cars were disassembled out back. If we saw any of the James family, as we came and went through the front of our home, they stared at us in a way meant to intimidate. They drove their stolen vehicles across our back yard into theirs. Again, for our safety, I decided to suck it up and tolerate the abuse.

~ ~ ~

The Bovine Smoke Society, six of us anyway, collaborated on a story inspired by a series of paintings I did while trying to capture some of the feel of my hospital stay. The Pain Doctors series didn't depict anything I actually saw or experienced, but the artwork had the emotional feel of the long medical episode, the temporal lobe seizures, and hallucinations, with an element of dark humor thrown in. We packaged the story and samples of the artwork as a proposal and sold the book to a publisher. *The Pain Doctors of Suture Self General* was an 11"X14" picture book for grownups. I was nominated for the World Fantasy Award for Best Artist in 1994, I believe, on the strength of the artwork I did for *The Pain Doctors of Suture Self General.*

Melody and I attended the World Fantasy Convention in New Orleans, and went to the awards banquet in the Clarion Hotel ballroom with a couple hundred others, professionals and fans of fantasy and horror. The place settings had Mardi Gras masks and tiny, souvenir bottles of tabasco sauce. I didn't think I'd win the award, the other nominees being all highly accomplished illustrators, so I enjoyed my dinner and the good cheer while fairly well at ease. When time came to announce the winner of the Best Artist Award, the Presenter said, "We have a tie, Jeff Potter and Aiden M. Clark." Too bad Jeff Potter hadn't come to the convention. He was tall, and I could have hidden behind him.

Standing to approach the microphone situated on a small stage past the dining tables, my heart leapt in my chest. With all those professional writers, artists, and editors watching me, I found myself at a loss for words. Like an idiot, I hadn't prepared anything to say. Ramsey Campbell patted me on the shoulder as I walked by. I liked his writing a lot and he'd shown great interest in my artwork over the years. Seeing his beaming face with a smile so like that of a little boy, I thought of a particular irony in my receiving the award. I knew what to say as I faced the crowd.

"As a boy, I hated school. Instead of being there, I wanted to run free and make things with my hands. My parents were disappointed in me for my performance in school. My brother and two sisters made high grades. Most of mine were Cs and Ds. I'm a slow reader, and had difficulty concentrating on it when young. My father, who loved to read throughout his life, didn't accept that I didn't love it too. For Christmas and birthdays, he gave me books I shamefully knew I wouldn't read."

From such a large gathering of fiction enthusiasts, I expected the revelation of my youthful heresy might draw gasps. Even so, the audience remained respectful.

"Although grade school was bad enough, junior high truly sucked. I began seventh grade at a brand new giant school that had no windows to speak of and several classrooms in one space separated by light partitions. Being a small human being, bullies targeted me. The next year, eighth grade, I rebelled against my parents and the society that kept me imprisoned in school. I didn't study and did no homework."

I'm sure they wanted me off the stage, but I wasn't finished. I had to get there quickly, or they'd usher me off.

"Tension among the students grew because desegregation busing had begun that year, so I kept my head down in a book. Not a school book, though. No—friends had introduced me to the writing of H. P. Lovecraft. His imagination got my attention. I sat in the back of class and read his fiction and all the associated horror pulp that came out in paperback that year, 1971."

I saw a few heads nodding and knew the audience could see where I was going. I relaxed.

"Of course, I failed the eighth grade. My father reacted as if I had seriously damaged my life."

I let that sink in for a moment, then held the award high and said, "Yet now I am honored to receive the bust of H. P. Lovecraft. What an influence he turned out to be. Thank you for the award."

I can still hear the applause that followed!

Afterward, no strange notions that the award might be taken away occurred to me. I didn't feel like a fraud. Instead, I felt quite grateful and worthy of the honor. Melody and I had glowing memories of the convention, of touring the French Quarter and New Orleans cemeteries, and hanging out with wonderful friends, creative minds and fans alike.

Later, when we'd returned to Nashville, while visiting at my parents' house one evening, I told Daddy what I'd said at the award ceremony, and how I felt about the honor.

He smiled, gave me a big hug, and said, "I'm proud of you and what you've accomplished with your art."

I barely held back tears of joy.

Frederick: 6

In early spring of 1887, Frederick had been an Assistant Surgeon for fourteen years. He and Mr. Swoon had been moved five years earlier to the hulk of the Turnswift, a much smaller, corvette class vessel, the hulk of the Quicksilver having become so rotten it had to be broken up. The overseer, named Sherman Peggett, had shown himself to be a much harder man than Mr. Milner. The newer hulk was not a receiving vessel for criminals, but of citizens of all types entering service with the Royal Navy. Although fewer felons filled her decks, life aboard the hulk hadn't changed much.

Mr. Swoon had turned melancholy over the past few years. In the last year, he'd fallen into a despondent state, complaining to Frederick that his visions had turned on him.

"I'm no longer allowed to linger in my beautiful gardens. Demons chase me away from them into a burnt landscape full of hulks and ruins. The larger the dose, the longer the delay before the demons come. I cannot sleep without it. I have no appetite. I suffer the cold even if the weather is warm. My blood runs sluggishly. See my dreadful pallor?"

"Yes, sir" Frederick said. "and please forgive me for saying so, but you've become irritable and unreasonable at times. You must give it up before you are truly harmed."

"Yes, of course you're right. I have tried. I must redouble my efforts." He offered Frederick a weak smile.

That was the last time Frederick had seen the man alive. The next day, Mr. Swoon failed to awaken from a rather large dose of chloroform.

The surgeon had created a leather hood that fit over his head, one with a snout-shaped projection below where his nose was situated when he wore the contraption. The snout had holes to allow the passage of air. He'd been wearing the thing to aid in administering increasingly large doses of chloroform for some time. The night of his death, he'd soaked a roll of bandages in the drug before putting it inside the snout area, and placing the hood over his head. Frederick discovered him in the morning as he reported to the infirmary to begin his day.

Seeing the man lying lifeless on the cot, Frederick felt a spasm of fear and pain, much milder, but not unlike what he'd experienced at his mother's death. Mr. Swoon had been good to him, his fatherly presence providing a sense of security. Yet the man had changed over time, giving Frederick the impression that the situation on the hulk had become somewhat precarious.

Frederick's old urges and dark thoughts about young women resurfaced. While struggling to push the disturbing desires back down, he also felt an unexpected excitement.

Aiden: 7

After winning the World Fantasy Award, my illustration business grew more rapidly. My paintings, always dark and strange, had become even more so since the hospital stay. I approached the work with a certain reckless glee and a sense of humor. Perhaps I had gained a perspective that added a disturbing undercurrent to the work; an appreciation for the power of the unseen and unknowable. Publishers of dark fiction seemed to like what they saw in my work. Most of the jobs I got were for books within the horror genre.

Unfortunately, Melody and I couldn't quite keep pace with the cost of living. Our biggest expense was insurance. Melody's job had always provided medical insurance, which could be extended to cover me as well for a reasonable fee. That's how we'd paid for the brain abscesses and the substance abuse treatment. Not part of a pool, now that she worked with me, we were on our own. Medical insurance became exorbitantly expensive, about $1500.00 per month. What small savings we had was used up paying the premiums.

Randy brought to a Bovine Smoke Society meeting news of an upcoming anthology of Jack the Ripper fiction that had opened up for submissions. "You should submit a story," he told me.

I took his suggestion. The research I did while writing that story would have a dramatic effect on my future I could not have imagined at the time. I borrowed a book from my cousin, Stephen. Unfortunately, I've forgotten the title and the author's name. The book was one of countless nonfiction paperback titles about the killer. In the text, I found the police reports for each of the victims. The possessions found with the four women killed on the street were cataloged in the reports. The list for Catherine Eddowes took me by surprise:

A black straw bonnet with green and black velvet, black beads, and black strings

A black cloth jacket trimmed with fake fur at the collar and cuffs and 2 outside pockets trimmed with black silk braid and fake fur

A chintz skirt—3 flounces with a brown button on the waistband

A worn green silk dress bodice with a black velvet collar and brown metal buttons down the front

A grey stuff petticoat with a white waistband

A very old green alpaca skirt

A very old ragged blue skirt with a red flounce and light twill lining

A white calico chemise

A man's white waistcoat with green revers; she had no drawers or stays.

1 thimble

1 mustard tin containing two pawn tickets: One in the name of Emily Birrell, 52 White's Row, dated August 31, 9d for a man's flannel shirt. The other is in the name of James Birrell of 6 Dorset Street and dated August 28, 2S for a pair of men's boots. Both addresses are false.

A pair of men's lace up boots with mohair laces, right boot fixed with red thread

1 red gauze silk (worn about the neck)

1 large white handkerchief

3 abalone buttons

1 blue stripe bed ticking pocket with waist band and strings

1 white-handled table knife

1 cork

2 unbleached calico pockets

1 white cotton pocket handkerchief with red and white birds-eye border

1 pair of brown ribbed stockings with white mended feet

12 pieces of white rag, slightly bloodstained

1 piece of white coarse linen

1 piece of blue and white shirting—three cornered

2 small blue bed ticking bags

1 short black clay pipe

1 tin box with tea

1 tin box with sugar

1 piece of flannel

6 pieces of soap

1 small tooth comb
1 pewter tea spoon
1 red leather cigarette case with white metal fittings
1 empty tin match box
1 piece of red flannel with pins and needles
A ball of hemp
A piece of old white apron.
A printed handbill
A printed calling card for Frank Carver, 301 Bethnal
Green Road
A portion of a pair of spectacles
1 red mitten

I showed the list to Melody. We were both reading in bed late on a Friday night.

"That's a lot of clothing to haul around," she said.

"She was wearing all that," I said. "So many garments and possessions, and the fact that she'd spent the two nights prior to her death in the casual ward of the work house, suggests she carried everything she owned on her."

"What's the casual ward?"

"Outdoor accommodations at the workhouse for the ill, the transient, and the known criminals."

"She sounds like a homeless bag lady."

"Yeah, a Victorian era bag lady."

The list spoke to me of a pitiful existence. Perhaps the most valuable item among her possessions was *a portion of a pair of spectacles*. Strangely, I could picture her existence as I fell asleep that night.

The next morning, as we made the weekly grocery list in preparation for shopping, Melody said, "We need sugar." I grabbed the legal pad we used and a pencil, and found myself writing *1 tin box with sugar*, one of the items in Catherine Eddowes's possessions list.

Well, that was weird. I stopped what I was doing, suddenly seeing more clearly the poor woman's poignant experience in my mind's eye. I imagined a novel that used the acquisition of the items in the list as the basis of chapters telling her story from childhood to death. What I'd learned about her life, the loss of her mother, then her husband, her estrangement from her own children as she descended into alcoholism, and finally her demise, could become a compelling emotional drama.

"You've got that far-off look in your eyes," Melody said. "What are you dreaming up this time?"

I told her about the idea.

"Are you going to write it?" she asked.

"Not yet," I said. "I don't think I'm capable of writing something that emotional."

I wrote a piece of Jack the Ripper fiction with a friend. We failed to make the deadline for the anthology. Later we sold the short story to a magazine. After that, the idea for the novel about Catherine Eddowes banged around in my head for almost two decades, the story I envisioned strangely more vivid than anything else I wrote over that time. I didn't know what to make of that until much later.

~ ~ ~

By the summer of 1995, our savings had run out. Melody got a job at the same bank she'd worked at before.

In December of that year, she became pregnant. We hadn't expected to become parents and I was afraid. At thirty-eight years of age, I felt like I'd just become an adult. "I haven't been sober five years yet," I said to Melody. "What if I relapse?"

"We're hopeful now," she said. "Everything seems to be working well in our lives. You say you still have no desire for drinking or drugs."

"That's right."

"You may be afraid, but you shouldn't be. You'll make a good father."

Melody was clearly ready to have a child, and that made me ready.

~ ~ ~

We attended the World Horror Convention in Eugene, Oregon in 1996. Melody wanted to see the Northwest, so we stayed after the convention, rented a car, and saw the sights. The state has vast areas of wilderness, temperate rainforest, old growth forests of primarily conifers, mountains that are sleeping snow-capped volcanoes, high desert, a beautiful coast with cliffs, dunes, beaches, rocky blow holes, and tide pools full of life. The human inhabitants seem to know what they have and do a good job keeping the place clean and wild. Certain areas of the state appear so primordial that finding dinosaurs roaming the landscape would seem quite natural if not for the time period and extinction issues.

We had a lot of fun at the convention. Oregon was spectacular—not just the sites, but the people as well.

I have the anti-social habit of talking to strangers. "You should leave people alone." Melody used to say to me. "No one wants to talk to a stranger." People not wanting to talk to strangers was particularly true in the South, where we came from. Dave Conover used to tell me, "You *harass* people. You can see by the way they look at you that they think you're up to something."

True, some strangers I spoke to in the South seemed to think I had a nefarious agenda. I never said things meant to upset them, though.

In Oregon, the strangers I spoke to didn't appear the least bit perturbed. On the streets, in a grocery store, and while waiting in line at the post office to ship my artwork back to Nashville, I spoke to several people.

"They don't even look me up and down before responding," I told Melody.

Most of the folks we met in Oregon seemed unguarded, unafraid, contrasting starkly with what we experienced in the East. Despite maintaining her stance that I bothered folks, Melody agreed that the people of Oregon were unusually friendly. Those we met running businesses seemed to adhere to the old adage—seemingly obsolete in the East—that the customer is always right.

On the flight back home, Melody lamented, "Too bad we can't live in Oregon."

"We could if we wanted to. It would be a great place for Little Bean to grow up."

Yes—I'd taken to calling our unborn, as yet unnamed, child "Little Bean." I'd always thought that infants, especially their oblong heads, looked like beans.

"I could never leave my family," Melody said.

Her family—mother, sister, and niece—lived about an hour north of Nashville in Russellville, Kentucky. Melody's father had died of a heart attack before I met her. I'd never known him. She'd always said I would have liked him.

That seemed like the end of the discussion about moving to Oregon—it was on that day—but apparently I'd planted a seed in Melody's thoughts.

Looking around once we got home, Nashville didn't look good to us. In recent years, the city had become a giant sprawl. To go anywhere, one had to be in a car because there were no sidewalks. The streets and neighborhoods remained terribly littered. Crime rose in Nashville, as most of the rest of the country enjoyed declining crime rates. The hot, humid summer, that seemed to get worse each year despite the protestations of global warming deniers, had just begun.

Shortly after we got back from Oregon, I looked at the garbage that had accumulated next door in the James's front yard and couldn't live and let live any longer.

I went over and knocked on their door. Mrs. James answered. "What?" she asked brusquely.

"Your front yard is full of rubbish," I said. "Will you clean it up, please?"

She answered with a silent glare, so I turned and left.

Following that, the driver's side window of our car was shot out as the vehicle sat in our driveway. Since the shot had come from the direction of the James home, I thought better of making any more complaints about what they got up to.

"Too bad we can't live in Oregon," Melody said while we sat eating a dinner of jambalaya that night.

"I can do my work anywhere," I said. "You work in a bank and I think they have some of those out there."

Melody looked at me like I had to be crazy for seriously considering moving across the continent. Again, she was the worrier who had married a risk-taker.

"Okay, let's make a list of the pros and cons," I said, putting down my fork. I got out the legal pad we used to make grocery lists. "What about leaving family behind, pro or con?"

She looked at me exasperated. "Con."

As we continued the list, Melody didn't take the effort seriously at first. She continued eating, and that gave me a chance to finish my meal. I ate faster than she did. A lot of her concerns revolved around what she thought would be best for our unborn child, so I began to concentrate on that as well. I used imagination to help tilt the scales.

"It would be nice if our child could grow up where there are sidewalks, bike lanes on the roads, wilderness to explore, extra friendly people to meet, clean air, clean water, the less hectic life of a small city, and less crime. We have virtually none of that here, except maybe the wilderness way outside of town. Even that's dotted with hulked cars and dead appliances people don't want to haul to the dump."

"Isn't the Green River Killer in the Northwest?" Still an avid horror fan, she posed the question with a crooked smile. I knew that she *did* actually worry about such things. The serial killer had not been caught yet.

"Yes," I said, "but you can't put that on the list because there are murderers in all parts of the United States."

The pros side of the list quickly became much longer than the cons side. Melody became excited in spite of herself. I saw that she'd forgotten about her jambalaya.

Following more discussion, she frowned. "Still, I'd have to leave Mama."

"Yes, we won't take her with us."

"I just don't think I'm ready." She resumed eating her now cold dinner.

Again, that seemed the end of the discussion.

~ ~ ~

Melody got up earlier than I did to get ready for work. Just about every night, I stayed up reading next to her in bed while she went off to sleep. One night, about two weeks after we'd returned from Oregon, I'd been reading for about half an hour when Melody turned over and said, "I can't sleep for thinking about moving to Oregon."

~ ~ ~

We spent a year putting our affairs in order and preparing our small, lavender house for sale.

Lysta Littlebean Clark was born on September 3, 1996. Yes—I had to give her name a bit of humor. Melody allowed the odd middle name because she could see that it ever so slightly eased my fear of the serious responsibility of parenthood.

"What if she grows up to love reruns of *The Love Boat*," I asked Melody while we bathed Littlebean in a small tub with a warm, moist washrag. "What if she insists I attend her high school basketball games? What if she's painfully serious? What if the weird in the world frightens her? How will I relate to all that?"

"Do you also worry that she might not like to read?" Melody

asked. She flicked water in my face.

I wiped off the water and frowned. She was clever to bring up Daddy's disappointment, since, of all his children, I'd been the one to make a career within the book publishing industry both as an illustrator and more recently as a writer. What did that say about parental concerns?

"You already know the answers to all those questions," she said. "That's why you included *The Love Boat.*"

She referred to the fact that I did not get her intense appreciation for television shows like *The Love Boat*, *The Brady Bunch*, and *Eight is Enough.*

"You love *me.*" she said.

Yes, I did.

Melody gently rocked Littlebean in the tub, and sang the theme song for the television show.

Lysta giggled.

"Don't encourage her to like it!" I said.

Melody gave me a wilting look as she slid the soapy washrag over our daughter's pudgy little hands and feet.

I hoped I'd love our daughter once the cute was gone. She'd been born with my blue eyes and Melody's warmer, darker skin color. Her hair began dark, but had turned blonde within a couple of months. She looked up at me with her big eyes, and wrapped her tiny fingers around one of mine, and my heart melted. I found myself making plans for her future, ridiculous ones.

"We should take her to see the seven wonders of the world," I said. "I should teach her to paint while she's a toddler so she'll have a leg up on all the artists of her time that will only begin to learn when they're teens or adults. We should make her multi-lingual. She should speak Japanese, Spanish, and German, as well as English."

Amazingly practical in those early moments of excitement, Melody said, "We should watch to see what *she* finds interesting first."

~ ~ ~

I could not shake the fear that Lysta would grow up to become someone uninteresting to me. I kept pushing the idea away. Still, the fretful thought nagged at me from time to time.

Of course the grandparents loved Littlebean. Surprisingly, Melody's mother, Mary, didn't mind the child's middle name. "It's silly,

but Bean was my mother's maiden name, so I suppose it will do."
She complained about our plan to leave Tennessee to live in Oregon.
Melody reassured her that we'd stay in touch over the phone and
come back to visit.

My parents didn't give us a hard time about leaving Tennessee.
Their children had always lived in different parts of the country. I'd
left home at fifteen to find a high school and college in San Francisco
that would provide a better art education than what the schools in
Nashville, Tennessee offered.

Right as we'd gotten everything organized for the big move,
Daddy was diagnosed with leukemia. I had second thoughts about
leaving. I was torn. We'd organized so much, not just in Nashville.
In Oregon, a friend we met at the World Horror Convention had
found us an apartment. I worried that I might never see my father
again if I left town. No one suggested we should not go, though, so
we continued toward the exit.

When not at the hospital with Daddy, Mama looked after Lysta,
while we got ready to leave town. Melody and I sold the house for
a better price than we'd thought we'd get. We packed up all our belongings in a self storage unit, and lived with my parents in the big
brick family home. Once Melody's two week notice at her work had
run its course, we said our goodbyes to family and friends. We rented
a truck and loaded it. We rented a trailer to haul our car behind the
truck.

Setting out in early March of 1997, we took turns driving and
entertaining Littlebean or encouraging her to sleep. Each night as
we became tired, we found a motel to stay in. The truck averaged
a frustratingly slow fifty miles-an-hour as we traveled a distance of
about 2700 miles. Unfortunately we'd packed most of our music,
and had only Melody's cassettes of albums by the Beatles to listen to
over and over. With time, just as I ceased to be aware of the smell of
previous renters' sweat in the truck's upholstery, I couldn't hear the
music coming out of the little boom box we'd brought with us. We
were sick of that truck cab, its uncomfortable seat, the bug-spattered
view out its windshield, and its rattling vents long before we arrived
in Oregon six days after leaving Nashville. Realizing we'd had it easy
compared to those who traveled west on the Oregon Trail one hundred and fifty years earlier, did not ease my weariness one bit.

We lived in the apartment for the first month and a half while we looked for a house to buy. A year and one week after the World Horror Convention, we occupied the home where I currently sit typing this manuscript. Well, I should say that it's not exactly the same one. The house is largely the same, though, and exists in the same location as the one we bought in 1997.

The place started out a simple, one story wood-panel house painted robin's egg blue on a piece of property eighty feet wide and one hundred feet deep. A six-foot-high wooden fence surrounded the back yard. The previous owners had planted thirty-two rose bushes, yellow and coral-colored ones in the front yard, red and white ones in the back. They'd also planted six rhododendrons along the back fence, all various shades of pink and purple, the tallest over ten feet tall. I learned how to take care of the roses and kept them blooming eight months out of the year. For a 925 square foot home in a modest suburban neighborhood, the place was beautiful.

Indeed, Oregon had banks, and Melody found work at one.

Lysta Littlebean grew.

The amount of work I received didn't slacken as I'd feared might happen. Instead, I enjoyed a steady increase in assignments from publishers as the years passed.

Our life in Oregon had just begun, and it got better by the day.

Frederick: 7

The new surgeon on the hulk, Alister Clamp, looked as if he were gazing at a bug in his supper when he looked at Frederick. Mr. Clamp's criticism of his assistant seemed endless. On his second day at the hulk he found eighteen ways to express his disapproval.

"You must shave closer," he said when Frederick arrived to start his duty, "and work harder to remove the stains from your clothing." After a moment, Mr. Clamp added, "Keep your nails trimmed short and remove the filth from beneath them."

He is establishing his own discipline, Frederick told himself. *Once he sees that I'll comply with his wishes, he'll be more at ease.*

At midday, Frederick returned to the infirmary after collecting incoming supplies, and entered the cell where they were stored to put them away.

"When you've been to the head, wipe your feet before returning to the infirmary," Mr. Clamp said.

"Should I go there, sir," Frederick said, "I certainly will do so. Just now, I was well abaft of the head."

"Do not use nautical terms. We're not at sea!"

"Yes, sir. Begging pardon, sir. I have the habit, forgetting that some don't know. I will do better, sir."

"I cannot understand you if you don't pronounce more clearly the letters H, T, and G in your words."

"I will make every effort to do so, sir."

"Look me in the eye when I speak to you," Mr. Clamp said, still trying to talk to Frederick with a bulkhead between them, "you impertinent wretch."

Frederick had an insult ready, and struggled to hold it back. He checked his features with his fingers to make certain no challenge could be seen in his expression, then stuck his head out the door, and looked toward the surgeon. "Yes, sir."

He pulled his head back in as Mr. Clamp approached. The surgeon crowded into the small cell, backing Frederick up against the bulkhead. He felt a small panic, and wanted to lash out at his superior. Gulping a couple of quick breaths, he succeeded in staying his hand.

Mr. Clamp glared at him, then looked to the shelf of medicines. "The labels on the bottles must all face the front," he said, reaching past Frederick to twist several bottles around.

Later, whilst reading Frederick's record of the week of Mr. Swoon's death, Mr. Clamp said, "Your writing is all flourish and no message. Trim your letters!"

"Do not smile when you make an incision," Mr. Clamp commanded in the mid-afternoon, as Frederick worked to remove a thick splinter from an inmate's heel. "Your eyes must show some sympathy to those under your care."

An inmate came to the infirmary with an aching head and a dark green tongue. Frederick consulted one of Mr. Swoon's small books titled *Tongue Colors in Health and Disease*, in hopes of learning something about the man's condition.

Mr. Clamp approached. "I cannot work with a man who will not stand up straight." He put one hand under Frederick's chin to lift his head, while jabbing the other hand into the small of his back. "And no more reading while you're on duty." He snatched away the text and threw it on a table.

Again, Frederick held his tongue, and kept his pride in check.

Just as Frederick's hours of duty ended, the surgeon said, "You must respond more swiftly to my commands. You must learn to anticipate my needs, so I don't have to ask you for everything. Because I may need you in an instant, do not sit during the hours you're on duty."

Frederick despised Alister Clamp. Everything about the man had become disgusting and hateful: his shiny red nose, the flakes of skin that fell from his head of graying hair, the creaking and popping of his joints, his bowed legs, light frame, and Scottish accent.

"No," Mr. Clamp said on his third day at the hulk, "you must shave close enough that your face is sanguine."

The surgeon had just begun. Over the next few weeks, Frederick tried to adapt, to swallow his pride, and take on all of Mr. Clamp's preferences, methods, and policies, no matter how silly they seemed. But as Frederick would eventually discover, his efforts were futile.

A cousin of Mr. Clamp's, a young man named Phillip Rodgers, came several times to the hulk. The surgeon showed the man around the infirmary in an instructive manner that seemed unusual to Frederick. At one point, while Frederick was lancing an abscessed cyst in an inmate's underarm, Mr. Clamp asked Mr. Rodgers to step in and take over the procedure.

Reluctantly, Frederick drew the small knife away from the operation.

"Hurry," Mr. Clamp shouted. "Get up and get out!"

Frederick gritted his teeth. He wanted to plunge the knife into Mr. Clamp's throat. Instead, he quickly set the instrument aside, and left the infirmary. He glanced at Mr. Rodgers as he went, and saw a look of embarrassment. The man would not meet Frederick's gaze.

That afternoon, Mr. Peggett came with two guards to escort Frederick to shore. One of the guards, a man named Garrison, had lost a finger to Frederick's knife, and had shown over time that he held a grudge. The other, a fellow named Hoffman, was new. Frederick didn't know him at all.

"You are dismissed from service," the overseer said. He held up a fine meerschaum pipe carved into the shape of a wild boar. "This was found among the clothes within your berth. It belongs to Mr. Clamp."

"I did not take that, sir." Frederick could feel his mouth hanging open. He imagined that he looked foolish and shut it, then said, "He is trying to replace me with his cousin."

"You will be put ashore. Your chest is already in the tender."

"Sir, I'm the *Assistant Surgeon*."

"You are a criminal."

"No, Mr. Swoon had me reinstated with rank. I shall have a certificate of service."

"You have no such thing. Mr. Swoon said he appealed to Mr. Milner on your behalf many years ago. The best the man would do was to give you some small pay. When Mr. Swoon came to me, I would do no more."

"My pension!"

He lunged toward the overseer, to beg for his livelihood, but Mr. Garrison and Mr. Hoffman brought him up short.

"You've received what you're worth. Now go, before I have you and your chest thrown overboard."

Frederick thought briefly of reaching for his knife. His left leg wobbled beneath him. The smell of the grave filled his nostrils, and he began to quake. The loss of bodily control took him by surprise, as he hadn't had a fit in many years. Mr. Garrison's scowl loomed as he grabbed Frederick's right arm and twisted the limb behind his back. Mr. Hoffman struck Frederick on the head, and grabbed his other arm, even as the world dimmed and went black.

The apparition he'd known in previous visions appeared for a brief moment, standing in a bright room with dead animals hanging from the ceiling.

Aiden: 8

As if from magic beans, Lysta grew. Her hair remained blonde for a short a time, then began to darken again. Whereever her bright eyes went, her fingers soon followed. Melody and I had always kept a myriad of fun objects about the house, such as small sculptures, pieces of hand turned pottery, historical artifacts, and human bones. Our new home was no different. Littlebean liked all that stuff and destroyed much of what was fragile. Melody wanted to store all the small objects away until Lysta became older, but I persuaded her that we shouldn't do that. I wanted to make certain our little girl grew up with her curiosity and longing to explore satisfied and intact. I continued to fear that she'd grow up with a plain and uninteresting mind. We did put away objects small enough to swallow, things like arrowheads, fossils, mini balls, and sea shells. We secured the areas under the sinks where we stored all our poisons. I allowed Littlebean to chew on my precious British Museum dinosaur collection. She particularly liked the pliosaur.

Her first word was "no," and I immediately assumed that she would grow up to have a negative outlook.

"You have no reason to believe that," Melody said. "Give her time and room to develop before deciding what to guard against."

Now, I was the worrier, and Melody had become the risk-taker.

We got Perry, a schipperke dog. He and Littlebean were toddlers together. For the first year in Oregon, I didn't get much done during the day. I had to wait for Melody to get home in the evening before I went into the studio to work. The next year, as an adult, Perry took over some of the entertainment and babysitting duties. I'd made a big safe play pen out of the living room, where Lysta and the pup could play together for an hour at a stretch, a precious amount of time in those days. With time, I no longer had to keep her confined while I worked. Perry and Littlebean napped together in the afternoons. If she got up and wandered off, he would come into my studio and look at me until I noticed him. If that failed, he gave me what we called his "polite bark." Then I'd go see what Littlebean had gotten up to.

Thankfully, Daddy recovered from leukemia. He and Mama came to visit. We drove around the state together, visiting sites, hiking a bit, the incredible beauty of the place leaving us in awe. Reflecting on their visit after they had gone home, I realized that Dr. William M. Clark had lost some of his seriousness. He'd become more playful. Much the way I'd discovered renewed gratitude for life following my brain abscesses and nearly killing myself with alcohol, I think his appreciation for life had been refreshed.

~ ~ ~

The Trillepetol continued to be an uncomfortable part of daily life. Having to make lists each day in order to remember everything I needed to do had become a real pain in the ass. With a child to monitor through most of the day, my naps to recoup energy in the afternoon became all but impossible.

Business had gotten good enough that I needed a better brain. I found myself forgetting to take my medication. Perhaps some of that forgetting was intentional. I suffered no seizures, so as time went on I worried less and grew more casual about whether or not I took the medicine. Still, I was nervous enough that I spoke to Daddy over the phone about not taking all my doses.

"You know it's dangerous to take the medicine inconsistently," he said.

"I'm more likely to have seizures taking it sporadically than not at all, right?"

"Yes."

"Yet I haven't had any seizures, so I'm better off quitting the drug entirely."

"I can't advise you on that. I don't treat family. Talk to your neurologist."

In Oregon, my prescription for Trillepetol had been continue through my new GP. I hadn't spoken to Dr. Reed in years, and didn't really want to deal with him having most of a continent between us. I also didn't want to find a new neurologist to consult.

"I have my answer," I said. "I'm not having seizures while taking Trillepetol inconsistently, and that's more dangerous than not taking the drug at all. I'll take my chances with not taking it."

He didn't sound pleased, but he also wasn't much of a worrier. "Good luck," he said, and let the matter go. So did I.

A couple months later, his Leukemia returned and he went into the hospital. The treatment for the disease involved chemotherapy that killed his bone marrow. Without the bone marrow, he could not produce white blood cells to fight off infection, so the hospital staff tried to keep his environment as clean as possible. Even so, he got a fungal pneumonia, which traveled to his head and could not be removed or stopped.

I got a phone call from Mama. "You should come home to see him before it's too late." Her voice over the phone sounded hoarse and broken. "He has about four days to live."

The family assembled in Nashville to comfort Mama and see Daddy, an altogether painful time. He seemed to be unconscious when I arrived in his hospital room and did not become more responsive. I wanted to say my goodbyes, to tell him that I loved him dearly. In the sterile hospital room with staff coming and going, and so many family members hovering around, I could not find the words. Even if I had, I didn't think he could hear me. I had to be content with the idea that he knew how I felt. With regrets for how I'd treated him over the years, especially as a teen, the notion wasn't reassuring.

Dinner at my parents' house the first night, was a family favorite: Marinated flank steak broiled rare, roasted potatoes, and asparagus or "pee stinkers," as Daddy used to call them. Although Mama had made the delicious meal as well as ever she had, nobody showed much enthusiasm to eat. We discussed the irony that the fungus growing in Daddy's head would kill him instead of the leukemia.

"That's another neurological disorder for the Clarks," I said. "That's three just in the immediate family."

When thirty-two years old, my brother Bill suffered a brain tumor that had to be surgically removed. I'd had the brain abscesses.

Carol seemed to think about that for a moment, a troubled look in her eyes as she considered the red juice that flowed from the rare meat on her plate. "What brain disease will Cindy and I get?" she asked sardonically. She pushed her uneaten meal away and sat back.

"Maybe the animals Grandaddy used in his research haunt us," I suggested, trying to lighten the mood and failing miserably. Cindy grimaced at me and pushed her meal away too.

Grandaddy's pioneering neurological research, mapping the

brain, involved unanesthetized animals—chimpanzees, dogs, cats—with electrodes implanted in their brains. Along with his laboratory investigations, he wrote several revisions of the standard textbook, *Anatomy of the Nervous System,* used in medical schools around the world. Grandaddy's research had gone on after his death. As a child, I saw the lab and the poor animals. Of course I'd been kidding to suggest the haunting, but I couldn't help thinking we owed something to those poor animals.

Daddy died seven days after Littlebean's second birthday. Watching that was one of the worst experiences of my life. Afterward, rarely did a day pass that I didn't think of him and notice something of his presence in my own. I saw his eyes in the mirror, heard his words on my lips, and found myself appreciating things in the world that I knew he would have found fascinating. In that way, he haunted me, a bitter-sweet experience, exquisite and priceless.

Never had I felt such a powerful need to get home to my family as I did after his death. The night I returned, I held Melody and cried, then hugged my baby girl and the tears dried up. Understanding more clearly than ever that life was all the more precious because it ended, and accepting death as a necessary part of the experience, I let my father go, and concentrated on my own family.

~ ~ ~

As the years passed, I had a few odd déjà vu episodes, and some lightheadedness accompanied by a strange smell. I knew that odor, yet only after I began to experience the inexplicable dread associated with the temporal lobe seizures, would I come close to admitting to myself that something was wrong with my brain. I preferred denial. Although the symptoms became progressively worse, I told myself that they remained light and not at all dangerous. I didn't want to see a doctor. I wanted the brain abscesses to remain a part of my distant past.

My business increased. I created a website, www.aidenmclark. com with store from which I sold original drawings and paintings, and archival reproduction prints of many of my best pieces of art. Eventually, when I'd gotten enough of my writing out in the publishing world, I made books available for sale in the online store; including a full color book of my artwork, anthologies to which I'd contributed short fiction, a couple of collections of my fiction, and novels that I'd written. Three anthologies, the Imagination Fully Dilated series, of stories inspired by my artwork were published. Along with the stories, written by all sorts of great writers, the artwork appeared in the books. Gratefully, I saw that excitement for my work was building, particularly among horror professionals and fans. I sold book proposals to various publishers, some of which involved my writing as well as illustration. One, a novel titled *Siren Promised*, that I wrote with Jeremy Robert Johnson, was nominated for a Bram Stoker Award in the Best First Novel category. Along with co-writing the novel, I gave the story about forty illustrations. I got the opportunity to illustrate and design two children's books. Lysta Littlebean liked those a lot.

Together, Melody and I brought in enough income to add a second story to our house, doubling the size of our home. We paid the contractors in cash and had no residual debt.

I had the illusion that life was well in hand.

Frederick: 8

Frederick awoke among the tall grasses along the south bank of the River Medway. The guards were on their way back to the hulk in the tender. As Mr. Hoffman rowed, Mr. Garrison went through Frederick's chest. He must have pried the box open.

Back on his feet, but still unsteady, Frederick watched as the man threw items from the chest out of the tender into the river: books, articles of clothing, small keepsakes from visits to Chatham and Rochester. Mr. Garrison fumbled with a small leather case that held surgical instruments, and it went overboard even as the man tried to prevent that.

Frederick waved his arms and shouted incoherently. His voice didn't work well after the fit, yet he also was at a loss for the words to adequately condemn the cruelty visited upon him.

Mr. Garrison pointed toward Frederick. Mr. Hoffman looked in the direction indicated. Frederick heard the guards' laughter. Mr. Garrison lifted a leather pouch from the chest and held it up in he air. "I have your purse," he shouted. "Mr. Peggett will be pleased."

The purse held what little Frederick had saved from his paltry wages over the years. He leapt into the water and began swimming. Mr. Hoffman increased the pace of his rowing and quickly Frederick knew that pursuit was hopeless.

He snatched the case of surgical instruments caught in an eddy of the river current, and made his way back to dry land. Standing on the river bank with a pit of misery opening in his gut, he watched his other possessions flow downstream. His purse went back aboard the hulk with the guards.

Savaged and feeling severely diminished, Frederick checked his arms and legs. Instead of missing limbs, he realized his prospects were gone. A week ago, his life had been in order. His demise had occurred rapidly. He had no faith in authority coming to his aid. Indeed, Mr. Peggett *was* the authority on that piece of the river. He and Mr. Clamp had neatly sewn Frederick into a canvas of lies and dumped him overboard without so much as a prayer. His life was over! He should never have trusted any of them. He would never trust anyone, ever again.

Making matters worse, he'd had a spell!

He had nowhere to go and nothing to do. Frederick sat on the bank, trying to think of what could be salvaged from the situation. If he got back aboard the hulk, he might retrieve his purse. To do so would involve great stealth and possibly violence. Mr. Pegget and the guards would show him no mercy. If caught, he'd be returned to prison. What he'd saved in the purse wasn't worth that.

As night fell, the chill March air and hunger got him moving. Frederick headed toward Rochester with few plans. He found and followed a well worn road, the moonlight providing ample illumination of the path.

After a short time, he heard a woman humming a tune up ahead. She made a half-hearted effort, as if the music was not wanted, so much as needed. Perhaps afraid of the dark, she merely whistled past the graveyard, so to speak. The voice seemed that of a young woman. His sister came to mind; healthy, happy Abigail.

He hated her. Her kind was highly prized and closely guarded, while no one but his poor mum had ever cared what happened to Frederick. The strange woman ahead on the road represented an arm of the body that had harmed him. She somehow belonged to the men responsible for his demise. Although he didn't know of any family belonging to either surgeon or the overseer living in the area, that didn't matter. The woman became Mr. Clamp's daughter, Mr. Peggett's ladybird, Mr. Swoon's pride and joy. All three men would pay for what Frederick had suffered that day.

He pulled a long surgical knife from his leather case. The woman, carrying a cloth sack, came into view around a bend in the road, her breath flowing in plumes behind her. She shivered and pulled her shawl more tightly against the increasing chill in the air.

Frederick looked around, saw nothing but darkness among the tall grasses that crowded the road. Trying to remain quiet, he sped up to catch her. She must have heard his footsteps because she looked back. Eyes wide, she screamed, turned away, and ran. She stumbled, dropped her sack, and pressed on. Frederick tripped as well—probably in the same rut—and fell in a heap. A woman's shoe lay beside him in the depression along with the sack. He threw himself to his feet and ran after her. Having lost a shoe, she'd begun to limp, holding her arms out for better balance. Without support, her shawl fell from her shoulders.

Frederick caught up with her easily. Her terror reached a vocal crescendo that nearly cut off his rage. Frederick wondered what he was doing and why for a brief moment, even as he brought the knife up and across her throat. He turned his body to avoid the spray of blood which appeared like a ruby treasure pouring from a great purse, somber red in the moonlight. Her scream had turned to a burbling gasp. She stumbled back. Her eyes bore in on Frederick's with an unanswerable question as she reached for her throat.

He didn't completely understand his need to cut her, and that didn't matter. Gaping in fascination at the bloody gash in her neck, seeing the pain and fear in her eyes, Frederick's pulse beat rapidly, his vision sharpened, and he got a surge of vitality. He felt the excitement most acutely in his loins.

With increased terror, her eyes focused briefly at the crotch of his breeches. He glanced down to discover the cloth bulging over an erection. Immediately, the fabric around the bulge darkened. Sexual release shook him as the woman slumped to the ground with a final rattling breath.

Once his racing pulse had slowed a bit, Frederick glanced around fearfully. He saw no one. The night had become still again. He grabbed the dead woman under the arms and hauled her into the tall rushes.

Except for a formative experience during his service with the Royal Navy, the sensations he'd known during his release were unrivaled. He would cut her up, but she would not be aware that he did so. What satisfaction in that?

Next time, he wouldn't be so hasty. Next time he would study his need more closely before he attacked.

Looking at her pale face, Frederick knew he was meant to feel bad about having taken her life. Although he felt nothing for her, he had a heady sense of accomplishment; taking something from others gave him power.

He backtracked along the road to retrieve the woman's shawl and the sack she'd dropped. Inside, he found a half-eaten loaf of bread and wool yarn. Frederick devoured the loaf as he left the woman's corpse and ghost behind, resuming his trek northeastward.

Aiden: 9

I continued to experience petty concerns about my daughter, unworthy ones, too small to matter, but which I couldn't shake. Littlebean's fascination for my computer, for instance, starting about age four, troubled me. For the longest time, I wouldn't let her go near the equipment. I feared she'd grow up so dependent on the technology that she wouldn't know how to have fun in the real world.

One night after Littlebean had gone to sleep, Melody and I were watching a movie I couldn't get into. I paused the film and turned to her. "I worry we've created a world for Littlebean that's too small and bland, one that might not provide the stimulation her mind needs."

"Are you thinking we should move?"

"I just want her to have lots to explore, like I did."

"Yeah, I know. I had woods to explore. Things weren't so *suburban*. You know we couldn't afford a home like the one you grew up in."

~ ~ ~

I'd spent much of my youth barefoot and climbing trees. After my father's residency at Columbia Presbyterian Medical Center in New York City in 1962, we moved away from all that concrete, brick, and asphalt to the forested small city of Nashville, Tennessee. I was five years old at the time. We lived in the house Grandaddy had built in 1935 near Brown's Creek.

When the house was new, the lot existed amidst farmland instead of other residential properties. The mailbox stood a half mile away along a dirt road. Since then the land had become a residential neighborhood. The area had no sewers and water flowed a bit too freely without natural filtration. That had been a problem in many parts of Nashville. The city experienced several epidemics of water borne illness in its early history. The Old City Cemetery has large sections that appear empty, but those gently rolling grassy areas are actually mass graves of those who died in the epidemics. Because the city took its water from where Brown's Creek emptied into the Cumberland River, the codes for my neighborhood regulated that residential lots should be no smaller than three acres.

My siblings and I had what seemed many centuries to explore the heavily wooded landscape of our home. The property had been part of a rock quarry before the Civil War, and some of the bedrock, where exposed on the side of a hill, had drill holes and blast marks over a hundred years old. Many of the trees, black walnuts, oaks of different sorts, and cottonwoods exceeded seventy feet in height. Between the time when Grandaddy had passed away and my family had moved into the house, the property had been neglected for a short time. In Tennessee, that's all that's needed for a wooded area to become overgrown. Vines, mostly grape and honeysuckle, knitted some spaces between the trees together, creating tunnel-like avenues through the woods and "rooms" where we children enjoyed exploring and playing.

The mass of growth also had covered over remnants of activities decades old. Buried in the weeds, tangled in the vines, my brother and I found toys from the 1930s and 1940s, an old, iron-rimmed wheel from a pony wagon, hand-made carts my Grandaddy had used to haul slabs of stone up from the creek to terrace the back yard and to create steps up and down the hill.

Our woods had owls, hawks, herons, chipmunks, hummingbirds, foxes, and gray squirrels, as well as flying squirrels.

Our greatest treasure was the creek. About ten to fifteen feet across, the small stream trickled over exposed limestone bedrock of primarily ancient sea bed, full of fossils. Minnows, amphibians, brilliantly-colored damselflies, crayfish, snakes, and snapping turtles made their homes at the creek. My brother Bill and I turned over every rock we could to see what we might find, despite our father's warning about snapping turtles. "If one bites you," he'd said, "it won't let go 'til it thunders."

The creek changed course a bit with flooding. In one stretch in particular, the water took a sharp left turn, eroding and undercutting a section of the bank that was over six feet tall. Over the years, several human burials became exposed there, one at a time. My brother and I unearthed the remains, buried about four feet down, and brought the bones up to the house. They were fragile, the soil having leached away much of their mineral mass. The skulls had broken into pieces. Daddy helped us put them back together using Duco Cement.

Along with the bones, we'd found bits of leather, scant scraps of what looked like wool cloth, and chunks of brass corrosion, probably buttons or insignia. Likely, the remains belonged to casualties of the Battle of Nashville that raged in that part of town during the Civil War.

I was maybe ten and Bill twelve when we made another great discovery. We dragged out of the brush a four wheeled device made of wood, with a small, rust-encrusted motor that had a four-foot-long, segmented pipe attached. A rotting canvas and rubber belt hung limply from a drive shaft on the motor. We carefully rolled the thing on its cracked rubber wheels up to the top of the driveway and waited impatiently for Daddy to get home to ask him about it.

When he arrived and saw the contraption, he laughed. "That's a go-cart Phillip and I made." Grinning, he shook his head as if in disbelief. "I'd forgotten all about that. Where did you find it?"

We showed him.

Phillip was his childhood best friend.

"What's that," I asked pointing at the weird, little motor with the long pipe.

"That's a washing machine motor. Our old Maytag broke and I took the motor from it. Takes a mixture of oil and gasoline. The hose is long so you can stick it out a window."

"We'll fix it up and ride it," Bill said.

"Yeah!" I said, jumping around with nervous excitement. I could imagine flying down the road on the thing.

"It's been exposed to the weather for twenty years," Daddy said, shaking his head. "The wood of the frame has rotted around the bolts holding it together, and that motor will never run again."

"We'll get it running," Bill said.

I agreed with my brother—we'd get the thing going.

"You can try," Daddy said. He left us to our work.

Bill and I cleaned the thing up that evening. The next day, we put fresh fuel in it and cranked the motor's foot-starter until our feet and legs hurt. In the buggy summer heat and humidity, we became miserable. We abandoned the thing numerous times, but always came back. The following day as we continued, we heard a tiny explosion inside the motor and a puff of gray smoke popped out.

"Maybe we broke it," I said, disappointed.

Bill looked at me like I was an idiot. He smiled. "We almost got it started."

His confidence rubbed off on me. We redoubled our efforts. Soon the thing made tiny explosions fairly regularly. Daddy came home and we showed him.

"You crank it," I said. "We're all worn out."

Being over six feet tall, his legs were a lot more powerful than ours. After a couple of tries, he got the motor to turn over three or four times before quitting. Then, a loud bang came from the exhaust, and a thick black smoke ring rolled from the end of the pipe. We cheered.

"That might have helped clean it out," Daddy said. He cranked again and again. Finally the motor started and remained running for a while. The smoke had turned from black to blue-white. The thing backfired every few revolutions, sending out thick smoke rings from the pipe.

As far as I was concerned, Bill and I had done a great thing. We had succeeded at a nearly impossible task through sheer persistence.

Daddy looked at us with astonishment. "I wouldn't have believed you'd succeed, if I hadn't seen you boys do it," he said.

We had impressed our father, and that felt good. Of course we'd never be able to ride the rotten contraption, but that didn't diminish our sense of accomplishment one bit.

~ ~ ~

That sort of wild childhood is what I wanted for Littlebean.

"We live in a nice neighborhood," Melody said, "much nicer than anything we could afford back in Tennessee."

She was right. Still, our little blue house in Oregon sat in a suburban development of little lots with the six-foot-tall wooden fences around each yard. Thankfully, the neighborhood's curvy roads, many cul-de-sacs, and dead-ends discouraged through-traffic. The quiet streets and the sidewalks helped me feel better about letting Lysta explore. We'd bought her a small bicycle when she turned six. I worried about her out riding on the roads of the neighborhood, despite knowing that the drivers in Eugene were by and large much calmer and more responsible than those in Nashville.

"Are we going to watch this movie?" Melody took the controller away from me and started the film.

I still couldn't get into the story. I became lost in thought.

The dangers of traffic in the neighborhood aside, I was most concerned about Lysta's emotional and intellectual development and her happiness. Although I came from a family of smart people, I thought their intellectual successes had more to do with a fascination for life instilled at an early age, rather than high IQs. My job was to help my daughter develop a mind of sufficient curiosity that it might sustain her through the rigors of life. I hoped I was up to the task.

Melody encouraged Lysta to garden with her in the back yard. They would go out with a bucket of tools, till the soil, plant flowers, and weed. Melody hadn't enjoyed gardening in Tennessee. "Too hot, humid, and buggy," she'd said. "And the plants need too much care."

Her tune changed in Oregon. "Here, almost anything will grow. Just drop whatever you want on the ground and it'll take root."

She and Littlebean spent hours designing and planting gardens. If I went out to look in on them, most often I'd find Lysta playing with ants, worms, and a certain black beetle that exuded an unpleasant odor. Buckley, our second schipperke that we'd gotten in the year 2000, liked those bugs. I think he introduced her to them. Sometimes, when they came in from playing in the back yard, both she and Buckley stank of those beetles.

Although not on our property, Lysta did have Amazon Creek that ran through Eugene, great lengths of the thin waterway passing through parks and a wetlands preserve, with trails dedicated to pedestrians and bicycles. Together, we explore different parts of the creek, and got to know the wildlife well, including salamanders, frogs, snakes, turtles, all kinds of water fowl, and raccoons.

"I like the nutria best," Littlebean told me, "because nobody else does." The big rodents had been introduced to replace the beaver that had been hunted out over a hundred years earlier. They looked like big muskrats, had orange teeth, and were considered destructive to the creek environment.

Lysta's first day of school, she turned to me as I dropped her off. "I don't want to go to school," she said.

I totally sympathized. At the same time, my stomach sank as I thought about my poor performance in school and the trouble that had brought me.

Her door was open and both Perry and Buckley tried to get out to go with her.

"You'll have to decide if you're going to school or coming home," I said, "because we need to shut the car door."

She looked at me like I'd disappointed her, and said, "I *have* to go to school."

In relief, I smiled. "Have a good day, sweetie."

I watched her shoulder her little backpack and walk away. Lysta had courage even with her trepidations. She was a risk-taker. I loved that about her.

I did see early indications that she liked the dark side. Watching a nature show with Melody, Littlebean saw an African wild dog grab prey by the neck and shake viciously. "Mama, why did it shake the deer?" she asked.

"Maybe to break its neck."

Later while playing with Perry in the back yard, Littlebean pointed out to us that he shook his toy animals the same way.

"Break its neck," Melody said.

Perry shook the fake rabbit.

"Break its neck, Perry," Lysta said, giggling.

Truth is, I didn't care if she liked the dark side of things. I avoided pushing her toward my interests. What I hoped to find in her was a willingness to become engaged with the world around her, to explore those things that drew her attention and kindled her fascination. I suppose I was watching to see how her imagination emerged. That made me feel a bit like a policeman, looking for evidence that my daughter didn't have what it took to get along in the world and have an interesting life. Of course, I would be the one to suffer punishment if he made the case. I even visualized the cop in my head, taking petty notes on a mean little pad. Not wanting to be that way, I asked myself why I couldn't just let life happen and be happy. No answer came to me, and my petty concerns persisted. I struggled to avoid projecting onto Lysta the unhappiness I had visited upon myself in life. I'd become *such* a worrier!

Littlebean did not frighten easily. She seemed content around the creepy things we had in our home, like Melody's collection of Day of the Dead figures, our library that contained all kinds of creepy books as well as volumes of surreal and grotesque art, and the mummified animal mobile I made and hung from the ceiling of my studio.

On Saturday nights, she loved to stay up late, lie on the sofa with her mother, and watch old horror movies. *The Birds* was her favorite film, perhaps because Melody loved the movie so much. On a trip to San Francisco, California to visit my Aunt Cherry, we stopped in Bodega Bay, saw the diner and the school from the film, and then went to the beach to have a picnic. As we sat in the gravelly sand with the warm sun on us, and ate sandwiches and chips, a sea gull landed nearby and watched us. Littlebean laughed. "It's gonna *get* us!"

"It's gonna get your sandwich, if you don't eat it," Melody said.

Then another gull landed, and another, and another. "Look, look, *look*," she said, giggling and pointing to each one that came to rest in the gravel. "There are eight, no, ten of them." All the birds paced at a distance, about ten feet away, staring at us with one eye at a time.

"They *are* intimidating," I said.

Melody shuddered. "I wonder if Hitchcock had this experience here?"

"You're *scared*!" Lysta said to us, grinning. She squealed with delight.

We all laughed so hard, the birds flew away frightened.

Again, the policeman inside me had been watching Lysta intently. Apparently, he didn't merely register petty concerns; I realized that she had the dark sense of humor I liked. I could see a bit of my father in her. Sure, she'd been exposed to the macabre along with everything else, but she'd chosen to embrace the morbid with a mischievousness I knew well.

Melody had the patience to take Lysta trick or treating. Halloween was a big pseudo-holiday around our home, with much preliminary talk about costumes.

"One year," I told Lysta, "My father helped me become the Mummy. Being a doctor, he knew something about applying bandages."

"Yes, yes!" she said. "I want to be the Mummy." She extended an arm, and came toward me, dragging one foot sideways.

We did as I'd done with Daddy; got rolls of gauze and roughed them up in the fireplace ashes. Littlebean used eye liner and pastels to give herself a creepy mummy face. Trying to remember how Daddy had applied the bandages, I wrapped her from head to toe over a black leotard she'd put on. Of course, when I was a boy, over an evening of begging from door to door for candy, I'd become unraveled some. That happened even after someone who knew what he was doing had bandaged me. Littlebean lost a whole lot more bandages than I had, but that didn't seem to upset her. She and Melody, all smiles, returned with pillowcases full of candy.

They dumped their treasure on the kitchen table and Lysta pawed over the sweets trying to decide what to eat. "I didn't take a single razor blade apple," she boasted.

"Don't give yourself a stomach ache, Littlebean," Melody warned as she left the kitchen. "You had a bunch already while we were out."

I saw a type of candy I'd always loved, and picked it up. "May I have this one?"

Lysta pulled away the bandages that had slipped down over her eyes to get a look at what I held up, a peanut butter taffy wrapped in orange wax paper. "Yes," she said with a smile.

"I'm sorry my bandaging skills aren't any better," I said.

She shrugged. "The real Mummy had some that got loose too."

The policeman inside informed me that Littlebean was easy-going, willing to roll with the punches, or the loose bandages, or whatever. I knew that would serve her well as she got older. After that realization, I worried less about what the big bad world would do to my sweet child. Deciding that the policeman inside had finished his job. I tried to dismiss him.

~ ~ ~

Having found a more easy-going attitude, I'd begun to feel more confident as a father when suddenly, I knew that the world wasn't what I should worry about. Instead, *I* was the real danger. I awoke one Saturday in a fevered sweat, feeling as if I were trying to get out of a body and a mind that I hated.

My thrashing in bed had awakened Melody. She turned toward me, and held my shaking arms. "What's wrong?"

"I dreamed I gained Littlebean's confidence," I whispered, my voice quivering, "then betrayed her."

I looked into the hall to see that Lysta's bedroom door remained shut. She wasn't up yet.

"She brought home a chicken as a pet, named it something with an "s," Sally maybe. Because she loved the bird, I slaughtered it and served it to her for dinner, only telling her it was Sally after she'd taken the first bite. She cried. She hit me and hated me, but eventually calmed down. I wooed her back into my confidence and love so I could find another way to betray her."

"Just a dream," Melody whispered.

"The feelings that went with it! I feel horrible."

"You would never treat her like that."

"No," I agreed, still troubled that I'd had the dream. I wondered if some latent cruelty lurked within me, and if and when that might emerge.

In the following days, I knew the policeman inside me was back on the beat. But now, I had the odd feeling that he was secretly delighted by the prospect of finding problems, and might even encourage them. Worse than that, I imagined that if he didn't find enough trouble, he'd start some of his own. He'd gone bad. I felt a danger inside me, almost as if someone else's personality were leaking into my consciousness. Since I saw no outward manifestation of the feelings, I eventually decided that my imagination had gotten the better of me and no more. The strange thoughts and feelings remained strong for over a year before diminishing somewhat.

~ ~ ~

When Littlebean reached the age of eight, Melody and I decided she was old enough to leave the neighborhood to ride bikes with her friends. I'd gotten her a bigger bicycle. With her help I'd assembled it in our garage. As we finished, Melody opened the garage door for the launch of the new vehicle. Littlebean hopped on and circled the driveway a couple of times. Thinking about my girl riding next to cars, even in a bike lane, gave me chills. As she angled toward the street, I called out to her. She stopped and looked back, the late afternoon sunlight golden on her perfect cheek and forehead.

"You stick to the sidewalks while outside our neighborhood," I said, "okay?"

"She's not supposed to do that here," Melody said. "The sidewalks are for pedestrians. That's why they have bike lanes on the roads."

"Yeah, Daddy," Littlebean said, "you want me to look like a putz?"

She'd gotten the Yiddish word from Jill Bauman, a good friend of ours, an illustrator from New York. Littlebean called her Aunty

Jilly. We didn't tell Lysta that the word meant "penis."

"When you were a child, your parents pretty much let you run wild," Melody said. "You told me you and your brother rode all over Nashville, your dog trailing behind you where ever you went."

I glanced at Lysta, then back at Melody. "You didn't have to say that out loud."

Melody shrugged.

But she was right, my brother, sisters, and I did run wild back then. Our parents gave us room to make mistakes so we could learn how to get along in the world. "Okay," I said, and Lysta rode off down the street.

"You have to have the courage to let Littlebean make mistakes too," Melody said.

"I hope her mistakes are survivable so she'll have the opportunity to learn from them," I grumbled stupidly.

~ ~ ~

While our neighborhood wasn't the exciting sort of landscape I'd grown up in, Lysta didn't seem to notice. She explored everything and everywhere. She knew all the best dedicated bike trails throughout the city. I had no idea Eugene had so many. Littlebean led the way when we went for bicycle rides as a family in the evenings and on weekends. She insisted that we get a bike trailer for the dogs to ride in so they could go with us.

Lysta saw agility training for dogs on television one weekend. "If we built an obstacle course for Perry and Buckley," she said. "I could teach them how to run it."

We went to the garage to look for raw materials to work with. First, she asked for a couple of inclines, a bridge, and a tunnel. Then she saw a metal rod and a five foot length of wooden I-beam left over from the construction of the upper floor of the house. "We could make a teeter-totter out of that," she said, and told me just how that could be done. She had the ideas, and worked with me in the garage to make all the pieces for the course.

Finally, her grandest idea: "Let's make a flaming ring for them to jump through."

"Their fur might catch fire," I said.

"I'll always get them wet first."

We had a long discussion before I dissuaded her from pursuing her flaming notion. Littlebean got a lot of ideas and wanted to see them all realized. She was creative after all. Despite my worries shortly after her birth, I did indeed find her interesting. More recently, I'd come to the conclusion that she had developed the emotional and intellectual curiosity needed to make life itself a source of fascination for her in the years to come. Others clearly found her as fascinating as I did. She'd made good friends in the neighborhood and at school. Again, I'd begun to put some of my fears for her safety and wellbeing to rest with the notion that her life was well-started.

Even so, the sense that something dangerous lurked inside me had not gone away entirely. Not the policeman gone bad. Something worse. I couldn't put my finger on it. Since the feeling was a bit like the dread that went with the still mild temporal lobe seizures I was having, I tried to dismiss it as merely a symptom, but I was also in the midst of denying to myself that I was having the epileptic episodes. Because I saw no evidence of danger in my interactions with Littlebean, I didn't talk to Melody about the feeling. Since I could not identify the threat, I continued to push it away.

Frederick: 9

Frederick stole clothing drying on a line behind a house along the river. He made a bundle of some of the clothing and placed his case of medical instruments within the folds. He moved on, crossed the River Medway on the cast iron bridge at Rochester, and walked late into the night toward Gravesend.

Bundled in the shawl that had belonged to the woman he killed, Frederick slept for a few hours in the rushes beside the River Thames. Warmer than the air, the water created a mist that helped hide his presence.

He awakened in the late morning. Walking toward London, he decided to knock on doors and offer the services of an itinerant barber surgeon. Dead on his feet and hungry, in the late afternoon, he stopped at a smithy in Bexleyheath. The blacksmith looked him up and down suspiciously. "You don't look like any surgeon I've ever seen."

Frederick wore ill-fitting clothes of poor quality, and suspected he had bruises from the struggle with the guards at the hulk.

"I was attacked and robbed along the road from Gravesend," he said. "The footpad tore my clothing as we fought. He took my purse, but I managed to keep my instruments." He revealed his medical case in the bundle he carried.

The man gazed at Frederick a bit longer, then said, "Thomas has a bad toe." He opened the door to his home and gestured toward a boy about ten years old, seated in a chair beside a warm fireplace. "This is my son."

Thomas had one foot naked and resting on the hearth. The big toe had become swollen and red. Pus oozed from around an ingrown toenail.

Frederick could see that Thomas would lose the toe if the infection wasn't stopped. He sat beside the boy, opened the medical case, and took out scissors and a small knife.

Thomas winced, but when asked, he lifted the foot into Frederick's lap.

"Sir, if you will," Frederick said to the blacksmith, "place the poker in the hot coals."

He trimmed away callous from the ingrown toenail, gently expressed pus from the wound until blood flowed, then cauterized the open tissue. Thomas gritted his teeth throughout the procedure, yet didn't utter a sound until Frederick had finished bandaging the toe.

"Feels better," the boy said with a forced smile. He wiped tears from his cheeks.

In exchange for his service, Frederick was fed, and allowed to sleep in a tool house.

The next day, he headed for London, arriving in Poplar before dark. Frederick felt comfortable in the environment. He'd had a room in Pennyfields Street while working as a lumper at the various docks along the Thames between his time in the Royal Navy and employment at St. Pancras Station.

Fairly certain that no one watched him, Frederick slipped over a fence and into the yard behind terraced houses along Morant Street, and took clothing from a laundry line. He dressed in a privy.

One fellow saw Frederick coming back over the fence. The man smiled knowingly, and kept walking without a word.

Dressed in better clothing, but still needing a waistcoat and jacket to complete his costume, Frederick moved over several streets, knocked on doors, and resumed his role as an itinerant barber surgeon. When folks looked at him suspiciously, he gave the same excuse he'd given the blacksmith, of having been robbed while on the road.

Frederick spent a couple hours in the home of the Bixbey family, a two room abode within a brick tenement. "A shilling for the household, Mr. Armes?" the man of the house said.

Frederick had made up the name on the spot. "Yes."

"To start," Mr Bixbey said. "a shave for me, and hair cuts for the boys, Harry and Edward."

Frederick took the stubble down off the man's gaunt cheeks and prominent chin, then cut the blonde hair of his two sons, who looked to be ten and twelve years old.

A girl about eight or nine years of age hovered, watching Frederick work. When done with the boys, he turned to her. "What shall I do for you, young lady?"

"That's little Grace." Mr. Bixbey said. "Show the man your

knees, girl."

She backed away, shaking her head, never taking her eyes off Frederick. He crouched down to be at her eye level. Grace opened her mouth and wobbled a bottom front tooth with her finger.

"I can take that out for you," he said.

She approached slowly, leaning forward and holding her mouth wide. Frederick tested the looseness with a digit, decided he didn't need a tool. He gripped the thing between two fingers and jerked it free. Wide-eyed, the girl stuck a finger in the bloody hole in her lower jaw. She smiled and looked for the tooth in his hand. He held it out for her. She took it, smiled, then raised her shift to show the boils on her knees.

A young, attractive ginger-haired woman entered the room as Frederick lanced the boils.

"My wife, Rose," Mr. Bixbey said. "Dearest, this is Mr. Armes."

"A pleasure, sir," the woman said.

"Yes, a pleasure." Frederick struggled to remain focused on Grace's knees, when he wanted to turn his full attention to the beautiful Rose. "And what shall I do for you, this evening?" he asked her, as he expressed pus from the last of the boils.

"Thank you, but I am not in need of your services, sir."

Disappointed, Frederick took a deep breath and tried to relax. Having the excuse to merely approach her with a blade, would have been a delight.

After exiting the Bixbey home, Frederick walked along the street to the entrance to a back lane. He shooed a cat out of a small crate, hid his few possessions in the box, and carried the thing with him to give an impression that he pursued an errand in the neighborhood. He tried to think about how he might look on a delivery of some sort, and acted accordingly.

Four people passed him as he moved along the back lane. None of them appeared curious.

Most of the gates to the yards behind the old terraced houses were barred. He didn't know exactly what he sought. He had precious little, though, so about anything he might scrounge or steal would be of use. A blanket would be a good thing to find, since he'd be sleeping rough again that night.

His situation brought back memories of the time following his mother's death, when he'd had no home, slept in doorways or among the rubble of rotting houses with other homeless children, and scavenged for whatever he could find to eat or sell. His uncle, Mr. Garrett Rodgers from Manchester, had taken in Frederick's older sister, Abigail, but not Frederick.

Her last words to him still hurt. "So, the street will see more of you," she'd said. "You've always been a bit of a waif, anyway."

He had indeed spent the bulk of his time in the street when not in school, and got into trouble, hoisting in the markets and stealing clothes off lines, yet when his mother was alive, he'd always had a home to return to at night.

Frederick hated Abigail and his uncle for abandoning him. He survived on the street by throwing in with other forsaken children, and spent many of his loneliest hours cold, hungry, and brooding about the warm, posh life at the Rodgers home in Manchester. Of course, Uncle Garrett was poor, and Frederick knew that nothing about the man's life spoke of luxury. That didn't lessen his young resentment one bit.

For a time, Frederick had earned as a crossing sweeper. Then he fell in with a group of boys, all between ten and fourteen. He learned to pick locks and pockets. After a few successful, but low gain thefts, he nearly got caught while trying to break into a warehouse at the London Docks. The Night Rounders did catch two of his friends on that occasion. A Magistrate gave those friends three months hard labor for their trouble. Frederick never saw them again.

A charismatic thirteen-year-old named Simon joined Frederick's group of boys. Simon had interesting ideas for combining fun and earning. First, he performed daring feats of balance and agility and challenged his mates to match them. Soon all the boys were tempting fate and daring each other. Excited by the activity, Frederick performed some of the most daring feats, and received several minor injuries. The boys climbed all over rotting structures in neighborhoods of abandoned houses. They leapt from one sagging roof to another, balanced on exposed timbers, swung and jumped from beam to beam, all at great heights.

One day, a gentleman passing by a ruined house the boys had infested, saw their antics. Clearly amused, he stopped and watched. Simon, standing on the footway and seeing the fellow, shouted to

Frederick who stood on his tiptoes at the end of a beam suspended thirty feet above an exposed floor. "We have an audience, Freddy. Entertain him. Jump!"

Considering himself one of countless, anonymous street children, seen as having little worth, Frederick became excited by the idea of having an audience. He thought for only a moment before leaping high into the air. As he did, he twisted around to face the end of the beam. As he was about to fall past it, he caught the end with his hands, then dangled by one arm, hooting and shouting. He swung, caught a lower beam, and leapt gracefully to the floor.

"Sir, what do you think of us?" Simon asked the gentleman. "We are the Regal Rats."

He'd made up the name then and there, but it stuck.

The gentleman spoke loudly so all the boys could hear. "I think you'll be performing one day at the Alhambra." He made a show of counting Simon, Frederick, and the other boys. "Eight of you?" he asked.

"That's right, sir."

"Here is a shilling to share with your company," the gentleman said, pressing the coin into Simon's hand. "That's pence ha'penny each. You be sure to share that."

"Yes, sir," Simon said with a winning smile.

The Regal Rats ate well that evening. Frederick and one of the other boys named Bertram each threw in a penny to buy a loaf of bread. Frederick ate his half of the loaf all in one sitting, an extravagance that made him sick to his stomach, yet one that he could not deny himself.

After that, Simon challenged his mates to try increasingly dangerous stunts, always in ruins with interiors exposed to the street. He stationed two of the Regal Rats on the road beside the ruin. They were to gape, gasp, and look wide-eyed, as if frightened for the safety of the boys performing within. With that, passersby who took notice of the performance occasionally gave an appreciative gratuity.

The occasional audience was like water for a thirsty boy. Frederick lapped it up.

Aiden: 10

Another dream gave me a fear that I was a danger to my own daughter. The look in a boy's eyes set it off, I thought.

The boy, named Daniel, about thirteen years old, lived in the house next door. He was short and sandy-haired, somewhat pimply. His mom, a single parent, seemed to be a drug addict, one of the maintenance variety; not much of a threat, never truly blotto. Still, she didn't earn an income, and wasn't much of a mother, as far as I could tell. She'd inherited the house when her father died.

Johnny Knoxville's pack of jackasses, the ones who had the extreme-sports/dare-devil/flirt-with-death-and-pain show on MTV, inspired Daniel and his young pals. I liked that show. Something about what Daniel and his friends got up to was disturbingly different, though. Perhaps I felt that way because I knew they didn't get paid for it, as well as the fact that the danger they visited upon themselves took place so close to my home and my child.

They had skate boards and bicycles of different types. They'd stolen shopping carts from the local grocery store, and made various types of carts to ride in. They dared each other to perform dangerous stunts, and made makeshift ramps, chutes and obstacle courses to try to survive while riding their vehicles.

In many ways Daniel had an unfortunate life. After his grandfather died, he probably got little adult care or guidance.

On behalf of his mother, he came over numerous times to "borrow" one type of food or another; eggs, butter, milk, hamburger.

"We have eggs for dinner every night." he told me once.

"Why?" I asked.

"Cause they're cheap."

I gave him an old computer and tried to show him how the thing worked. I let him borrow tools and video games until he failed to return them. He became increasingly surly, reminding me of the James family back in Nashville.

The fun Daniel and his friends had became messier by the day, sometimes making its way over the fence into our yard. I had numerous talks with the boy about toning their play down.

126

"I don't want to spoil your fun—I did all kinds of crazy things like this when I was your age—but I had a lot more room than we have in this neighborhood. You've damaged the fence and rutted the part of my yard next to yours. It's becoming a mud pit. Do what you want to your yard, but not mine, okay? Keep it over on your side and I'll be happy."

"Yeah," he said. That was all he had for me.

One day I saw him up on the roof of his house, tossing flaming rags down onto his friends as they rode bicycles through a short maze. The way the cloth burned told me he'd soaked the rags in an accelerant, like gasoline. Although I thought about Lysta's desire to have our dogs jump through a flaming hoop, and felt bad about squashing Daniel's fun, I'd had enough and spoke to his mother.

"Daniel and his friends are throwing flaming rags around the yard. Please do something about your son's dangerous behavior so I won't have to."

She pretended to be horrified. Her voice succeeded in expressing outrage, but her slight stupor didn't allow the emotions to be reflected on her face. Still, the boys didn't throw fire again.

Daniel attempted to turn his mom's beater of a car, which had sat inoperable in their driveway for over a year, into a part of his obstacle course. He and his friends used a sledgehammer to beat the vehicle into a shape that they could attach ramps onto. On that day, Melody was at work, Lysta in school, and I'd gone out running errands. I came back to find the boys hammering away. They'd totally destroyed the car, having broken all the glass, crushed the roof and dented every inch of the body. As I arrived, Daniel was hitting the trunk so hard, sparks flew. No doubt the vehicle still held fuel. I got scared and hurried over to stop them.

"I'm calling the city to have this car hauled away. I don't think you want to be here when the police arrive."

Without challenging me, the boys wandered off in sullen disappointment.

I did sympathize with Daniel. In many ways, his life sucked, but I couldn't let him endanger my family. I did contact the city and they sent out a crew to haul the hulk away.

The next day, I saw Daniel watching Lysta riding her bike along our road. The look in his eyes was pure resentment. He didn't know I watched him. I feared what he might do in retaliation for what I'd done to squash his fun, yet I tried not to let that get to me.

"Lysta," I said at dinner, "stay away from Daniel for a while. Just don't go near him and his friends if you see them, okay?"

"I don't have anything to do with him, anyway," she said.

"Good."

That night, I dreamed that I stalked Lysta as she rode her bike through our neighborhood. She was a little bitch who had everything, while I had next to nothing. Her asshole of a father thought he could buy my friendship, but he didn't really give a shit about me.

I decided I was somehow channeling Daniel's feelings, because in the dream, Lysta was my neighbor, not my daughter. Even as I wondered about that, she became my sister. I hated her, and looked for a way to get her alone so I could cut her.

I forced myself to awaken. Melody hugged me while I struggled and cried out.

Lysta came into our bedroom. "What's wrong?"

I felt the need to harm her, and I liked that feeling. The hatred from the dream had followed me back to the waking world. Even as I looked at the fright on her face, I felt a weird satisfaction.

"Get out!" I shouted. "Quickly, run—get out."

Littlebean stared at me in horror.

"It's okay, sweetie," Melody said. "Your father's had a bad dream is all."

Without another word, Lysta turned away and left the room.

Melody eventually rolled over and went back to sleep.

I couldn't sleep. About four in the morning, I went to Littlebean's room, opened the door and looked in on her, determined to run if the desire to harm her awoke inside me. Thankfully, the feeling had passed. She didn't stir. I left her alone and returned to bed.

The next day, no one said anything about my nightmare. That's what they believed I'd had, and I agreed. Lysta didn't seem to have hurt feelings. I tried to let the incident go, but I'd become frightened. Several days passed before I ceased to brood about the dream.

Within the year, Daniel and his mom lost the house because she hadn't paid the property taxes. They moved away and I never saw them again, but I wondered from time to time if Daniel was okay, if he had a life, if he was happy.

~ ~ ~

Somehow, while I wasn't watching, Lysta had become increasingly interested in what had been an ordinary, everyday aspect of her life: my artwork. She started with questions about age eleven.

She'd come upstairs to my studio. I was at the drafting table, working on a sketch for the cover art of Simon Clark's novel, *Vampyrrhic,* an image that depicted a little boy reaching into darkness after a toy while unaware that a ghoulish form in those shadows reached for him. Always careful not to bump my table while I worked, Lysta stood back a little bit. "Why do you like such creepy stuff?"

I sat up straight, put my pencil down, and turned to her. "You like creepy things, too."

She came closer. "Yeah, but I don't make them."

"Well, I suppose I'm a little odd. I grew up around a lot of creepy things, and your grandfather, my father, liked that sort of stuff too. Some of that maybe comes with being a doctor because his father, your great-grandfather, enjoyed morbid things as well."

I'd become hopeful as she brought up the subject. "Do you want to make creepy stuff, too?"

"Well, in art class the other day, I was going to draw something awful. I stopped because I don't want anyone to think I'm weird."

"What kind of awful?"

"Siamese twins." She grinned nervously, shifted uneasily on her feet. "I saw it in one of the books in the walk-in closet."

The one she referred to was titled *Anomalies and Curiosities of Medicine,* a large hardcover tome published in 1900, filled with descriptions and illustrations of different types of deformities of human disease and anatomy.

"Some of the books in that closet belonged to my father's father. When we were boys, your Uncle Bill and I looked through all his old books. Although they were full of gross stuff, I liked them. I guess I think the world and life has a lot of scary stuff, and taking a liking to some of that takes away the power it has to frighten."

"Like illness or being deformed?" she asked. "I wouldn't want to have a sister stuck on the side of my head. It's gross and scary."

"I see what you mean. Why'd you want to draw it?"

"Cause I wasn't afraid to, and...I don't know...it's interesting. I wonder what the Siamese sisters would say to each other." She looked a bit embarrassed, as if she wasn't certain she'd made an appropriate use of her imagination.

"I think it's fun to think about things like that. Some people won't understand. If a person thought you were weird for being interested in it, then they don't know you. The world is full of people who decide what others are all about without getting to know them. If someone treats you that way, they're missing out on making a wonderful friend. I'd feel sorry for a person like that."

"So how'd that book get here?"

"I brought it here after my father died, along with a couple others; the one about the history of medical illustrations, and some of the old medical textbooks. They used to be in my Grandaddy's study, sitting on a shelf that also held two human skulls. When I was a boy and had a new friend visiting the house, I'd say, 'You want to see my grandfather's skull? It's on a shelf in the room where he died. All that was true, but not the way the new friend took it. If I showed him the two skulls, I explained about Grandaddy's work, and admitted that neither one had ever been under the skin of his head."

She grinned again, then wrinkled her nose. "You were funny."

"Funny looking!"

Since I wasn't drawing, she leaned on my drafting table and considered my sketch. "I could draw that," she said. Somehow, I knew she didn't mean to be competitive. She meant that she'd be comfortable drawing something like I'd drawn, something that creepy.

I got the impression, Lysta Littlebean was a closet goth, like her mother. We'd always had goth friends, like Lorelei Shannon, who collaborated with me and Cousin Stephen on the duology *The Blood of Father Time*. Lorelei wore a lot of black, dyed her hair odd colors, and drove a hearse. Melody thought of her as particularly cool. Even so, Melody would never for a moment consider presenting herself in a way that might make someone look at her oddly.

I think Littlebean was asking for my permission to be weird.

"You should draw whatever you want. Don't worry about what people *might* think. If someone has a problem with you, let them work up the guts to tell you about it."

Her nervous grin had disappeared. Instead, she wore a confident smile.

After that conversation, Lysta drew more often. I did not expect what poured out of her imagination. As her father, I wasn't particularly objective, but I'd say that I found her subject matter, compositions, her budding style, her ideas, and the sense of humor evident in her work engaging and unique.

Lysta Littlebean Clark had the weird gene that Grandaddy, Daddy and I had, the one that sparked an appreciation for the bizarre and a sense of humor about the dark and disturbing. Not only that, she loved art!

I taught her to paint. In my studio, we collaborated on paintings, drawings, and sculptures! I got a new, oversized drafting table so we could work side by side.

One painting that we did together when she was thirteen, I considered to be quite good. We'd done a sketch of figures with giant mouths chasing and devouring one another. As we painted together at the new drafting table, the piece became weirder and funnier.

I got so worked up, talking and laughing with her about our piece of art, I had a seizure. As the smell and the dread came on, I gripped the edge of the drafting table. I couldn't see Lysta for a time. Instead, I seemed to be carried in a boat over a river, and roughly dumped on the bank. I had the sense that I'd lost everything, that I was alone in the world with no future. Again, I felt as if I were remembering something I didn't really recognize.

Then Lysta shook my arm. "Daddy, look at me. *Daddy*, are you okay?"

She seemed to relax when I focused on her.

We resumed painting, but the spell had been broken, my good humor gone.

"Don't tell your mother about what happened to me, okay?"

She nodded absently as she put her finishing touches on our masterpiece.

Even then, I wouldn't admit to myself that the seizures were a problem. I told myself that I'd merely had an elaborate daydream.

The truth, though, exerted some pressure. I worried about having a seizure while driving. Since I worked at home, I didn't need to go out much. Littlebean rode her bike to school. I decided to cut back even further on my driving.

I focused on my daughter and her growing talent instead of my health. As she grew, she became my compatriot, my artistic confidant, a co-explorer in the landscape of artistic expression.

I felt I had died and gone to heaven.

Frederick: 10

Well past his fortieth year, Frederick avoided risks to his physical well-being if possible. Resisting the urge to climb fences, he didn't find anything useful along the alley until he saw a window at the back of one of the houses with a slightly crooked sash. No lights shone from the house to which it belonged. Frederick tried and found the gate locked. He took his possessions out of the crate. Carrying them, he climbed the fence as quickly and quietly as he could, and made his way to the window. As he pushed, the lower sash reluctantly slid upward within the jamb. He entered what scant moonlight revealed to be a single room dwelling. The one door seemed to be locked from the other side. He discovered a few shriveled potatoes in a bin, and part of a loaf in a bread box. Although the potatoes had sprouted and the bread had become hard and dry, he devoured them.

A layer of dust told Frederick that whoever lived there hadn't been home for some time. He ate, relaxed on the dusty bed, and reflected further on his time with the Regal Rats.

If he'd ever loved anyone besides his mother, Frederick had loved Simon. He had not lifted Frederick and his other mates entirely out of the gutter, but he'd tried.

Simon eventually took their act to the streets around Leicester Square. Instead of scampering about in ruins, they performed in the road. Again, two boys gaped, pointed, and called attention, while their fellows dashed about among the traffic. Frederick and his pals leapt through the gap between the legs of walking and trotting horses or the wheels of carriages in motion. They capered over the backs of horses, climbed moving carriages and wagons, leapt from one vehicle to another, deftly avoiding the whips and swats of the drivers. Gripping spokes, they cartwheeled down the road attached to hansoms and growlers. If those driving or riding the conveyances became upset, or if a constable got involved, so much the better. The two boys calling attention to their fellow's feats also solicited donations. During times when crowds made their way to various performances at the square, the earnings doubled.

Among the Regal Rats, Simon's greatest competition for the

boldest, most daring feats had always been Frederick. The two worked out increasingly dangerous street antics. With a sense that the larger society had tossed him away and preferred to ignore him, Frederick continued to feed on the attention he got. His goal was to shock audiences into remembering him. His craving for the attention grew so strong that he pushed Simon for more.

"Let's set up for the crowds leaving the halls as well," Frederick said.

"Too dangerous after dark," Simon said. "Not enough light, and you know how the pavers sweat once the sun goes down."

"We'll be more careful." Frederick turned to the other boys to make an appeal. "We can do it for the money, can't we, Rats?"

He'd touched upon a motivating force. The boys were doing better than ever keeping themselves housed and fed, but they wanted more comfort. Currently, they sat around an abandoned saw mill where they slept at night. The business had closed down after a fire burned half the structure.

"Bertram and I found lodgings in Great Windmill Street as might take us all," Alex said. "We just need enough chink."

"Winter is coming," Quint said. "Would be nice to have a warm place."

Several of the others nodded hopefully.

"Squint, he always complains when the weather turns cold," Simon said. He waved his hand in the air as if he could dismiss the idea entirely with one gesture. A long silence followed while the Regal Rats continued to gaze at their leader. Simon clearly became uncomfortable. "We'd be too tired out to do another show so late," he protested. "That and the dark—I won't lead you boys into harm."

"Well," Frederick said, "if you're frightened…"

Finn poked at Simon with a look of challenge.

"Come on," Alex said. "Like Freddy says, we can do it."

Simon glared at Frederick, yet reluctantly agreed to do a street performance the evening of the following Saturday.

When the day came, the chill fall weather had left moisture on the paving stones. The air had become still. A haze of coal smoke hung over the Leicester Square area. As the audiences attending performances exited the theaters and music halls, the pall of smoke seemed to dampen their mood. The Regal Rats' antics in the road were largely ignored.

"Walk the wheel," Frederick said to Simon. "That always gets the crowd excited."

Simon frowned. The leader of the Regal Rats was the only one among the group who could balance on the moving wheel of a hansom cab. The feat required a carriage moving at just the right pace, and a confederate to draw the driver's attention to the right side of the vehicle, while Simon mounted the left wheel and took rapid steps on top of the turning rim. He dropped off the wheel onto the pavement as soon as the driver noticed him. Although the action didn't last long, those watching loved the feat, and it always increased their earnings.

Simon shook his head. "Too dangerous."

"Is that all you have for us tonight," Frederick asked, "cowardice?"

Several of the boys watched to see what Simon would do. Their leader looked up and down the lane. His eyes fixed on a hansom cab approaching from the south. "Squint," he said, "you catch the driver's eye."

Simon spit on the pavement at Frederick's feet, then scampered with Quint into the road to meet up with the cab. As the carriage came close, Finn and Alex did their best to draw the attention of the crowd moving along the footway to the action in the street. Frederick saw the head of the hansom driver turn toward the right. Simon made his move, grabbing spokes near the rim and allowing their movement to pull him up onto the wheel. In a fluid motion Frederick had never been able to get right, Simon found his feet on the wheel rim, facing the direction the carriage traveled, and began walking backwards in rapid, mincing steps. Gasps, oohs, and aahs from the crowd on the footway drew the driver's attention back to the left.

The man was quick. Seeing Simon, he struck him with his whip.

Frederick had seen Simon dodge whips many times, and didn't want to believe his eyes as he watched his friend stumble. Simon's face reflected confusion and frustration. His arms pinwheeled briefly as he fell in front of the wheel. The rim passed over Simon's neck, and the carriage kept going. Those watching on the footway flooded into the road, surrounding the broken boy, and obscuring Frederick's view. That was the last he saw of Simon.

Frederick experienced a pang of loss that reminded him so much of what he'd known when his mother died that he immediately pushed the feeling aside, and walked away.

~ ~ ~

In the days that followed, the Regal Rats looked at him with scorn. Even so, he tried to lead them. Their performances lacked a certain vitality. They had lost their spirit. None of them had the charisma to gather much of an audience. Frederick told himself that Simon's death wasn't his fault, but fearing that he deserved to be the next to fall maimed or dead, he quit the street company.

He returned to scavenging for a living. Trying to find a position in industry at age fifteen, he found that he'd become too large to perform most child labor, and wasn't considered mature and trustworthy enough for an adult job. He worked as a pure finder, selling dog shit to tanneries, and tried his hand as a tosher in the sewers beneath the city. Once he'd had enough of going hungry, he lied about his age and joined the Royal Navy.

The agility Frederick had gained with the Regal Rats proved invaluable while learning the ropes of the HMS Challenger. The experience did not help him avoid the block Simon's ghost had swung at his head. When he'd first begun to have his fits, he'd known they were Simon's revenge.

Frederick hadn't thought of those boys in a long time. Remembering their feats of daring, he hoped he still had enough agility and stealth to reach his next goal. For the few things he'd need to purchase, Frederick would continue to earn as an itinerant barber surgeon. He'd search out a chemist's shop or a surgery, break in, and steal chloroform and morphine. Then he'd find a secure location where he could hide a young woman, perhaps one of the abandoned storehouses along Bow Creek. Homeless squatters would be a problem with any abandoned property, but he'd deal with that when the time came.

Killing that woman on the road had reawakened his need for a certain type of satisfaction. Since she'd died too quickly, his desire had been stimulated, then frustrated.

He stroked his prick. Instead of finding release, he found the edges of a fit. Odd thoughts and feelings, as if belonging to someone else, flitted through his mind. He cast them off and redoubled his effort to find release. As he pictured a gaping wound and stroked harder, faster, the bed banged against the wall. That stopped him.

Frederick hoped the noise had not revealed his presence in the house. He imagined those living in other rooms deciding to investigate, finding him, and the possible consequences. His gut churned uncomfortably as he thought about having to get up and flee. After a while, with no one coming for him, Frederick relaxed.

Finally, he slept.

Aiden: 11

As quickly as I'd come to see Lysta as my compatriot, she'd decided I wasn't cool. Actually, I could see that coming for over a year, as she became increasingly impatient with Melody and me. At fourteen years of age, she told me, "Don't call me 'Littlebean.' That's a kid's name."

I didn't like her boyfriend, a kid named Sean who had a hard time looking me in the eye. The truth is, I didn't like him because she preferred to spend her time with Sean rather than creating artwork. She hadn't painted or drawn with me, or on her own, since she met him six months earlier. She hadn't been home much either.

On a Saturday when her plans to meet with Sean fell through, I asked her to help me start a painting we'd sketched out and had been planning for almost a year. In a bad mood, she merely shook her head.

Then I said exactly the wrong thing. "Lysta, you shouldn't abandon your talent right as it's beginning to develop."

"I'm more interested in other things these days. The art I've done is just silliness. I've got better things to do."

I could not imagine what those things might be, yet I knew enough to back off. If I gave her room, she'd return to her creativity soon enough. I sure didn't like the way she looked at art in that moment.

I threw myself into my work and tried to give Lysta room to grow into a young adult.

~ ~ ~

That year, 2010, Lazy Fascist Press published a collection of my short fiction. The publisher, Cameron Pierce, then approached me at BizarroCon and asked, "Would you write a novel for us?"

In his mid-twenties at the time, he seemed very serious and earnest for such a young fellow. His writing was a lot more playful than he was. I liked what he wrote and what his publishing company chose to put out in the world.

We were surrounded by other people, mostly writers, who were all talking, laughing, and having a good time. The volume of nearby voices made conversation difficult. The event takes place just outside of Portland, Oregon at a weird hotel with surreal murals on most of its walls. The place had been a work farm during the Depression and later a nursing home. The structures are slightly institutional, but old-fashioned and fun to explore.

With Cameron's invitation, suddenly I was no longer at the event—at least my mind was elsewhere.

I'd had four novels published at that point, all collaborations with talented authors. The novels I'd worked on alone, I hadn't tried to get published because I didn't consider them good enough.

Coming from a publisher I respected, the invitation seemed like a gift. To take full advantage of the opportunity, whatever I wrote had to be an ambitious undertaking. Immediately, the novel about Ripper victim Catherine Eddowes, comprised of chapters based on the acquisition of the items found with her at the murder scene, presented itself and would not take "no" for an answer.

I pitched the idea to Cameron then and there. He could barely hear me, so I suggested we step away from the crowd. As we stood in a slight drizzle outside the hotel function space referred to as the Ad House, I gave a better description.

"Yes," he said, "write that book."

~ ~ ~

Being a piece of historical fiction, the research required to write the novel about Catherine Eddowes discouraged me, as I'd known it would. Progress on the project remained slow and grueling during the first week of work. By the end of the second week, the effort had become somewhat easier. Then the accumulation of knowledge about my subject matter began to snowball, and progress in getting the story down accelerated rapidly. The novel was written and edited within two months.

I'd researched historical settings and events for fiction before, but none of the environments had seemed particularly familiar to me. Somehow, I felt accustomed to the environment of Victorian London. Moving characters around on the streets of the city, in the homes, and work environments had a natural, unplanned flow I didn't expect. Writing dialogue felt more like listening to what my characters had to say. Although carefully plotted out, the amount of discovery I experienced while in the creative process was greater than what I'd known in previous writing efforts.

The novel, *Of Thimble and Threat*, came out in 2011.

I went on to write more historical fiction novels for Lazy Fascist Press, two that took place in the United States, a southern gothic titled *A Parliament of Crows*, and an early western, *The Door That Faced West*. But Victorian London called to me. The haunting feeling that I'd *been there* at some point in my past intrigued me, and I missed the gritty environment. I returned by writing the second novel in what became my Jack the Ripper Victims Series, *Say Anything but Your Prayers*, the story of Elizabeth Stride, who died at the hands of the Ripper an hour earlier than Catherine Eddowes.

The third in the series, *A Brutal Chill in August*, explored the life the first victim, Mary Ann "Polly" Nichols.

~ ~ ~

One afternoon, while caught up in the odd déjà vu feelings I got during some of my research, I had a light seizure. Although I didn't lose awareness of my studio, images/ideas/thoughts—something akin to a sexual fantasy perhaps—flowed through my head as if from someone else's mind. I imagined a deep, bloody gash in a human thigh spread open. *That is a beautiful vagina*, I found myself thinking. *I'd put my penis in the wound if it were sharp enough. No, I want a knife for that. A knife will bring much more satisfaction.*

I truly didn't know what to do with those thoughts. The sexual fantasy wasn't the sort I cared to have. Along with the images, I felt the dread I'd known from previous temporal lobe hallucinations.

I could no longer deny that the seizures had returned. Unfortunately, that didn't mean I intended to do anything about them.

~ ~ ~

Lysta fell in with a bad crowd. At least that's the way I saw them. Truth is, I never really knew much about her high school friends. They were a bit secretive, and that's what alarmed Melody and me. Lysta stayed out after school. Sometimes, she didn't show up for dinner. She wanted to stay the night at girlfriends' houses all the time. When she did come home, she often smelled of pot or cigarette smoke.

Melody and I tried to give her room. At the same time we made an effort to keep up with her; calling her cell phone, asking her to let us know where she went and what plans she had. Lysta kept her phone turned off except when she used it. If she got our messages, she rarely called or texted back. I became afraid she might be doing drugs worse than pot while away with her friends.

"You can't just do whatever you want, whenever you want." I told her.

We sat for a nice spaghetti dinner together in the kitchen, something that didn't happen as often as Melody and I liked. "We need to know where you are all the time. We have a legal obligation to take care of you."

"I should be able to make decisions on my own," Lysta complained. "I'm almost an adult."

"You don't have the experience to be an adult." I regretted the statement immediately, not because it wasn't true, but because I could see in her eyes how the words affected her. I might as well have said, "You're stupid, and ugly, and no one will ever love you."

Melody had gone to the refrigerator for the pitcher of ice tea. Standing behind Lysta at some distance, Melody pretended to pull a zipper across her lips.

"You're an ageist and a hypocrite!" Lysta said to me with as much bite as she could muster. "You lived on your own at sixteen."

While Melody poured tea into our glasses, I gave her a withering look. "I thought we agreed not to talk about certain things."

Melody grimaced as she sat back down. "Sorry," she said.

"I'm right *here*," Lysta said.

Her impatience, the contempt in her eyes, how could I break through that?

"She also said you were a bad kid and your parents sent you away."

Fuck! Enough truth existed in what she'd said to damn me unless I explained, and I didn't know if Lysta should hear about that time in my life.

"I wasn't a bad kid, just not nice at times." That didn't sound persuasive.

Lysta sat silently, her eyebrows raised in challenge, and a self-satisfied hitch in her lower lip.

Melody poked at her food and kept her head down. She'd opened a can of worms and she knew I wasn't happy with her.

"I tried to become more independent too early, like you're doing."

Lysta pretended to consider that, then asked, "Were your parents being mean or giving you the room you needed?"

She'd never known Daddy—truly she'd been too young to re-member spending time with him—but she'd gotten to know and love my mother. I had to wonder if she thought we might send her away, or if perhaps she wanted that.

I shook my head, frustrated. "It was complicated. Yes, actually, I got what I wanted. Look, all children have to grow up and move away. Sometimes they do things to make that move faster. Sometimes parents want to hold on in ways that makes things worse."

"Like you're doing?"

I knew I'd have to tell her something about my teen years. My rebellion against the world, especially against my parents, had begun the year before I decided to do no schoolwork.

"Maybe," I said. "Could be I'm worried about you because of the things I did."

Now, she had a smug look on her face, like she didn't think I'd ever risked much in life for adventure.

I remembered a Halloween party we'd had at the house back in Nashville. A lot of our friends had children then. They brought their kids to the party, but the children went out back and had their own party without the adults. I went to check on them, asked if they want-ed to take part in the games, the ghost story-telling, and such.

The oldest girl, named Susan, turned to me and said, "No, thanks. My parents don't know how to have fun. They're not at all cool."

"Well, there are a lot of other cool people here at the party," I said.

She looked at me like she couldn't possibly believe I spoke the truth. I had the impression that she thought her father, an old friend of mine named Joe, wasn't capable of risking anything for adventure.

Joe had lived with me for a time in San Francisco during the early 1970s. Although a self-destructive time, we'd been involved in all kinds of great sex, drugs, and rock and roll. She knew nothing of the adventures, some truly *cool* ones, in which her father had partic-ipated.

And I could not tell her about it. I left the children out back and returned to the party, where I felt particularly cool for having survived my early adventures and for not drinking.

Sitting across the dining room table from me, Lysta had the

same expression of contempt the girl, Susan, had shown. And just like with Susan, I felt like I shouldn't tell my daughter about the iniquities of the past.

Nobody was eating the delicious spaghetti dinner I'd cooked. I debated getting up from the table and leaving the conversation, yet I hesitated, knowing the problem wouldn't get any better unless I risked something.

"In seventh grade, at age thirteen, I got involved with kids who had wrangled certain freedoms from their parents—some had motorcycles, some were allowed to smoke or stay out all night with friends whenever they wanted—that sort of thing—and I wanted those freedoms too." Lysta tried to interrupt, but I was quicker. "Most of the kids had more independence because their parents both worked or were divorced and didn't have the time to monitor their children as well as mine did."

I'd actually had great freedom throughout my childhood to make all the mistakes I wanted, and, boy, did I ever.

"You smoked, didn't you?"

I ignored the question, and the desire to ask if she ever smoked.

"Like you, at age thirteen, I wanted to see myself as an adult."

"I'm fifteen."

"I grew my hair long—you've seen the pictures—and started hanging out with hippies on the steps of the Parthenon in Centennial Park."

"Sure, you smoked pot too, I'll bet."

"Yes, and much worse," I said.

Lysta's mouth closed and I knew I had her attention.

"All that frightened my parents, and they tried to control my movements, so I steered clear of them the best I could. I didn't go home some days after school and some nights, and they had no idea where I was."

"You're even more of a hypocrite, now."

"Yes, I'm a hypocrite wanting to have a say in who you hang out with, but I know from experience the kind of trouble you could get into."

"But—"

"Wait, and I'll tell you even worse."

She closed her mouth again.

"The police arrested me several times, once for running away from home, once for possession of marijuana, and once for taking LSD with a kid who had a bad trip and ended up in the hospital."

I didn't know Lysta's eyes could get that big.

Melody shook her head and got up to clear the table.

"Another arrest for armed robbery—"

"You're *not* serious!" Lysta cried with a shrill laugh.

"—of a drug store." I held up my hands and smiled nervously. "I was innocent, but I guess I'd gained a reputation as a druggie in school and in my neighborhood, partly because of who I hung out with. The clerk at the drug store, who'd been robbed at gunpoint, said the perp looked like me. The police held me until the clerk saw my mug shot and said I was not the one."

I paused.

"More," she said. Lysta seemed to think she had fun at my expense.

"I hitchhiked all over town, also out of town with friends to see concerts and outdoor music festivals. Some who picked me up, robbed and abused me."

"What do you mean?"

I shook my head and, thankfully, Lysta let go of the question.

I couldn't tell her that one guy who picked me up raped me. Unfortunately, I had my first orgasm during the experience. I had to wonder what the response meant since it occurred while one I didn't find the least bit attractive treated me cruelly. With no ready answers, I became distrustful of my body and mind. A couple of bad LSD trips following that and I found myself with a shattered personality that I had to rebuild over the course of several years. Having survived the deep end had helped a lot with those situations.

"By the time I was fourteen years old, I'd found a slightly better class of friends. Some were artists. We'd get high smoking pot, and collaborate on weird artwork."

Lysta nodded her head knowingly, and I resisted the urge to ask if she'd smoked pot.

"'All I want to do is to hang out with my friends and create,' I screamed at my parents. The truth is that a lot of my unhappiness came from an addiction to being high. That was a large part of why I did so poorly in school. I failed the eighth grade and had to take it over again. I wanted an art education, and Nashville public schools gave me little of that. Being cruel to my parents, I said the most horrible things to them I could think of, just to hurt them."

Perhaps because she could see the regret that rose up in me as I spoke, Lysta's face took on a sad frown. Although she did say things to hurt us, she never seemed proud of that, and I could see that she struggled not to, even in the heat of arguments.

Melody worked quietly at the kitchen sink.

"Things got so bad between us, I suppose they *did* want me gone. They still loved me, though, and tried to give me what I wanted. They sent me to San Francisco to live with my Uncle Mac. He and Aunt Cherry had divorced, and he agreed to take me on as a roommate and help me find a high school that would give me a better art education. The next year, one of my art friends came out and we got a place together. I was still addicted to being high. Pot started making me paranoid, but I just kept at it. I drank along with doing the pot to dampen the paranoia. At sixteen, I made a lot of bad choices."

Lysta looked a bit apologetic as she said, "Yeah, but you had some adventures, and got an art education."

"Yes, I did. I also suffered a lot for those bad decisions. I had addictions to overcome, and a lot of shame for all the stupid and occasionally dangerous things I did while high and not thinking straight."

"I'm not like that," she said defiantly.

"I wasn't either until I got involved with drugs."

"Is that what this is about, me doing drugs?"

"It's about your ability to make decisions. Like I was, you're too young to decide *everything* for yourself."

She folded her arms and glared at me, then got that distant, sullen look about her she'd had at the beginning of the conversation. As I looked at her, I imagined one day having to pick her up downtown at the police station, and finding a tweaker shell of what had once been my beautiful and talented daughter. Although that extreme vision wasn't likely, I knew I'd never be able to help her avoid such things if she didn't trust my judgment. I thought hard about what my parents had done to draw me back in.

"We won't watch you every moment. We won't control everything. We'll let you go places with your friends and stay out late on weekends. Won't we, Melly?"

"Yes, as long—"

I cut Melody off. "We won't question you about what you've done while away. Just let us know where you are, and allow us to say "no" *sometimes.* We don't want to squash your fun, *your* adventures."

I became upset as I reached the end of what I had to say, my voice cracking a bit with emotion. "I don't want you to end up with the sort of problems I caused myself. I was lucky to survive my adolescence."

I looked away to keep from gathering tears. Lysta got up and came around to my side of the table, placed a hand on one of mine. "I'll try to do a better job than you did," she said with a playful smirk.

She'd broken my gloomy spell with humor, the little turd! In mock outrage, I grabbed for her. She dashed away laughing.

"Are you two going to eat?" Melody asked.

Lysta and I both said we would.

"Then I'll heat your dinners in the microwave."

We'd all been sitting at the table, quietly eating for a time when Lysta broke the silence. "I'm glad you're lucky. I'm glad you survived."

I smiled at her, and she smiled back. I hadn't seen her wear such an unguarded expression for many months. I relaxed, deciding that revealing my past to her had been a good risk.

That wasn't the end of our problems with Lysta. She fought fiercely for independence all through high school, but the conversation had broken the fever that had grown up between us.

She got back to her artwork. We even collaborated on two cover paintings for Deadite Press books, one for an edition of *The Rising: Selected Scenes from the End of the World,* by Brian Keene.

Frederick: 11

Most everything had gone according to Frederick's plan, and the rest seemed to fall neatly into place. By mid-April, 1887, he found an abandoned storehouse along Bow Creek, as he'd hoped. The main entrance to the building had sagged dramatically from rot in the roof at some time in the distant past. Fear of further collapse kept all but homeless persons and adventurous children from wanting to enter the structure.

Frederick broke into the Poplar Hospital and stole the drugs he needed from a storeroom.

He befriended Thomas Beaumont, Lars Gutstram, Alfie Watkins, and Neville Strainger, all mucksnipe lushingtons easily tempted by a taste of something more powerful than drink. In exchange for each receiving a daily supply of gin containing a dose of morphine, and a loaf of bread, they kept the squatters and urchins away from the derelict storehouse.

The structure had a cellar broken into several dank, musty rooms. The foundation stones that formed the walls of the cellar had been designed to keep water out when the creek flooded. The stout floor above had been built to hold great weight. Few sounds originating inside escaped to the outside.

Frederick outfitted one of the rooms with a table, into the top of which he'd cut slots to hold numerous leather straps. One wall of the chamber supported a long shelf on which he placed several lamps and his instruments. He put three padlocks on the room's heavy single door. The doors that led into the cellar from the storehouse above, he nailed shut from within. He came and went through an old coal chute.

Frederick stalked a woman he'd seen strolling sadly through the Newham Recreation Ground three nights in a row. He chose to see her sadness as a sign that her life wasn't worth living.

From a small court beside a tenement south of the river in Stoney Street, he stole a barrow with high side rails and wheeled the thing back across the Thames on the New London Bridge. Frederick added wooden slats to make the railings solid walls. He loaded a couple of blankets and a three foot long, oak board into the barrow, and wheeled the conveyance into a fenced yard along Churchill Road that he knew the young woman passed on her way to and from the Newham Recreation Ground. Hemmed in by tenements, the road bent slightly and narrowed beside the gate, limiting the view and approach to the area from either side.

Waiting for her to happen by and fearing she might not make her routine stroll, Frederick chewed his nails. He'd never understood why anyone would chew fingernails until then. Once he'd begun, he chewed several down to the quick. Finally, they hurt so much he stopped.

Frederick heard footsteps on cobblestones, then saw the woman coming through the bend, her attitude still somber, her head down.

He allowed her to pass his hiding place.

She wasn't the daughter of a man of means, but he had to get his practice in somehow. Unlike his sister, Abigail, the young woman didn't deserve what he'd do to her. Still, he tried to imagine all the petty and mean things she might have done in life as he quietly dashed out from the shadow of the fence gate and struck her a great blow to the head with the oak board. He embraced her to prevent her from falling, and pressed a handkerchief soaked in chloroform to her mouth and nose.

Frederick glanced around uneasily as he dragged her toward the gate to the yard. He loaded her into the barrow, threw blankets over her, and hauled her back to the storehouse.

Frederick took the young woman from the barrow, slipped her down the coal chute into the cellar, and followed her.

He lit a lamp and placed it in the room he'd prepared. Frederick picked the woman up, carried her into the room, and secured her to the table with straps around her neck and all four limbs. He gave her an injection of morphine, and dosed her again with the chloroform.

As he began the work of taking off her lower left leg, he couldn't help comparing the experience to the first amputation he'd performed.

~ ~ ~

Frederick served aboard the HMS Challenger during the combined English, Spanish, and French occupation of the city of Veracruz in late 1861. The Mexican garrison had evacuated the nearby fortress island of San Juan de Ulúa. The city offered little resistance.

A rowdy bunch after a long sea voyage, many of the British Royal Navy sailors got drunk and started fights. With the HMS Challenger at dock, the orlop deck served as an infirmary. Frederick, alongside the surgeon, Mr. Wistwater, struggled to attend all the illnesses and injuries of the sailors. Several Mexican civilians were brought aboard to receive treatment for wounds received in violent clashes with drunken members of the Royal Navy.

An encounter with a young Mayan woman had a lasting impact on Frederick. She had suffered a gash in her left thigh and a blow to the head. On the day she was brought aboard, Mr. Wistwater had been too busy with other wounded to help her. "Do what you can for her," he said, "but don't waste your time."

Delirious and no doubt largely unaware of her surroundings, the woman moaned and writhed in pain. At first because of her small size, Frederick believed her to be a young girl, perhaps ten or twelve years old. He decided that she'd stand about four feet tall. She had brown skin, straight black hair, dark, almond-shaped eyes, and a hooked nose.

Quite pretty, in her way, he thought.

Frederick found a space for her on the deck. He pulled her skirt up to get to the wound. While he cleaned the six inch gash in her thigh in preparation for dressing the injury, she continued to squirm and her legs opened. The odor of her sex organ hit him nearly as hard as the block, *Simon's revenge,* that had swung loose from the ship's rigging and struck him in the head two days earlier. Frederick gagged, and turned away, yet something about the odor drew him right back.

The pictures he'd seen of the female sex organ in scientific publications left too much to the imagination. He'd had sexual intercourse with prostitutes, but had been too shy to ask to see where he placed his manhood.

Having a desire to see more clearly the Mayan woman's sex, Frederick wanted to spread her legs wider. He glanced around the infirmary to make certain no one watched him. Mr. Wistwater busied himself pulling pot shards from a young soldier's wounded arm. Occupied with their own various agonies, the infirmary inmates paid no attention to the Assistant Surgeon. He could see that the Mayan woman was too delirious to be aware of what he did. She made no protest as he spread her legs.

Her sex organ had grown a fine black hair. A secondary set of delicate, dusky pink, hairless lips peeked out from inside the larger ones.

Frederick became fascinated and aroused. Although the sight and the smell of her sex filled his head with desire, he knew he would have to find release later, and without further exploration.

"Be done with that Indian," the surgeon shouted.

Frederick stood quickly, thinking Mr. Wistwater watched him. No—the man remained occupied with the young soldier.

"Take her out," he grumbled, as he sutured a wound.

Frederick wanted her to stay. He sought an excuse to explore her further. "If you please, sir, her wound looks to be infected. She might have to lose the leg."

Mr. Wistwater glanced at the woman. "She doesn't get a bunk or hammock. Do you hear me? If she's at all improved tomorrow, she must be taken out."

Her wound wasn't better the next day. She did regain her senses, though. Frederick brought her food and water. She smiled and spoke to him. He couldn't understand her language. The trust she displayed in allowing him to inspect her leg had a profound effect on Frederick. An English woman, unless a prostitute, wouldn't have tolerated his probing so close to her sex. The Indian clearly knew that he could see between her legs. His arousal prompted him to touch her sex, yet he held back.

Over the course of the next few days, her leg wound began to smell of putrefaction. Frederick alerted the surgeon to the need to amputate. He looked forward to the procedure in part because he would be afforded an even better view of the woman's sex as he assisted Mr. Wistwater.

"She's your pet," The surgeon said. "You do it. I've taught you what you need to know."

Frederick was proud to be so trusted, but frightened of failure. Still, he began to assemble the instruments he'd need.

Mr. Wistwater stopped him. "You'll have to wait until we've finished with the men."

The hot day wore on. The sick and wounded kept arriving. The Mayan woman became delirious again.

"Please sir," Frederick said late in the day, "allow me to perform the amputation on the Indian before it's too late."

"Make it quick, then."

Frederick fetched two young seaman to help him. They got the tiny woman onto a table, and he set out his instruments: a tourniquet, a long surgical knife, a bone saw, and sutures. He raised her skirt and got his glimpse. The smell competed with that of the wound, nearly too much to stomach in the enclosed heat and humidity of the orlop deck. Both boys turned their heads away from the sight of her crotch and wounded thigh and remained that way, dutifully holding onto the woman's extremities, despite an evident desire to have nothing to do with her.

Frederick placed a patch of leather in the woman's mouth and a tourniquet around the wounded thigh, below the buttocks. Then, as quickly as possible, he cut around her thigh, through to the bone, leaving flaps of skin that would be gathered and sutured to close the wound.

The Mayan woman awoke and looked him in the eye in the middle of the procedure. As she noticed the boys holding her, terror and understanding gripped her features simultaneously. Her eyes became wide and filled with pain, but they also held a terrible resignation. Seeing her reaction, Frederick's heart beat faster. He felt an exuberant surge of emotion, a feeling not unlike, yet more powerful than what he'd got while playing for audiences as part of the Regal Rats.

Regretfully, the Mayan woman became insensible again.

While he quivered with excitement, his hands remained steady as he quickly tied off the exposed blood vessels, took up the bone saw, and swiftly cut through her femur.

He glanced over his shoulder to make certain Mr. Wistwater wasn't looking his way. Seeing that the boys still kept their eyes averted, Frederick plunged his index finger into the woman's warm sex organ. Pulling it out, he found the digit coated with blood. Red oozed from between the lips of her crotch as he watched. Although hairy, the cleft had become so much like the swollen gash that had been in her leg, he experienced an odd déjà vu-like association between the two. His engorged penis pressed painfully against the fabric of his trousers.

His left leg quivered, then began to shake violently. The smells of the woman's wound and her sex became much darker, more ancient and foreboding. Together, they became the smell of the grave. The infirmary tilted and he lost touch with his senses.

Simon's curse had visited Frederick for the first time.

He awoke sitting on the deck, leaning against the bulkhead. Mr. Wistwater stood at the table the Mayan woman rested upon. He worked on stitching the skin together around her stump. The surgeon glanced down at him with a look of disgust. "I cannot entrust you with such tasks if this is how you will perform. Go to your berth and rest."

Frederick looked toward his crotch. Relieved to find that his erection had fled, he got up and did as he was told.

Those with berths near his own slept, awaiting the ship's bell to alert them to take up their watch duty. With loud snoring all around, Frederick decided they'd be unaware that he lay in their midst, pleasuring himself.

Thinking about the Mayan woman's sex organ, he stroked his manhood. About to spend, the image in his mind's eye switched from that of the woman's sex to that of her wound. The release, much greater than any he'd previously experienced, forced a gasping groan from him. Startled from sleep, two of his shipmates lifted their heads to look around. Frederick had covered himself in time. He pretended to sleep and his shipmates dozed off again.

The next day, he hurried to see the Mayan woman in the infirmary, well before the hour he was expected to begin his duty. Two shipmates were lifting her on a litter as he arrived.

"She's off to shelter in town," Mr. Wistwater said.

Frederick followed the litter and helped his two shipmates negotiate the tight passageways of the ship to the upper deck. As they emerged into daylight and sun beams reached the woman's face, she opened her eyes. She saw Frederick, frowned briefly, then took his hand and smiled.

She still thought kindly of him, even after what he'd taken from her. That realization coupled with the arousing experiences of her emotion and flesh would stick with Frederick for years to come. As he watched her leave the ship, borne on the litter, he hoped she'd survive. Then a thought arose unbidden in his mind: *One day, perhaps I'll get to take another piece of her.*

Once she was gone from his life, his desire to cut other women, particularly young ones, emerged. Although he wanted to imagine cutting his sister, Abigail, he hadn't seen her for so long, he couldn't quite picture her in his mind, so he focused his attention elsewhere.

In a crowded market in Jamaica, he almost stabbed a young woman. Bambpaul, a black shipmate, had pointed her out. "She's the Governor's daughter," he said.

"Pretty girl," Frederick said.

"Glocky from the heat, though. Look at the way she's dressed."

The young woman wore a white bonnet, and white silk from head to toe, with only her hands and face, pink and shiny from the heat, uncovered. In her tight bodice and full skirts, she clearly suffered.

Frederick presumed his shipmate knew that a proper English lady had to dress that way, heat or no heat. He obviously made a sport of laughing at people. Frederick thought that one day Bambpaul's jesting would get him into trouble.

The young woman wiped sweat from her brow with a delicate handkerchief.

Frederick thought he might like to put her out of her misery, but he knew he could not get away with that. Yet a quick slice from his knife along her lower back, just enough to draw blood, the blade quickly withdrawn, hidden, his slow, confident exit from the market—*that* he might pull off.

Leaving his shipmate, he stalked her for a time as she considered the mangos a toothless Quadroon woman offered for sale. Right before committing the act, Frederick noticed someone eyeing him suspiciously, a bald dark-skinned man with a keen eye. He hadn't seen the fellow until that moment. Frederick became certain the man was her personal guard. His heart took a few extra, uncomfortable beats as he realized frightfully that he'd nearly made a terrible, fateful decision.

On that day, the thought of a future in prison or of being hanged dissuaded Frederick from responding to his need to cut a woman. To get along in the world, he knew he must quiet the budding fascination. Since the urge was linked to sexual desire, he tried not to indulge in carnal thoughts or picture in his mind open wounds. He became increasingly successful at ignoring the need to pleasure himself, as well. Frederick had been somewhat chaste through most of the years he worked at St. Pancras Station. Then he'd noticed that young women were traveling alone, he'd found the dog, and everything changed.

~ ~ ~

Frederick heard footsteps coming through the floor above him, no doubt Alfie Watkins, patrolling through the empty storeroom as directed. He was old, but large and intimidating. Hopefully, the man wouldn't decide to look in the cellar against his instructions. Of course, he'd have to break in, yet the man was powerful enough to do that in short order. The promise of more gin or an extra taste of morphine had always secured his compliance. He'd also been useful in keeping the other three men in line.

As Frederick finished cutting through the soft flesh of the leg, just below the young woman's knee, he felt his erect penis throb in beat with the pulse of his heart. Although the tourniquet held back the majority of the flow, her blood ran like liquid rubies from the incision. He undid buttons and allowed his engorged organ to jut into the open air below the flow. Each drop of the warm liquid lightly kissed his manhood.

He adjusted one of the lamps on the shelf for better illumination, and used suture to tie off the blood vessels. Taking up his saw, he cut first the small bone, and then the larger. Her left lower leg dropped from the stump, and fell from the table onto the dirt floor.

Frederick inserted two fingers of his left hand into the woman's sex organ, then lifted the digits to his nose. He found the odor disappointing.

Then the smell of the grave, the aroma of the Mayan's sex, mixed with that of her wound, filled his head. Frederick welcomed Simon's curse because it brought with it the right smell. Yet the onset, coupled with his imminent sexual release, was ponderously slow.

He felt a presence within his mind, perhaps the apparition from past spells. *Let him watch,* Frederick thought, the idea that he had an audience adding extra excitement.

As his left leg began to quake, he gasped, leaned back, and thrust his hips forward. Without encouragement from his hands, his red-spattered penis jerked and spent in the open air. His seed, trailing tiny wisps of vapor in the chill air, arced onto the young woman's bloody stump. His fluids mixed with hers.

Frederick shuddered in the depths of emotion. He'd destroyed something valuable, taken something beautiful from the world. Someone had loved the completeness of the young woman, and he'd taken part of that away.

Still holding his fingers to his nose, Frederick went to his knees. The presence in his thoughts reacted with horror, redoubling Frederick's satisfaction. As the vision began, he embraced it, wanting to feed on the apparition's outrage.

He found himself in a room full of oddly shaped furnishings. Several people sat around the chamber, all looking in Frederick's direction and laughing. Although he liked the idea that he had an audience, something was different about the experience. Instead of seeing the apparition, Frederick knew that he looked out through the hypocrite's eyes. He felt an odd, sentimental commitment to those assembled, an uncomfortable connection with them that left him intensely vulnerable. Memories, probably belonging to the hypocrite, surfaced within Frederick's own mind of finding a penis shaped object, perhaps made of gutta-percha rubber, within a strange collection of rubbish.

Did those assembled also know what Frederick had done? Probably not, but the hypocrite did, and that was enough.

Then, Frederick became aware of himself again, lying on the dirt floor. He rested for a long while, the need to release the tourniquet and close the wound impinging upon his pleasure with increasing urgency.

Finally, he rose and set about to preserve the life of the young woman strapped to his table. She still had a lot more to offer.

Aiden: 12

In 2015, Lysta began college at Oregon State University, and went to live in the dorms. Not knowing exactly which way to go, she studied art and science.

Even though I felt relief that she'd survived her childhood, I still worried about her, and I missed her presence at home. Her weekend visits weren't nearly enough.

Perry had died in 2011. We got a puppy that looked like a rat terrier to harass Buckley so he wouldn't grow old too quickly without his pal. At the time, Melody was reading *Of Thimble and Threat.* She named the pup Conway after Catherine Eddowes's first husband, an author of gallows ballads and a major character in the book. Later we got another Schipperke that she named Jasper after a character in my novel *A Parliament of Crows.* The alfa-dog of his litter, Jasper was a handful. I felt like I'd signed on to be a parent all over again. He got into a lot of trouble, tore up many things, including the entire sprinkler system out back. Variously, we called him Little Shit, Jasper the Rasper, and Jasper the Bastard.

Melody would imitate Glenda the Good from the movie *The Wizard of Oz*, and ask, "Jasper, a're you a goo'd dog or a ba'd dog?"

Although a handful for the first year, he did turned out to be a goo'd dog.

Print-on-demand, the ability of printers to produce as few as one paperback book at a time, had become a successful service offered to publishers. With the advent of computer tablets, ebooks had finally become popular. Because making ebooks available for sale costs little but the human energy required to create the writing and the files, and print-on-demand helped do away with the need to warehouse regular books, the trend among publishers was to avoid the overhead costs of publishing altogether. My service of producing cover artwork and interior illustrations for books represented overhead. While illustrations remained an important way for both ebooks and those printed using POD to distinguish themselves, publishers wanted to pay less and less for the work. They also wanted more for their money, say cover art as well as interior illustrations for the same price or less than they'd paid previously for a cover alone. Increasingly, I felt like I was on a treadmill, cranking out artwork for little return.

Several publishers treated me roughly. As I asked one for a better fee for my services, he said, "I can find younger artists hungry for jobs who will work for next to nothing."

"So why try to hire me at all, then?" I asked.

The answer was clear, yet that didn't promote the argument the publisher wanted to make, so he didn't really answer.

I took fewer low-paying illustration jobs and concentrated more on my writing. I'd had lots of validation of my visual art efforts over the years. I didn't make a killing on the writing either, but my publisher treated me well, and the work still felt like an adventure.

As I considered how best to start the fourth book in the Jack the Ripper Victims Series, one about the life of Annie Chapman, I visited family in Tennessee.

Randy and Zoe Fox organized a small party for me and a bunch of our good friends at their house in East Nashville. That was the older part of town that had a lot of neighborhoods with fine old houses. Not fancy ones, just homes from a different time, before condos and McMansions. Their house was a nice brick place built in the 1930s, with unpainted woodwork and polished floors, stained and varnished to show off the grain. When I got there, Randy had western swing playing in the background, its lilting tones like jazz with cowboy hats. Troy Guinn, John Davis, and Beth Gwen had already arrived. Having come down from Louisville, Dave Conover had been with Randy and Zoe much of the day. He'd brought with him an edition of *The Star*, a London newspaper.

"I thought you might like to have this," he said. "I got it in an online auction several years ago."

"Thank you," I said, then saw how browned the paper had become and the date on the edition. "Wow, September 13, 1888, five days after the murder of Annie Chapman. That's an incredible coincidence; she's next in my series."

"I thought she might be. There are reports about the murder in it."

"Thank you!"

Randy turned the music down. We sat talking in the Fox living room, and snacking on foods Zoe had made. Despite being thrilled to see my old friends, as we caught up on each other's lives, the newspaper, which rested on the coffee table in its protective plastic sleeve, kept drawing my attention. I wanted to know what the old text said, yet sitting and reading the thing wouldn't be much fun for the group. I made more effort to be present with my friends. Soon, I forgot about the paper.

Each of those friends had a great sense of humor and a lot of imagination. Several of them had been members of the Bovine Smoke Society. Nearly all of them were writers, artists, or both with whom I'd collaborated. Although I didn't get back to Nashville for a visit but every three to five years, when I did, the years fell away and our conversations, our humor, and fondness for one another flowed naturally as if we'd never been apart.

Inevitably, the story-telling began. I encouraged Dave Conover to tell his tartar cup story, a food poisoning episode he had while on the streets of Los Angeles. He told the self-deprecating tale with such humor, we all choked on our own laughter.

Of course that inspired more of the same. When my turn came, I told my Packing-Penis story, one I'd told friends in Oregon over the years.

"My brother, Bill, and I grew up with Robby and Devin, the children of a producer for a record label. The producer was an angry man, puffed up on a sense of his own importance. He talked a fair amount about having grown up poor. He spent a lot of money and said he didn't want to deny his children anything. The boys were spoiled. The father tended to leave money lying around the house, and he threw away lots of perfectly good things. They had a dog that knocked over the trash and dragged the rubbish around their yard.

"One day—I guess I was nine years old—I saw fifty or more demo 45s spread across the lawn, all of a new song by a popular musician. I took some of the 45s home, feeling cool for getting to hear and own the music before anyone else did.

"After that, I checked their garbage from time to time to see what I might find. One day, I found a giant penis in the rubbish."

I nodded at the surprised faces around the room.

"Yep, I couldn't believe my eyes. It was at least ten inches long and hollow. I immediately picked the penis up, laughing, showing Bill, Robby, and Devin. They wanted to inspect it, but I wouldn't let them near the thing. The giant penis was *all mine.*"

"Not a real one!" John shouted, and everyone laughed.

"No, *of course* not. You could feel through the smooth outer surface something like foam rubber inside. The penis had to be packing material of some sort—right?—something used as a cushion to protect a valuable object during shipping. It just happened to be that shape, and a rosy, pink flesh color."

"A dildo!" Randy said, giggling like a little boy.

"Now, remember, I was young. No one in the world *I knew* would intentionally make a giant penis." I had to controlled my laughter so I could go on with the story. "No—this had to be a Packing Penis!"

Knowing where the story headed, I couldn't help laughing. Out of control, I fell against John who sat beside me on the sofa. I got up feeling dizzy and dislocated. My friends all laughed, which gave me time for my head to clear before continuing.

"They chased me, trying to take the penis away. That's how valuable it was!

"'I have a great idea,' I shouted as I ran. When we got to my house, I took them all into the kitchen and said, 'I'm gonna make it piss.'"

That drew horrified looks from my friends.

"'How are you gonna do that?' Devin asked.

"'Food coloring and water.'

"It took us a while to get the yellow color just right. We made a tall pitcher of the stuff. During all the giggling excitement, Mama discovered us making a mess in her kitchen.

"'What are you doing?' she asked.

"'Making fake urine,' I said."

By now, I had to pause each sentence to allow the laughter of my friends to subside before continuing.

"She looked at the penis on her kitchen table with surprise.

"'Isn't it great?' I said.

"'Where did it come from?'

"'The garbage at our house,' Robby said."

"Didn't she try to take it away?" Troy asked.

"Well, I don't think she knew what it was. Mama had led a rather sheltered life in some ways. Even if she did know, my parents had taken their child-rearing cues from Dr. Spock, and didn't want to give their children sexual hang ups.

"You guys know that strip along the creek on my parent's property?" I asked.

Some nodded their heads.

"Teen boys around the neighborhood hid their girlie magazines there. I guess because that strip was across the street from the rest of our property, kids thought no one owned it. Bill and I found *Playboys* and *Penthouses* in plastic bags stuffed into tangles of honeysuckle or in a couple of hollow logs down there. When we brought the magazines up to the house, Daddy would sit down and look at them with us."

"So she let you keep the penis?" Beth asked. I could see she didn't believe me.

"Worse, she allowed me to take a piss with it! We went outside, cut a slit in the tip all the way through to the hollow interior, then filled the penis up with fake urine from the pitcher."

I had to wait for my friends' outbursts to settle down again.

"I put my mouth up to the hollow at the base of the shaft and blew as hard as I could."

"You put your mouth on it?" Beth asked, outraged.

"Yes," I said.

Her mouth remained open, and her eyes blinked as if she had to make sure she truly saw me. "That's *so* gross. You had no idea where it had been."

"I turned on my brother and friends as a stream of yellow water squirted from the head of the penis, and I chased them around the yard."

I could hardly get the words out for laughing. Somehow, I could be heard over the guffaws of my friends because they clearly followed the tale.

"I let them spray me with the penis too. We kept filling it from the pitcher. We played with it all afternoon, carrying it proudly about the neighborhood. No one tried to take it away. In the early evening, Bill and I returned home, and I placed the packing penis in a prominent spot on a shelf in the living room. We played with it on and off for a few more days, always returning it to the place of honor in the most important room of the house."

I let my voice trail off. Right when Randy had stopped giggling and looked as if he'd ask a question, I cut him off. "Then, one day, maybe a week after we found the penis, it mysteriously disappeared."

"Your parents!" Beth said.

I turned to her, shrugging. "Back then, I might not have known where it had been, but I have a good idea now. The question is, where did the penis go? I asked around. Even my parents said they didn't know what had happened to it!" I said that as seriously as I could, yet I couldn't hold myself together. They burst out with fresh guffaws, and so did I.

I laughed harder than I had in years, since the times when I'd hung out with these same friends before Melody and I had moved to Oregon. Letting go without feeling foolish, I felt myself slip sideways, as if out of my own body.

I smelled the odd odor that accompanied the temporal lobe seizures, and the familiar dread gripped me.

The Fox living room and my friends vanished. Instead I stood in a darkened area, lit by small lamp flames. I saw a penis jutting forth toward a woman strapped to a table, and thought dumbly, *That's not the packing penis.* I assumed the organ belonged to my body, although the one in the hallucination wasn't circumcised.

The best orgasm of my life took me. Only as I ejaculated on the gory thing, did I recognize that the woman's leg terminated in a stump, bloody from recent amputation.

At the sight, I felt my balls shrivel and hide. I tried to scream, to no effect. I tried to claw my way out of that place, but had no control over my body. My mind rebelled, replacing the visual aspect of the hallucination with a wall of white-hot blankness; an angry, fearful rejection of what I saw.

Then, I heard Dave saying, "He's got a huge hard-on."

The Fox living room had returned. Randy had a phone in his hand. "Is he coming out of it?"

"Yeah," Troy said. He held me propped up against the side of the sofa.

I was on the floor. My left elbow hurt.

John Davis hovered over me. "Can you see me, Aiden?"

"Yeah," I said.

"I think you had a seizure," he said. "Are you all right?"

"I think so. Banged my elbow."

He smiled. They all smiled, and Randy put the phone down. Troy helped me up and put me on the sofa. I felt ashamed for scaring them.

"Has that happened before?" John asked.

"No," I lied, "My doctor warned I might have seizures after the brain abscesses."

They all knew about that episode in my life. Not a one of them was much of a worrier, and they found their way back to good humor fairly quickly. Randy put on some more music that I recognized as a collection of country music with a horror theme he called Haints, Hangins, and Hillbillies.

I was shaken. Not since the first temporal lobe hallucination had a seizure frightened me so much. The sense that I'd actually participated in some abhorrent cruelty toward a young woman didn't go away. For the first time in many years, I needed a drink, but I knew better than to start down that road.

I hid my distress and went on with the evening. Thankfully, no one seemed to notice. My years of training as an alcoholic had turned me into an excellent actor.

Frederick: 12

"You mustn't move," Frederick said, as the young woman began to emerge from insensibility. "The accident left you with a spine so tender that with much movement, you might become permanently crippled. The driver of the coach that struck you has been caught and taken to the police station."

She moaned, and strained at the straps that bound her to the table.

"You must trust me. I am the Surgeon's Mate." Frederick didn't know why he'd used the old term for Assistant Surgeon, since he'd much rather be known by the more formal title. "Try to become calm. The straps are meant to prevent you from harming yourself. We don't want you to sever your spine. With the blow to your head, your eyes are too sensitive for light, so we have applied the bandages to prevent you from going blind. Because your hearing is sensitive too, we placed you in a quiet room. You might become chilled, but that too is for your own good."

Frederick watched her assemble her mouth to speak through the small opening in the bandages across her face. "Ma fatha!" she said, her words slurred almost to the point of incomprehensibility. "Misser Cha'les O'en."

"Mr. Charles Owen?"

"Ye',"

Delighted to know her father's name, Frederick immediately tried to picture the man learning about the loss of his daughter. In his mind's eye, the man wore in a fine suit and top hat, even though Frederick knew by the clothing she'd worn that the young woman, Miss Owen he presumed, was from a middle class family.

"Your father has been found, but the doctor doesn't want you to see him yet for fear that too much emotion will create problems."

"Ma' leg hu'ts."

"Your left leg was badly mutilated in the accident, and had to be removed."

Again, she strained against her bonds. She gagged on the fluid in her mouth.

Fear that she might choke to death spoiled his delight with her response. He was relieved when the coughing ceased. She turned her head to one side, and the saliva and mucous flowed from her mouth. "Noooo," she moaned, the agonized word oozing out miserably with the fluid. While he continued to enjoy her reaction, the moment had been somewhat lost.

"You must rest. I will give you another dose of the palliative."

Frederick prepared and administered an injection of morphine. Within a few moments, Miss Owen's moans grew quieter and she ceased to strain against her bonds.

He wanted her to trust him without the comfort of the drug. Perhaps he might find his way to that following the next amputation.

~ ~ ~

After removing all Miss Owen's limbs, Frederick knew that the first amputation, that of her left lower leg, had been the most satisfying, his sexual release during the process the most complete. Somehow, the spell, with its attendant erotic smell had completed the experience. The hypocritical gaze of the apparition in his vision, looking over his shoulder, so to speak, had been a welcome, added benefit. Frederick took pleasure from the idea that he'd shocked that presence more than any audiences he'd had on the streets while with the Regal Rats. Real or not, the apparition seemed a weak, little man. The depth of his sentimentality left him hopelessly vulnerable. If the presence were one born of madness within Frederick, he told himself that the lunacy seemed of a particularly harmless variety.

Yes—the first amputation, that of the woman's lower left leg, had been the best. After that Frederick had suffered one frustration after another.

Simon's curse, which always seemed to bring him the smell of the grave, had not visited since the first amputation. The aroma of the woman's sex organ was inadequate, in part because it wasn't combined with the odor of wet gangrene. Also, without the fit, he had no audience. He wanted the apparition to witness.

As he'd found with the dog, the removal of her upper legs wasn't as satisfying because the functionality of the limbs had already been compromised. The same had been true for her upper arms. When he told Miss Owen of the loss of her right leg, her response, subdued in comparison with what she'd had for her left leg, surprised him. For the briefest moment Frederick wondered if she'd liked that leg less. Then he'd realized that her reaction must be much like his own; once her functionality had been compromised with the loss of one leg, the loss of the other had less emotional impact.

Frederick had been unable to allow the woman to rise from sedation sufficiently to truly communicate with her. What trust he gained from Miss Owen seemed merely a product of her belief that he portrayed her situation accurately. She depended on him to see her through the difficulty, while rarely seeming to have an inkling that she diminished in size and function with each passing day. The best he'd got from her was clear gratitude whenever he promised more morphine.

As Frederick prepared to decapitate her, he told himself that the next one would be fully aware of her condition. She would know he took her limbs and he'd regain her trust following each amputation.

Once he'd killed Miss Owen, Frederick cut her torso in two. He wrapped all her parts in sections of blanket and dumped them into Bow Creek late at night, close to where the waterway met the Thames. He thought he saw Alfie Watkin's big shadow watching him from around the corner of the storehouse building. Looking more closely, Frederick didn't find the big man.

Even if he saw, he won't know what I'm dumping. The shapes give nothing away.

Frederick assumed the river would carry the body parts to separate locations and that his connection to the woman, her fate, and her ghost would be severed. As he thought about that, though, he began to worry that she might be gathered together and identified.

Next time I'll dump the parts in different places.

The idea seemed to spawn a recurring nightmare in which he wheeled his barrow through the city at night. The vehicle held an unlimited supply of body parts, which he delighted to sprinkle liberally, yet secretly about the city and in the river. What began so happily, inevitably turned unbearable, as someone caught him dropping a limb. A chase would follow. Dogs would join in pursuit. Frederick feared the canines more than the humans.

He always awoke from the nightmare in a cold sweat.

~ ~ ~

Frederick spent the next fifteen months creating a better plan to exact his satisfaction. His efforts as an itinerant barber surgeon brought enough income to pay for his few needs, and those of his four watchmen.

The Storehouse had worked well. So many properties had fallen into ruin along that part of the waterfront, the city could not keep up with condemning them all. The condition of most of the derelict structures went unchallenged. He had little concern that the storehouse would be razed or that the owner would invest in any changes to the property.

Frederick came and went through the coal chute hidden in the foliage at the northern end of the structure except on the occasions he delivered supplies to his lushingtons. As time passed, his relationship with them changed uncomfortably.

"We aren't fed enough," Thomas Beaumont complained, "and we could do with whiskey instead of gin."

"We set the terms of our agreement some time past," Frederick said. "I don't see that anything has changed except your desire for more. If you want to leave, do so."

Thomas bared his broken teeth. Although broad in the shoulder, his short stature and bowed legs removed any menace he might have had.

"Thomas, here, he has refined tastes and a big appetite," Neville Strainger said, giggling uneasily. He was a rail thin man who frequently stank like a rendering pot. "Me, I should take pig wash and all sorts if you'd dose the gin a bit better."

They had clearly become unsatisfied with the arrangement, and that worried Frederick. Alfie Watkins watched the two men with barely disguised contempt. Lars Gutstram had kept his distance during the exchange.

A few days later, Thomas and Neville began to pry—literally— into Frederick's business in the cellar of the storehouse. Alfie had caught them trying to break loose one of the cellar doors. He had beaten the two men and driven them away.

"I needed those men," Frederick said. "I should send *you* away!"

"N-no, sir," Alfie said, his big guileless face wide with fear. "I—I can do the job by myself. I don't need them. Don't need Lars either. The more you have keeping watch, the more likely what you do will come to light."

Deciding that Alfie must know about the murder, Frederick turned away quickly, trying to decide if he could succeed in killing the big fellow. He didn't think so. No—he must flee, and start over elsewhere.

Alfie put a hand on his shoulder to stop him, and Frederick reached for his knife. The hand pulled away from his shoulder quickly.

"Please, sir, listen to me," the big man said somewhat pitifully, as Frederick spun around, and looked up at him. Perhaps because Alfie was such a large capable fellow who rarely showed much feeling, the look on his face had a greater impact. Frederick had never seen a sadder expression. He relaxed.

"I've never had much in life," Alfie said. "That's my own doing, I s'pose. Soon I'll have a lot less. My sister's husband, Mr. Loveridge— he's a veteran Indian—says the lumps in my gut are a cancer. I drink for the pain, but your medicine is best."

"Do you mean veterinarian?"

"S'what I said." Alfie looked frustrated. He pressed his lips together hard before continuing. "I have nothing but what you give me. I don't want nothing else. Please don't turn me away."

"How long have you had the lumps?"

"A year and more."

Slow growing, Frederick thought. "How's your strength, your appetite?"

"Still strong. I could lift you with one hand. Mr. Loverridge says I got a bit of time, yet."

Frederick realized he couldn't hope for better in a protector, at least for the next few months.

"We keep Lars," he said.

"Yes, sir," Alfie said. "You won't regret."

Thomas Beaumont, and Neville Strainger did not come back, despite the need for morphine they'd developed. When asked how that had been achieved, Alfie said, "I told them there are worse things than doing without." He didn't elaborate, yet the look in his eyes gave Frederick confidence.

The efforts of Alfie and Lars ran like clockwork as long as they got their morphine.

Frederick restocked his supply of drugs from the storeroom in the Poplar Hospital. He rounded up lumber, lath, plaster, and paint, and finished the room in the cellar to make the chamber look as much as possible like a hospital room. Lying upon his table with the neck strap in place, he determined what of the room a person in that position might see. Then, he added a new door and door casing, and trimmed out the corners of the room closest to the door. He found making expertly mitered joints on the cornice molding, where the walls met the ceiling, the most difficult.

Even as the men who worked for him craved the morphine, so Frederick itched to get his hands on another young woman. He counseled patience to himself. If he wanted to meet his goal, everything had to be just right.

~ ~ ~

In early August of 1888, Frederick waited at night behind a privy in the rear yard of one of the terraced houses along East India Docks Road. The young woman using the facility had been inside for some time.

As he waited for her to emerge, he had an idea for encouraging gangrene after an amputation, one inspired by the reek of the privy itself. Most physicians believed that disease was born along on *night air*, such as what the privy exuded, and that when those with a weak constitution inhaled the noxious fumes, illness followed. Frederick had lived in miasmatic conditions throughout his life, and had succeeded in avoiding most of the illnesses that odor transmitted. He had received a terrible infection of the left wrist while on the receiving hulk, Quicksilver. The corruption had found him as he removed a lead ball from the gut of a man who'd been shot trying to escape. The exposed fecal material from within the fellow's torn large intestine had got into an open cut on Frederick's wrist. The infection had nearly necessitated the removal of his lower arm.

The woman, exiting the privy, interrupted his thoughts. He leaned around the corner to get a look. She held her lamp at an angle that allowed him to see her more clearly than before. The quality of her clothing told him she wasn't a servant, but indeed a member of an upper middle class family, as he'd thought. Although not the daughter of a man of means, she did represent a step closer to his goal. As she bent to straighten the flow of her skirts, Frederick slipped out from behind the privy and struck her on the head. He dragged her out of the yard, placed her in his barrow, dosed her with chloroform, and wheeled her back to the room in his storehouse.

Aiden: 13

Two months after I returned home from visiting family and friends in Tennessee, I fell into a deep funk. I moped about the house unable to devote my attention to any projects. The television shows Melody and I watched regularly didn't hold my interest. When she spoke to me, I rarely gave more than a two word answer. I ignored Buckley, Conway, and Jasper when they wanted to play.

We were in the last weekend of September 2015, and the heat and lack of rain from the long, hot summer persisted. My prospects seemed as dry and unpromising as the parched soil of our back yard, cracked from the drought and supporting mostly weeds. Rain wasn't in the forecast.

Lysta had decided not to come home that weekend, and she seemed up in the air about the next one as well.

"What's going on with you?" Melody asked me on Saturday.

Normally, I wouldn't remember what day it was, but the universe had scheduled a super blood moon total eclipse for the next evening, Sunday, September 27, and folks had been talking about it online all day. I had some small excitement to see it.

"I have no work on the horizon. There's less good work to be had than ever before. I don't feel like I'm contributing much."

"We're fine," she said. "My pay check takes care of us."

Following the financial crash of 2008, Melody's bank failed and she became unemployed. She'd gone back to school, gained the skills of a sterile processing technician, and got a job at a local orthopedic surgery center. The pay was much better than what she'd had with almost twenty years in the banking industry.

"Don't pretend you have to do the manly thing of bringing home the bacon," she said, chuckling.

I hadn't had a drink in twenty-five years. In that time, Melody had rarely seen me depressed. I'd been one of the lucky ones—once I stopped taking that depressant, I stopped being chronically depressed.

"It's not that. I worked hard to build up my illustration business. You know that at first I did work for markets that weren't markets.

They paid nothing, yet I got exposure. Once I started to get paying work, I gave it everything I had, even if the earnings were small. I feel weird turning down work now, but publishers want too much for too little. With thirty years in illustration, I deserve more, not less. Even though my work is better than ever, I feel like a has-been. With Lysta gone, and little work, I'm thinking my time has passed."

"Do more writing. You love it. Rub your damn buckeye and buck up."

Yes—I still carried a buckeye for good luck. I wished at that moment I could call and speak to Jack Daves. He was one of the funniest guys I'd ever known. Although a conversation with him would have pulled me right out of my funk, he had died in 2004. I missed him and his good humor.

Despite Melody's admonishment, my thoughts remained gloomy through the day as I tried to work. Jill Bauman called from New York to talk. When I told her about my mood, she said, "The coming eclipse is to blame." I didn't argue with her.

Lying in the bed next to Melody that night, resting only fitfully, felt a bit like the sleepless nights of the epic hangovers of twenty-five years earlier.

Sunday, Melody went to hang out with her friend, Kelsie, for the day. "I'll be back for dinner," she said.

I stayed home to continue my research of Annie Chapman's life. As I worked at my desk in the studio, looking for information online, the weirdest things unnerved me. I discovered that the building on the property where her lifeless body had been found housed a woman who ran a cat's meat business. I researched "cat's meat" and found reference to cat's meat men, vendors of pet food, who made rounds through neighborhoods selling mostly horse meat not fit for human consumption. To indicate that the meat was for animals, the cat's meat vendors died the flesh green or blue. Reading about all that echoed uncomfortably in my head, strangely resonating like old memories, false ones. They reminded me of those I'd had during my temporal lobe seizures in the hospital twenty-six years earlier, when I remembered doing things in places I'd never been. Since they came on with a large dose of dread, I feared another seizure loomed.

I took a break from the research to relax. I went downstairs, and lay in bed to read from a book my friends John and Laurie McNichols had given me, *The Ghost Map, The Story of London's Most Terrifying Epidemic—and How It Changed Science, Cities, and the Modern World* by Steven Johnson. The subject matter fit in well with all the research I did on Victorian London, but on that day, the reading didn't help me relax. I learned from the text that although hundreds of thousands of people had died over the centuries from cholera, science had determined that survival of the disease was a simple matter of keeping the sufferer hydrated. Dwelling on all that death that might have been avoided with sufficient water, I thought of my own inevitable demise. I thought of my father's death, and that of Warner Felton, a man who had been a good friend of my father's and mine. One of the few regrets that truly nagged at me, was not saving Warner's life. When I felt low and stupid, like I'd been feeling for some time, I thought about him, and wished I could have done better.

~ ~ ~

Warner Felton came from Memphis, Tennessee. As a guitarist, he'd played sessions during the early days of rockabilly and rock and roll. Then, he'd gone to Europe and studied classical guitar with the best in the world. He rose in prominence within the field and eventually played Carnegie Hall.

I'd been a child when I met him, maybe ten years old. At the time, he was a Musician in Residence at a university in North Carolina, but he also led a nomadic life. In his 1960 Cadillac with a camper grafted onto the back, he traveled from city to city, developing classical guitar societies. His wife Suzanne, a classically trained singer, and their young daughter, Naomi, went with him. Warner seemed to me an opportunist, yet I also knew he brought great value into the lives of virtually everyone he encountered.

Daddy joined the classical guitar society Warner helped start in Nashville, Tennessee, and they became good friends. While in Nashville, the Felton family made our home a base of operations, parking the camper/Cadillac in the driveway and joining us for meals. Following wonderful dinners my mother created, we had great music and conversation.

Whether he played the guitar or simply spoke, Warner's hands stayed in motion as he expressed himself. A widely traveled, charismatic man with a lot of energy and interests, he told great stories.

As sidelines to help facilitate his adventures and earn extra income, he'd become a photographer and scuba instructor. The skills helped him organize vacation adventures to tropical destinations for some of the people he met in his travels. He often took part in those vacations along with his clients. I would later get the impression that perhaps he'd also taken up photography and scuba to help him get closer to women.

My whole family became scuba divers and went on a couple of Caribbean vacations with Warner. With my training in scuba, I've been fortunate enough to dive in numerous locations in the Caribbean, Mexico, California, and Hawaii.

At some point in the late 1960s or early 1970s, Warner and his wife, Suzanne, divorced. She moved to San Francisco to work with an opera company and took Naomi with her. I moved to SF in 1973 to study art, went to Symbas Experimental High School in a warehouse commune called Project 1 just south of Market Street, then entered a BFA program at the San Francisco Art Institute. Warner moved to SF to be close to his daughter when I was in my second year of college.

He got in touch with me, and told me he'd gotten a job and a place to live.

I'd never known him to work a 9 to 5 job. "What kind of work?"

"I auditioned at the fancy French restaurant at the downtown Sheraton Palace Hotel. They hired me on the spot to play for tips in the dining room. In my spare time, I'll serve papers for the San Francisco courts, do some freelance photography, and find a situation to teach scuba."

"That's a lot," I said.

"The city is expensive, and I like to stay busy. Speaking of which, your father says you're busy in school. How's it going?"

"Well, I'm at the San Francisco Art Institute. My major is painting. A lot of the courses involve four or six hour-long studio classes. I paint and draw for hours on end in front of students and teachers. Some of my teachers are good, some are arrogant pricks. Same with the students."

"Ha! I know about that from studying guitar. What do you do in the evenings and on weekends? What do you do for fun?"

A lot of what I did was drink, smoke pot, and work on my art. At that point, I'd only known him in the context of my parent's home and the guitar society he started in Nashville, so I didn't want to admit to all the intoxication. "Most of the time, I work on painting and drawing. Sometimes, I go out and do stuff with friends."

"I tell you what," he said, "If you bring the pot, I'll provide dinner and wine on Sunday nights at my place. I'll also give you classical guitar lessons, if you want. You have a standing invitation. What do you think?"

Somehow, I wasn't surprised that Warner smoked marijuana.

"I like it." I took him up on his proposal, and got together with Warner just about every Sunday night. Although I enjoyed the experience of learning, I never got any good at playing the guitar.

The time of the hippies was beginning to wind down in San Francisco. Disco music had been in full swing for quite a while and would not go away. Punk rockers were just beginning to make an appearance on the streets, in the bars, and music venues. Gay pride was on the rise. The city was full of creative folks, and had a lot going on.

The police were lax in some areas. I was able to buy alcohol throughout my time in the city, though I arrived at the age of fifteen. Wild parties with sex, drugs, and loud music were allowed to run all night. Weirdness, most of it quite delightful, was rampant on the streets. Drugs, particularly marijuana, was tolerated. With all that tolerance, San Francisco attracted a lot of predators of various sorts. Charles Manson had been one of them several years before I arrived in the city.

As a young teenager, I was approached and offered money to participate in porno films. A couple of times, a luxury car with shaded windows pulled up beside me as I proceeded along a sidewalk. The door would open and remain that way for a time. I suppose the suggestion was, "If I'll offer you a ride in my fancy car, just think what other luxuries I might share with you." When I didn't respond, the door would shut and the driver of the car would speed away, perhaps looking for a more willing victim. I steered clear of the manipulative guru types, and the sexual predators, but fell prey to a more forthright set of criminals: muggers. Nothing serious, just my pride injured. Although terribly self-destructive, I enjoyed a great adventure in the city, despite the dangers or, in part, because of them.

I lived in seven apartments/flats during the six and a half years I was in San Francisco, most of them in old Victorian houses with aesthetic features missing from most dwellings today; more complex woodwork, curved walls and windows, patterned ceilings, wainscoting, hand-crafted banisters with lathe-turned newels, old porcelain and brass kitchen and bathroom fixtures, and lots of stained glass. I loved all that.

Warner called on me frequently for assistance of various sorts, mostly to help him haul stuff around. In exchange, he photographed my artwork, using portraiture-quality slide film for good color accuracy.

"You should archive all your paintings, drawings, and sculptures with photography," he said. "If you want, I'll teach you how."

I got a camera and he helped me learn how to use it with a tripod, lights color-balanced to the film, umbrellas to help diffuse the light, and a polarizing filter to minimize glare. All the artwork I produced for the next twenty years would be photographed in that way. A good thing too, since in the 1990s I scanned the slides of the images and had digital files I could sell to publishers of work I'd produced as far back as my first year in college. One painting a teacher had told me was crap, I sold to three different publications. I also sold the original piece and archival reproductions of the artwork. Nice crap, that.

Warner helped me quite a lot and I felt enough gratitude that I jumped when he needed help. Like me, he moved a lot within the city. Everybody did back then, as rents went up with no control. In a closet of one of the apartments I helped him move into, we found an old guitar in bad shape, abandoned by a previous tenant. The hollow body had bolts running back to front, holding it together. With the instrument's slightly bent neck, the string action close to the body was almost an inch.

"Well, I have a new concert model," Warner said, holding the thing out and inspecting it as if it were a fine instrument.

"You can't seriously play that thing," I said.

"You wait and see."

"Why, when you have really fine guitars?"

"Not ones I can take to the beach."

That evening, worn out from hauling his stuff into the new place, we sat around drinking wine and smoking pot. "Back when I taught your family scuba, I remember watching you swim," he said.

"I've never seen anyone so comfortable in the water."

I thought of my experience in the deep end as a small child, and decided that had probably removed what fear of water I might have had.

"I've been thinking," he said, "if you assist me in teaching scuba classes and organizing dive trips, you could go along for free."

I jumped at the opportunity. We did dive trips along the California coast. Some, like dives at Santa Catalina and San Clemente Islands, involved boat trips. Just off those islands in undersea forests, I swam among giant kelp plants that rose fifty to a hundred feet through wriggling columns of slanting sunlight, and I got to see bioluminescent algae during night dives.

When our trips were onshore, sometimes we'd camp and have cookouts on the beach. Tired from a long day and somewhat sleepy from a good meal, perhaps one with fresh abalone, we'd sit around a fire, talking, smoking pot, and drinking. Warner would whip out the concert model. As he'd pointed out, the instrument was the only guitar he owned crappy enough to be exposed to sand.

"Let's do a sing along," he'd say.

Tired, stoned, and drunken, the clients on the dive trip might grumble a bit, but they'd take part in a half-hearted way. Since Warner kept his professional worlds somewhat separate, often the clients didn't know how well he could play. Performing such hits as "She'll be Coming Round the Mountain," "The Streets of Laredo," and "On Top of Old Smokey," Warner encouraged their disinterest.

"I'm trying to offer some entertainment," he'd protest playfully, as their voices slowly died out.

He'd pluck awkwardly at the strings, maybe fumble and drop the guitar. He'd apologize for his ineptitude, and allow the instrument to fall silent.

Then he'd let a little time pass. Sometimes you could hear someone snoring. Folks got up to relieve themselves and return.

At the deepest lull, when the fire had died down some and no one spoke, he'd start something on the guitar so quietly, the sound barely registered. Slowly he'd bring up the volume and the speed of his playing. He'd explore some fast-paced flamenco, say, "Malaguena," as those around him stirred, sat up, and looked at each other in astonishment, their eyes round, awake, and gleaming orange in the fire light. Warner would sit with a quiet smile and play for another half hour or more. Nobody snored through that.

I knew about his skills with the guitar, but what an introduction to his talent those people got. What amazed me more than anything was that he pulled off such performances with that horrible guitar that had been abandoned in a closet.

At the base of high cliffs in Sonoma County, California, we were free diving (snorkeling) with one of Warner's classes when he ran into trouble. We'd buddied up for the class, diving in pairs. Warner seemed to always choose the prettiest female to be his buddy. I don't remember who I was paired with that afternoon. Screaming drew my attention across the water to the sight of Warner's buddy flailing and crying out. I swam toward her through two foot chop and ten foot surge. By the time I got to her, she'd become limp on the surface of the water. I shook her a bit and she perked up, fear in her eyes.

"Warner," she said.

I looked down and saw him a few feet away, underwater. He'd become tangled in the bull kelp and appeared lifeless. His pale face remained three feet below the surface. I dove, grabbed the strands of kelp, and found them too slippery to break. I had no dive knife and had to get the one strapped to Warner's ankle to cut him free.

Through the surge and chop, I hauled him to a muscle-encrusted rock jutting from the surf about fifty yards away. To get to shore would have been another fifty to seventy yards further and a more difficult swim and crawl through a maze of half submerged boulders. I got him up onto the rock, his back draped over the sharp prominences awkwardly. He remained lifeless, his usually expressive hands pale blue and reminding me of those in Picasso's painting, "The Old Guitarist."

A guy onshore, not a part of our dive party, shouted at me, "Perform artificial respiration and CPR."

I couldn't do the AR yet. I'd expended all my energy getting Warner onto the rock, and I needed what breath I could get to keep from blacking out. I was a smoker back then and not particularly strong.

As I considered CPR, my mind reeled at the thought of crushing his spine against the jagged rock and sharp muscles. I tried to get him into a position that might help me perform the procedure, but there was little room on the rock, and I had not regained much strength.

By now the stranger from the shore had made it to the rock. "Fucking idiot," he said.

I helped him position Warner better and he performed AR and CPR.

Nothing helped. The brilliant spark that was Warner had gone out. I'd failed a great and talented man, his family, and his friends.

The stranger glared at me as he left, and I shriveled up inside.

A coastguard helicopter arrived and hauled Warner away. I never saw him again.

Later, I dreamed someone told me he lived somewhere on the coast, south of San Francisco. I got on a wobbly tricycle to ride down to see him. The tricycle fell apart along the way. I encountered endless encumbrances, washed out roads, stormy weather, dangerous traffic, before arriving at my destination. Stumbling and staggering, I reached the door behind which I'd find the man. I knocked, and a stranger answered. "Oh, you just missed him, but I don't think he wants to see you."

At the time, I felt like a *fucking idiot.* Truth is, I'd felt like that since I was much younger. My family is full of smart folks. My sisters and brother all did extremely well in school, while I did poorly. I'd always felt like the dumb member of the Clark family.

Two weeks before Warner died, I'd gone with him to take a safety diving course where I learned all that I needed to know to save his life. I'd barely passed the exam at the end of the course. Nothing could have better confirmed my stupidity than the loss of Warner Felton.

~ ~ ~

Needing to get away from all the self-recrimination, I got out of bed and went back upstairs to my studio, determined to distract myself with work. I hadn't let my own internal dialogue get to me for a long time. My imagination is powerful and useful, yet it frequently tells me things about myself that are clearly untrue. Over time, I'd proven to myself that I had the capacity to use my brain. Bullshit messages such as "You're not smart," didn't usually hold much water anymore.

I'd left a bunch of items from my trip to Nashville in a pile near the top of the stairs. Yes—I'd been so depressed, I hadn't completely unpacked in over two months. My backpack still needed to be emptied out. I picked it up and started going through each pocket, putting away business cards, travel receipts, a book Randy had loaned me. In the largest section of the backpack, I found a cardboard stiffened, plastic sleeve. I pulled that out, turned it over, and discovered the edition of *The Star*, the London newspaper from 1888 that Dave Conover had given me.

As excited as I'd been to receive the gift, I'd forgotten all about it. At present, the desire to read the text drowned out the grim voices in my head. I stood at my empty drafting table and slipped the newspaper out of the plastic sleeve. Yellowed to a warm grey/brown, the paper had a slightly brittle feel, yet remained strong enough to handle without tearing. Although thrilled to touch something from the time and place of the period I'd spent so much time researching, the newspaper brought on that odd déjà vu feeling I got when I pictured Victorian London while writing. That feeling became associated in my mind with the hallucinatory false memory experience. I realized in that moment that the haunted feeling I got as I wrote about London had probably always been the edges of a temporal lobe seizure. But why would thinking about that city move me toward convulsions?

Would I have to give up the series to avoid having seizures? I had great sympathy for the victims of the Ripper. Their humanity had always seemed forgotten in the furor to figure out which asshole had killed them. I wouldn't give up the series easily.

A strange notion occurred to me, along with a question: *Does the Ripper haunt me?* Had my efforts to give the victims back some small humanity pissed off their killer? Did he somehow know what I was up to, and he meant to stop me?

That seemed ridiculous. Still, the question hung there in my mind, unanswered.

I spread the newspaper out on the drafting table. A single large broadsheet folded twice, the thing measured roughly three feet by two feet. In its time, September 13, 1888, five days after Annie Chapman's death, the paper cost a half penny, referred to as a ha'penny. I opened the first fold and read the front and back pages first. Advertisements for bird seed and Player's smokes appeared in the top left and top right of the front page. All the advertisements for overseas travel in the left-hand column had pictures of ships with sails, some square-rigged, some lateen. The "What We Think" editorial section had a distinctively liberal or *progressive* slant, in contrast with the same newspaper of today, owned by a powerful right-wing interest.

The "In the Police Courts" section on the back page had articles about an organ grinder playing his music too late and disturbing the peace at night, an attack on an artist in Bow Street, a woman stabbed by a Japanese man, and an Australian man thrown to his death from a train.

Then I opened the paper to the two interior pages. The name "Whitechapel" on the right-hand page caught my eye. I read the articles about the five-day-old murder of Annie Chapman. The only thing new I discovered was that someone had suggested to the police that they should take pictures of the pupils of Chapman's eyes in case the retina had captured an image of the murderer at the moment of death.

Further on, I read about the Pimlico mystery, involving severed limbs found along the Thames. I knew this had something to do with the torso mysteries contemporary with the Ripper killings. The police did not consider the Ripper homicides and the torso murders to be committed by the same killer. Between the years 1887 and 1889, someone left a headless, limbless torso in each of two locations in London, and another one had washed up on the banks of the River Thames. Other parts of bodies also turned up on the banks of the river over time.

The newspaper reported that a Mrs. Potter of Westminster had come forward believing the limbs found in Pimlico belonged to her daughter, Emma, who she referred to as having a rather weak intellect. The seventeen-year-old girl had wandered away from home a few days earlier.

I'm not certain how, but I knew the limbs didn't belong to Emma. The knowing brought on the most intense dread I'd ever known. I took a step back and almost fled the studio.

Instead, I abandoned the article half-read, and looked to the left-hand page. Trying to relax and stave off a seizure, I looked for something pleasant to read. I found an article about a Professor Baldwin, an American, who had come to London to demonstrate the new parachute he'd invented. He would perform a daring feat September 14, the day after the date of the newspaper edition.

"Yes, if the weather tomorrow is fine as it is today, I guess I am going two miles up in a balloon and coming back again in my parachute."

I figured that would be safe, light-hearted reading and continued. The man, clearly a Victorian-era science-geek, spoke of the science behind his effort. Likely, he'd come to London to impress folks who might help him finance his endeavors. The article felt like some steampunk fiction to me until he talked about the aerodynamics of his invention.

"Now, the object is to get as flat a surface exposed to the wind as possible, so that when the parachute oscillates the air on the side that is tilted up may readily escape, and the equilibrium be restored. But my parachute, non-rigid as it is, must to some extent be dome-shaped when inflated."

As I read his words, I thought back to my own experiences with parachutes. A series of pleasant memories unfolded, and I gratefully explored them as I sensed that would further reduce the risk of seizure.

I'd never skydived, but I did make parachutes for my piglet doll. Daddy's sister, my Aunt Alice, had given me the stuffed doll when I was three. Melody and I referred to him as Ancient Egyptian Piglet because he was old, threadbare, and bursting out stuffing at the seams. As a child, I took him on a lot of adventures, and he got into some fixes all on his own. The plastic adhesive bandages and repair stitches, particularly those over his heart, were the result of an argument he had with my dog, Fritz. He sustained damage in homemade glider accidents, trips down the stairs, off balconies, and rooftops. Because he became so discolored, I painted him with the first set of acrylic paints I ever owned, sometime in the mid 1960s. Not knowing much about mixing paint then, I used the acrylic straight out of the tube of yellow ochre because that was the closest pig-color in the set. His feet were repaired with velvet cloth. One was pink, the other black. His missing eyes were drawn on with permanent magic marker.

Not that she'd wanted to, but I never let Lysta play with him because he'd become so fragile. At about ten years of age, she awoke us in the night with a scream. Melody and I both got up and went to her bedroom. I turned on the light.

"There's something on the chest," Littlebean said, "hiding with the dolls."

Melody had recently moved all her creepy dolls to the top of a chest in the corner of the room. Lysta liked the scary toys, so I found her reaction confusing. Nothing seemed amiss.

"Go back to sleep, sweetie," Melody said.

I cupped Littlebean's cheek in my hand and gave her a reassuring smile.

Melody turned off the light as we went out.

We hadn't gotten back in bed before Lysta screamed again and we returned to her room.

"Don't turn on the light," she said. "Look."

I could see her arm in the dimness that filtered in through the bedroom window. She pointed at the chest.

A cross glowed faintly in the dark. I turned on the light and discovered that the illumination came from Piglet.

Then I remembered where the cross came from. I loved monsters in grade school. Hell, I was still into monsters. Back when I was a kid, black and white monster movies appeared on television at four o'clock after school. I loved those old movies. Wanting to keep Piglet safe from vampires, I painted the cross on him with what must have been some of the first commercial glow-in-the-dark paint.

I explained all that to Lysta.

"That's cute," she said.

We all went back to sleep.

One set of adventures I'd had with piglet in the 1960s involved parachuting. I'd made the devices from string and old bedsheets which my mother intended to tear up for cleaning rags. With Piglet harnessed into a parachute folded just right, I took him up as high as I could in a Tennessee State Forest fire tower and threw him off to see him float gently to the Earth. I had to make several attempts. The first parachute wobbled so much, my stuffed friend nearly met his end. The strings and cloth got into such a tangle around him that he and the contraption dropped like a stone the last fifty to seventy-five feet. I researched parachutes and learned to put a hole in the top of the canopy. That allowed the trapped, compressed air to spill not from the sides, which created oscillation, but through the aperture in the top of the chute, which acted something like a thruster, providing stability and direction during descent.

I resumed reading professor Baldwin's words in The Star since my reaction to the article seemed harmless enough. "By means of flaps, operated by pulling on cords, I've gained the ability to direct my descent to some degree. I hope to one day make a parachute which will not oscillate. It isn't perfect yet. I mean to improve it a lot by degrees. But it is good for my two mile trip tomorrow."

Then I had a frightening realization: The guy didn't know about putting a hole in the top of the chute. As I knew I couldn't turn the page to see what happened the day when he performed his feat, I got a cold feeling in my gut and my skin prickled.

I quickly moved to my computer, and made a search for him online.

On Wikipedia, I discovered that he'd fallen to his death. An article from *The Illustrated London News* said that the crowds on the Alexandra Palace grounds drew back to avoid the falling daredevil. The engravings accompanying the text showed the crowd—one of the largest ever assembled for such an event, the writer explained—ringing an empty space on the ground that had a featureless dark spot at its center.

What the fuck? If I'd failed Warner because I was stupid, here I'd found a situation in which my smarts might have helped. The irony seemed particularly cruel. If I'd arrived in London a few days before Baldwin's performance, I might have found him, and told him to put a hole in his *damned* chute. If need be, I could have demonstrated its effectiveness with a *fucking* handkerchief!

The day had become one big load of sad shit. Unable to get away from thoughts of death, I felt worse by the moment.

The daylight had almost past. With the onset of dusk, the studio had darkened, and I looked forward to Melody coming home any minute and saving me from myself. Goddamn, I needed her embrace.

I could not keep my thoughts from circling back to how I might have approached the professor. I got up to read his words again in *The Star*.

As I stood at my drafting table, leaning over to read the tiny print, the weird, dark smell that came with the temporal lobe seizures filled my head. More than ever, the odor seemed like something rotting in the grave, but now with a load of shit heaped on. I stood up straight and grabbed for the edges of the table as the room shifted dizzyingly. Something of another reality seemed to peek at me from the shadows. Then, the studio disappeared...

Aiden/Frederick: 1

…And I found myself cutting a woman's head off with a long, thin blade.

In horror, I let go of the knife, but it remained—I had no control of my hands!

The blood had a purplish hue. My hands appeared strange, the color of the flesh paler, rougher, the nails wider. The taste in my mouth was strange and unfamiliar.

The weird seizure smell, more powerful than I'd ever known the odor to be, came from her—she reeked of rot and old shit. Her shoulder stumps oozed pus and a brownish fluid.

I'd packed human shit into each of her four stumps, those at her hips and shoulders, before closing the wounds!

How the fuck could that be true? Yet the knowledge, the memory, though seeming distinctly different from my thought processes, stood out in the forefront of my mind.

As if to turn away, I recoiled violently from the vivid quality of what I knew must be hallucination. A mere spasm passed through me, and still, I faced the hideous scene. The dread that came with the seizures became electric and sizzling like what I'd experience during bad LSD trips.

Oh… the fit… and her sex!

That ecstatic voice in my head didn't "feel" like my own. I did not feel that ecstasy! If an internal voice could be said to have an accent, the one behind the distinctively male thoughts also sounded/felt different from my own.

The woman's eyes rolled aimlessly, becoming large in her grim face as I continued to cut through the translucent flesh of her throat and into the tough tissue of her larynx. I didn't want to know her. I tried not to think of her as a living being.

My left leg quaked against a gritty, unseen floor, and the cut became jagged.

I take your treasure, Abigail, your precious, bright rubies.

Again, the voice sounded silently inside me, though as if addressing the woman. Reading the attitude behind the words, I found all that is petty, small, and mean swimming like crocodiles in a strangely placid, liquid mind, also not my own.

His arousal overshadowed my dread. Yes—I'd begun to think of the other presence as male. I had difficulty separating my thoughts from his.

I know your hidden sex, the inside of you, what you've kept secret and protected.

He hated her.

He took what he wanted. Diminishing her made him larger, less vulnerable.

Without my bidding, my left hand rose to my nose and I smelled the odor of a filthy vagina on my fingers. That, the smell of rotting meat, and the sight of blood as I cut gave me a pounding hard-on. Just as having my first orgasm while being raped deeply disturbed me, I didn't want to feel sexually excited under the circumstances, yet my penis bobbed urgently in the open air beneath the edge of the table top as I leaned over the young woman.

The blade passed through the vessels in the left side of her neck. Blood gushed out in sluggish spurts. When the gash in her neck had become wide enough, the wound somehow took on the aspect of an aroused vagina. My hand set the knife down and then rose into the flowing liquid. Doused with red, the hand moved to my penis and began to stroke. Without intending to, I brought the organ out from beneath the table, leaned back and thrust it forward toward her neck. Unlike my own, the organ had a foreskin. I heard and felt myself groan with pleasure. With the warmth and wetness of the blood providing an exquisite sensation, and having taken the life of another human being to get it, I knew the lowest form of betrayal, and was thrown into a deep deluge of shame. I recognized the disturbing mix of emotions as being at the heart of the dread I'd felt since my first seizure.

I wanted out, but somehow I knew I couldn't just hold on and wait for the experience to end. No temporal lobe seizure had hold of me. I'd arrived at a deep end-reality too cruel to endure, one with no obvious route of escape. I found no bottom from which to kick off!

At the moment of orgasm, I wanted the wall of white-hot blankness to descend, as it had at Randy's house. Instead I felt muscles contracting in pulses and watched as ejaculate squirted over the bloody vagina in the young woman's neck. Simultaneously, her eyes rolled up and became still in her head.

As I shook with terror, the other experienced deep ecstasy. With thoughts of a sister—neither of them my own—and a small, dark woman, echoing, changing, blending in my mind, the body I attended quaked and shuttered uncontrollably.

I fell back onto a dirty floor, and lay for a moment gulping breath. Then he addressed me!

Oh, little man, she'd been another disappointment…until you….

Coughing, choking on phlegm, laughter—his reactions to stress and emotion interrupted his train of thought. Though disconnected from my consciousness, I felt them. I saw/felt/heard/touched/tasted him, and my thoughts shrank back in terror.

I'd regained her trust—she'd given me the look I craved and remained quiet—but I knew she loved me only for the morphine. But…having you to shock. I've not had an audience since I was a boy.

At last I'd become certain that I wasn't entirely me. I'd become someone else. With little presence of mind to think about how that might have been possible, I responded to the most immediate experiences as time pressed on.

I knew something of his mind, at first a mere trickle below his immediate responses.

Frederick Bledsoe. Yeah, that's right, fucking *Bledsoe. The* name—*I couldn't believe it! He thought of himself as the Assistant Surgeon. I knew him to be a monster, had known that since my earliest seizures, but had considered him a phantasm, a product of my diseased brain or distressed psyche, until now.*

Ahh…I know what Swoon knew, without the chloroform. *He chuckled.* Have you come to chase me from my garden? Simon might have done, but not you!

I didn't answer. He thought his feigned amusement hid a fear of insanity.

As if meditating, I did my best to empty my mind. I hid in a dark corner. That's ridiculous, of course. No such place existed in his head that I could see. I knew now that I saw, did, and experienced everything he did, and had no control. Still, I imagined a dark place and pictured myself retreating there.

Frederick lifted the woman's head and began sawing.

Although I tried not to feel and interpret, I knew his chuckling to be

187

a nervous response. He would not chuckle if he thought he were alone.

The head came free and rolled to one side on the tabletop. He laughed, the sensation grinding painfully against the revulsion I truly felt.

The body I inhabited, still stunned by the throbbing pulse of orgasm and seizure, staggered to a chair and sat. One of the three lamps on a shelf had gone out. In another, the flame had guttered down low, creating an eerie flicker that seemed to animate the face of the head on the table.

As the convulsions subsided, I did not find my escape. Weeping without tears, I clawed and tore without hands to get out, to get home to Melody and Lysta. I could only hope to ride another seizure back out and home, because I could not continue inside Frederick.

He laughed through it all, yet I knew he did so to deny a new fear; that somehow I was actually his conscience, that I'd finally rebelled, pulled away, and meant to exert control.

I gained some small hope from that. I did my best to empty my mind and retreat further.

Frederick wrapped the head and torso in cloth and tied the packages with cord. He put them into a large, heavy oilcloth sack that had a long rope attached to it. While at it, he checked the reeking interior for other body parts. I felt an intense gag reflex—mine or his, I couldn't tell, since our response to the odor may have occurred simultaneously. The sack contained only the head and torso.

His memory held recollections of carrying assorted women's limbs to various places in the city late at night to dump them. One arm he left somewhere on Lambeth Road. He liked to think about the reaction of the one who found it. He'd gone far upstream to the Chelsea Bridge to dump the other arm. One leg, he dropped off the Blackfriars Bridge. The other, he'd disposed of at an excavation for a construction site somewhere along the Victoria Embankment.

Tired and sleepy, he went to the shelf beside the table, and dowsed the guttering lamp flame. He picked up the remaining lit lamp, made his way out of the room and into a much larger space.

Finally assessing the environment as best I could, I decided it looked like a cellar of some sort. Where the fuck am I? *I wanted to ask, yet I lowered the heat under my boiling urge until the desire barely simmered. I had to be patient.*

He moved to a pallet in a stony corner, set the lamp on a masonry block beside the makeshift bed, and lay down.

Frederick expected that I came and went. I wished for that with all my heart, but it wasn't happening. I kept my mind as still and quiet as I could, hoping he would not figure out that I'd become a fixture in his mind.

Waiting for sleep, Frederick thought through his plans to get rid of the dead woman. He believed that he would not only dump the body parts, but that he'd be dumping the woman's ghost as well. Tomorrow, in the dead of night, he would haul the bag up a coal chute, put it in a barrow and wheel it...

As he was dropping off to sleep, I saw in his mind's eye where he would make his dump—the unfinished Tower Bridge stood in the distance!

And I knew where I was: London.

Frederick intended to dump the body in the Thames.

From what I'd seen of the city in his mind's eye, the place didn't look like modern London. His clothing and tools suggested incredibly that I had arrived in the nineteenth century.

With my excitement and a rapid increase in heart-rate, he shifted uncomfortably, but wasn't roused from sleep.

I struggle to relax as questions flew unanswered in my thoughts. Had I somehow truly traveled through space and time, or had I landed inside the head of an insane fellow with a delusion so complete, his mind held strictly memories to support it? Of course, such speculation was laughable, given that I couldn't decide which was more fantastic, the idea that I occupied another body or that I'd traveled through time.

Though still doubting what stared me in the face, I began to think about the opportunity to explore London of the period. While excited about the prospect, I knew enough to be fearful of what the society offered in the way of callousness and brutality.

But I could not deal with all that yet. I needed to know more about Frederick.

As he slept, I got to know him. His memory became more permeable the deeper he dozed. The flood of his life experience hit me like a tidal wave until I learned to flow with one surge of memory at a time.

Yes—he was the one who first visited me during temporal lobe seizures twenty-six years earlier, the one I'd mistaken for a nurse when he seemed to enter my hospital room. I knew what he'd said to me back then. "You don't like looking at it, but it'll have its way with you as mine has with me."

Somehow, he'd known of the discomfort I'd felt when I looked at my brain in the MRI film. I don't know how. He was epileptic, and his seizures had revealed me to him in some way I couldn't fathom. Likewise, I didn't understand why I'd known about him. And now—how could I know his thoughts, occupy his body? Had the brain abscesses somehow created a conduit between us? Why Frederick? Was he a member of my family? Did he represent a past life of mine? I didn't believe in past lives, yet I didn't believe in time travel or mental possession either. Still the past-life idea did help explain the déjà vu feeling I'd gotten while writing about Victorian London.

I learned of his murders, his time and positions at both hulks, St. Pancras Station, and in the Royal Navy, and his experience with the Regal Rats. His hopes had been struck down so frequently in life, I might have felt sorry for him if he had not become a monster. I knew how the formative sexual/amputation experience he'd had with the Mayan woman, coupled with his hatred of his sister and society had turned him, but I also suspected he'd had little conscience even before that. Nature or nurture, chicken or egg?

Speaking of chickens—the horrible dreams I'd had while Lysta was growing up, particularly the one about feeding Littlebean her pet chicken, seemed reflections of Frederick's desire to gain a young woman's trust, then betray her. He'd been bleeding into my consciousness for a long time.

With the amputations, the homicides reminded me of the unsolved torso murders contemporary with those of Jack the Ripper. No doubt the murderer had dumped at least one victim in the Thames because a torso washed up downstream in Rainham, and at least one body part had washed up in Pimlico.

At present, a dream Frederick was having leaked into my thoughts at weird moments. I saw him freerunning the rigging in an abandoned ship at sea with a boyhood friend, Simon. I knew of the boy from memories of the Regal Rats. Barefoot, Frederick balanced impossibly on the tip top of a mainmast in a terrible lightning storm. His beaming friend dangled from a stay, shouting insults. Simon made a rude hand gesture and slid down the cable. Frederick leapt to the stay and ran along the top of the cable to the foremast, chasing his mate. As if on level ground, the two did somersaults down the shrouds, racing to see who got to the forecastle deck first. All the while, despite a lashing wind and rain, they laughed.

I also learned that Frederick meant to kill again. He had been stalking the teenage daughter of George Noble, the General Manager for the Midland Railway, learning about her schedules and looking for a good situation to abduct her. Ultimately, he planned to leave the young woman's remains under a railway viaduct, since all of Frederick's loss had begun with the railway taking his home. I knew of that viaduct from reading about the Pinchin Street torso mystery of 1889.

I felt the edges of a seizure coming on. Frederick's left leg began to shake, and I became hopeful. I felt the roll and pitch of the ship on the sea in his dream. To my disappointment, though, the seizure symptoms faded. Frederick's leg ceased to quiver.

Simon, in the dream, swung a block at me, but missed. Even so, I reflexively tried to raise a hand to ward it off. The arm and hand of the sleeping body I occupied moved a bit. Although I felt the pitch and roll of the ship at sea, I still saw the darkened room around me, and hadn't anticipated that I also existed within Frederick's dream. The block had not swung toward him. Since he busied himself, chasing his friend back up a shroud, I knew that my mind had given the limb impetus. Stupidly, without seeing the big picture, I thought that if I'd seen the arm move, Frederick's eyes remained open. Who slept with their eyes open?

But, then, I wasn't asleep. Control of the body belonged to me!

Sure enough, I struggled into a sitting position. The ship had taken Frederick and his pal far away by the time I got to my feet. Some movements, like opening or closing the eyes occurred more automatically—I didn't have to think much about making that happen. Others seemed more mechanical, like bending the torso, or moving an arm or leg. I had to "ask" those parts to move at first. Frederick's muscles responded sluggishly.

Luckily, he'd fallen asleep with the lamp still burning on the masonry block beside the pallet. The candle within had burned down low. Within a few minutes, the tiny remnants of the wick would drown in the melted wax. Carefully taking up the candle lamp by its handle, I explored the cellar, several rooms with two crude stairways that led to doors nailed shut. I found the coal chute, and saw boards, like rungs of a ladder, fastened inside it. Thinking I might be able to climb out that way, a desire to go out and see London tugged at me. Fear made me stay put, and not just because the city was dangerous. I knew that whatever I did that night, I must be on the pallet again by the time Frederick awoke. He should not find out what I was up to.

Hell, having no idea how to get home, I didn't know what I was up to.

As the candle guttered, I returned to the pallet and lay down.

I felt foolish for falling into a trap. Not because I thought Frederick had intended to draw me in. I had the impression he didn't know any more than I did. No—as unnatural as my situation seemed, I saw myself as something like an insect in a Venus fly trap. I did feel like a lowly bug at that moment. While I might like to blame someone else, the plant that swallowed me had no guile.

I should never have gone off the seizure medicine!

I thought of Melody and Lysta, and tried to picture them in my mind, but they were so far away, I couldn't see them. Then the thought occurred to me that they did not exist. Not yet, anyway.

Frederik's eyes released tears as I wept.

Having finally discovered the damn good *reason for the intense dread I'd felt in seizures over the years, I could not sleep. I lay in a cold sweat, not knowing when Frederick would awaken to begin the next forbidding day.*

Aiden/Frederick: 3

When he awoke, Frederick undressed and put on finer clothes; a pair of gray trousers, a brown checked waistcoat over a white shirt, a black, knee-length frock coat, and a soft, gray felt hat. His black leather shoes were worn through on the bottom, but because he'd recently had a shoe-black work on them, the tops appeared to be in good shape.

Again, I had no control over Frederick's body.

He slipped a cord through the handles of a medical case and tied it in a loop that he put over his shoulder as a strap. He carried us, and the medical case up the rungs inside the coal chute and into the light of day. I got my first glimpse of London, a weed-choked area between two rotting buildings. The air was hazy with exhaust from coal-burning as I'd expected. Frederick's throat and lungs took the foulness without much trouble. I thought the slight chill in the air might indicate fall or early winter. Then I remembered something from my research for A Brutal Chill in August, *my Jack the Ripper Victims Series novel about the life of Mary Ann "Polly" Nichols. The eruption of Krakatoa in the Dutch East Indies in 1883 had tossed so much debris into the upper atmosphere that a brief global climate change occurred on Earth—a little ice-age. If I'd arrived during the time of the torso murders, 1887 to 1889, I would be right in the middle of that period. The Times had reported that witnesses saw snow in London, late at night on July 11, 1888.*

Frederick untied the cord, removed it from the medical case, and placed it in his coat pocket. As we emerged from between the buildings, I saw a small, filthy river or creek to the left. Young, muddy boys— mudlarks perhaps—busied themselves trying to uncover something partially submerged in the muck along the bank.

The position of the sun, merely a brighter spot within the bitter white haze of the sky, suggested that one-third of or two-thirds of the day remained, depending on whether I faced north or south. As Frederick seemed to notice the orb, I knew instantly that I faced south, the time to be about 3:00PM, and that he was in the habit of staying up at night until the wee hours of the morning to pursue his interests while most people slept.

He walked around to the sagging front of the building. I saw ship's masts, the sails on their spars stowed, rising above low brick buildings across the road. Knowledge of the area flowed readily from Frederick's mind, and I knew the ships were moored at the East India Docks.

I knew roughly my position within the city. The waterway where I'd seen the boys was Bow Creek. I wanted to go explore the docks, see the activity there and the ships, but I could only do what Frederick did.

He approached a large man standing in the shadows of a leaning wall. Instantly, I knew the fellow's name to be Alfie Watkins. He stank of old sweat, mildew, sad alcohol yeast, and stale tobacco smoke. His threadbare clothing and worn-out felt hat were hopelessly stained. Gray toes peeked out from between the leather uppers and the splitting soles of his shoes.

Frederick opened his medical case, took out two bottles that looked like they contained about a pint of clear liquid each.

"I gave you a bit more today, and will in the future if you'll stop dipping into Lars's share." He looked Alfie in the eye.

"Yes, sir," Alfie said. "Thank you, sir."

Frederick handed over the bottles, then turned and entered a thin, brick-paved road that passed between short buildings, some that looked like residences. The people we passed, all laborers, wore clothing that I could not easily place in time. Certainly they belonged to the nineteenth century. Some of the men wore bowler hats. The women were done up from head to toe, although some had sleeves rolled and the collars of blouses undone.

Frederick walked by a two story building on his left that held a public house named simply The Crown. Children's singing came from somewhere amidst the buildings in that block, enough voices to give me the impression they'd gathered for school, though none of the larger buildings looked anything other than industrial. On the right, I saw large storage tanks among warehouses and a building with a sign that indicated the structure was a galvanized iron works.

I knew we headed toward appointments offering barber/surgeon services to recurring clients Frederick had begun rounding up ever since he'd been back in London. At present, absorbed in trying to make a determination of the exact time period, I paid little attention to what went on inside him. Short of Frederick picking up a newspaper and looking at the date, I wondered what telltale signs he might encounter *that would tell me more.*

You like the gristle and marrow of life, *he thought at me.*

Feeling as if I'd jumped right out of his skin, I thought for a moment I might be free. That brief illusion passed, though, and I found myself as firmly planted as ever.

Yes—you like the gristle, but your sentimental nature doesn't allow you to chew on it. You want the marrow, yet won't suck it from the bones. Too proper for that, I suppose.

Although I knew what he was getting at, I kept my thoughts quiet.

I've known that about you since we first met, long ago. You're weak, and small. With that, you think ill of *me!*

I understood that he expressed overall impressions that had come off me in waves in his seizure visions. He did not know how or why he'd received those impressions any more than I understood how I'd known the things I did about him. I still did not understand the mechanisms that allowed me to know what he thought and felt, how he knew what I thought and felt, and why some information didn't pass between us easily or at all.

For purposes of offense as well as defense, I needed to figure those things out.

You fumble in the dark!

By that, I knew he followed my speculations. But how well? How transparent were my thought processes? I couldn't tell.

Concerning his assertion that I liked the grit and grime of life, yet didn't want to get my hands dirty, he called me a hypocrite because I didn't approve of his hobbies.

You toy with a desire to maim and kill, while I have the courage to commit the deeds.

Yes—I'd always liked the dark and disturbing. I enjoyed using the unsettling, the violent, the grotesque, and intimations of death in my art and writing to challenge the thinking of my audience. I suppose that's because I liked such things challenging my own thinking. Like a lot of people, I'd gained a complacency as I progressed through life, and a bit of terror, real or imagined, shook things up nicely.

Concerning an appreciation for imagined death, destruction, violence, and pain, I suppose mine began in childhood. As a boy, I feared failure, weakness, shaming, and regret, but most of all physical pain. I remember thinking that feeling tough enough to survive it all actually helped me succeed. The Vietnam War raged during my childhood and adolescence. I feared having to grow up and go into that fight. Still, I became fascinated with what the terror of that sort of struggle might be like. I fell in love with war movies, and found myself willing—no, wanting *to see the blood and gore. I think I believed that if I could face the horror in make believe, it might help me if I ever had to face the real thing one day. And maybe I felt one up on others if what shocked them didn't shock me. Was that why I got fake vomit and plastic ice cubes with flies in them to torment my mother and sisters?*

You're still a bit of a boy, aren't you! Have you breeched to long trousers yet?

His statement was true enough. Too bad he didn't have anything child-like left in him. Just as I needed to eat, drink, breathe, and stay warm, I wanted, no needed *to play and laugh. Much of that laughter was at the grim aspects of life.*

Oh, you're good at whistling past the graveyard, hiding from your fear of death.

Joking about pain and death didn't amount to denial of the seriousness and inevitability of those aspects of life. I'd always preferred to thumb my nose at the darkness rather than become depressed. I suspected that causing others pain and killing represented, in part, Frederick's means of thumbing his nose at his own suffering and eventual demise. His method wasn't the least bit funny.

"I like your combination of humor and horror," Daddy had once told me, "especially in the Pain Doctors paintings." He referred to the series of disturbing, yet humorous medical scenes I'd painted after the brain abscesses. "Humor and horror both require that audiences be caught off-guard," he said.

That got me thinking about the circumstances in which I laughed. I decided that I was usually in a position filled with emotion and possibility, one that left me feeling at least a bit on edge and slightly vulnerable. I chose to go into those situations with abandon, a willingness to see what happened, to take developments as they came, to risk. I craved laughter. I craved joking with friends and seeing how far we could push one another before having to pull back; just how inappropriate we could get using sarcasm, satire, and irony to create droll, morbid, grotesque, and self-deprecating humor. Those social encounters were risks. My friends could have easily taken offense and turned angry, become enemies. Yet I tended to choose friends who didn't take themselves too seriously, those I could safely joke around with and nudge emotionally. We all knew not to take the joking too far. I trusted them, and they trusted me…mostly! Some risk remained.

Those interactions were a bit like riding a rollercoaster. I got on the ride because I wanted the feeling of being in danger, while knowing that hundreds of people survived the thrill every day.

Craving good humor seemed a healthy way to have my world shaken up. I believed that when our self-satisfied assumptions about the world were shaken sufficiently, gratitude for life and learning, and a child-like innocence were at least partly renewed.

Concerning my appreciation for the reality of surviving actual death and destruction, I remembered my father's attitude following his success in fighting off the first bout of leukemia. He'd *been renewed, as I was after surviving brain abscesses and alcoholism.*

I am renewed when I take and spoil. You're the same.

Yes—at times in life, feeling small and diminished, I'd tried to take power from others, but that had never been more than a temporary patch of the hole that needed filling, and I'd never felt good about it.

Over the years of displaying my horror pieces in convention art shows, occasionally someone heavily leathered and pierced sidled up to me and spoke conspiratorially about the wonders of pain. At one event, I met a woman into S & M who persistently, perhaps hopefully, questioned me about my proclivities. "Some of your paintings are so sinewy, they look like you painted them with your penis. Was the rough surface painful against the tender flesh? Did you like it?"

I fielded numerous similar suggestions with good humor, yet I finally had to gesture to my artwork, and say, "This is all fiction. I'm into the fiction." While I respected everyone's rights to harm themselves or other consenting adults, I wouldn't encourage them.

I'd become intimately acquainted with pain, knew its value, and had no desire to seek it.

Although Frederick's interest was obviously different from those I met at conventions, his misunderstanding of my fascination with the macabre had a similar feel. He wanted to turn me into a co-conspirator, or be done with me.

But I wasn't going away. Would that I could've.

No—this asshole didn't know much about me if he thought my interest in horror meant that I wanted to see others hurt. Knowing the hardships in life and surviving them had given me new appreciation for even the simplest moments day to day. Since the ordeals of twenty-five and twenty-six years earlier, I'd been less in a hurry, had lived much more in the moment, and could find pleasure almost anywhere.

I was a survivor, and Frederick was a bitter idiot. I would get out of my predicament and stop him from killing again if I could. If I survived and somehow got home, I might never crave having my complacency shaken again, assuming I had any at all!

I knew my reaction confused him. He wanted to find the edges of me, and gain total control. Now, he fumbled in the dark.

Frederick wanted to ask where I came from. Clearly, what he'd seen of my memories confused him. Having read Jules Verne's novel, A Journey to the Centre of the Earth, *and several other lost world-type stories, he toyed with placing me in such a fictional context and wondered briefly if those tales held more truth than he'd known. He had the strangest tendency to think of me as one from the past. Somehow, that seemed possible, yet a visitor from the future wasn't.*

He didn't ask me where I came from for fear of looking weak. He'd been surprised and distressed to find me still in his head when he awoke. Even so, he didn't want to acknowledge to himself that he couldn't understand what mechanisms had brought us together, let alone admit that to me. No—Frederick frequently tried not to feel much as he moved forward in life, and that's why I'd been unaware of his emotions earlier. But then his feelings of discomfort had emerged as he tried to engage with me. For me, his denial created an uneven blind spot in the rearview mirror of his feelings. Sometimes, I didn't know what went on inside him. Other times, I did while he didn't.

I pitied him a bit and he must have felt some of that, because he tried to insult me.

You're a lushington, too weak to get along in the world without your mum to tuck you in and say a kind word. Worse, you're a mandrake, a disgusting backscuttle. You'd rather stir shit than enjoy a nice fish. You know it's true.

The insults fell flat. Neither accusation shamed me. He must have had an information dump from my mind similar to what I'd gotten from him in a tidal wave the night before. Also like me, he must have figured out how to follow the smaller surges and currents of memory. He'd discovered that I was an alcoholic, and that I'd experimented with gay sex. I refer to my experience that way because I'd never really been into men, yet the opportunities had come up and I was horny, especially as a teen. During my adolescence, I had an encounter with an older teen. I chose to go to bed with him and immediately regretted the decision. He forced himself on me painfully once we were alone—the second rape I'd experienced. I would have been about fourteen years old.

Frederick had focused on that event, and the prior rape that occurred when I was hitchhiking because I'd been weak and easily overpowered. Those experiences hadn't changed my attitude about homosexuality in general. I didn't consider it immoral. In San Francisco, around age fifteen, I took advantage of numerous opportunities for gay sex because I had queer friends, both male and female that I loved, and, again, I had that horniness. While having sex with another man, I always had to fantasize I was with a woman.

I was confused and frustrated. So were my male partners. Why couldn't I get into it? I thought I wanted to be bisexual. Instead, perhaps I thought that if I were gay or at least bisexual, that would somehow make sense of having had my first orgasm while being raped by a man.

Some of the parties I went to in San Francisco back then turned into orgies. Yeah, that's a dated expression. Still, "orgy" is the best word to describe what happened; sex in every room, men and women doing all kinds of things with each other. I'm not certain why, but having the mix of male and female, the homosexual sex worked better for me. That may have been because my attention was truly on the women involved. That was in the mid-1970s, when San Francisco was full of hippies who believed in free love, before AIDS had come to the city.

At Project 1, the warehouse commune where I went to high school, I got involved with a few adult women while I was still in my middle teens. One in particular was a thirty-five year old named Marlene. Sex with her felt right. I found her mature, attractive, affectionate, and passionate. The lovemaking, though exciting, remained casual since I wasn't truly lover material, being emotionally immature. I had no illusions about that.

Marlene was friends with the owners of the Erotic Art Museum, a volunteer there, or something like that. For whatever reason, she had access to the place.

"I have a key to get us in after hours," she told me. "Let's go look at the exhibits and make love on the sex furniture."

We did that a couple of times, having a lot of fun together. Marlene had a beautiful shape. She felt good, smelled good, and had a pleasant way about her.

Eventually we went our separate ways. I always had good feelings about my time with her.

Thirty years later, in 2003, I visited my illustrator pal, Jill Bauman, Aunty Jilly as Lysta called her. I'd gone to stay with her for a few days at her second floor apartment in a house in Queens, New York before we both went on to attend Necon, a conference of mostly genre fiction professionals in Providence, Rhode Island. We spent much of our time at her place collaborating on several pieces of art.

One evening, while Jill and I were painting, Melody called. "A woman named Marlene left you a message and a phone number," she said.

I didn't make the connection between the name and the person from my past. I took the number and made the call.

Discovering the Marlene I'd known from San Francisco on the other end of the phone line, my pulse increased and I became excited.

I went into the room Jill had given me to use, closed the door for some privacy, and sat on the folded futon/sofa I'd been using as a bed. The creepy clown in one of Jill's paintings on the wall stared down at me with a big grin of delight as I spoke with Marlene. Small talk didn't last long. Her tone became somber and she got to the point quickly.

"What I did to you years ago weighs heavily on my conscience," she said.

"What you did?" I said, confused.

"I am a psychologist now. Some of the patients I see are victims of pedophiles. I know what that does to young people."

I was just beginning to catch up with her meaning. She thought she'd treated me badly.

"What I did—" her voice cut off, and I heard the emotional weight of her words in her uneven breath on the other end of the line.

"Marlene — " I started, and she cut me off.

"I'm sorry I harmed you. I'd been reluctant to look you up for a long time, afraid of what I'd find, but I decided that if you needed *help, I should try to find that for you."*

"Please stop," I said, gently, and I had silence while I composed my thoughts. I saw in my mind's eye the beautiful woman I'd spent time with years earlier. Although Marlene sounded the same, I realized she was currently sixty-five years old. Since I could not see her, I experienced an odd dissonance between my rather fixed internal vision of her, and what I knew must be her changing appearance. Without the ability to see her facial expressions, the dissonance was compounded further by the fascinating and unsettling realization that what she felt about our time together and what I felt, her regret versus my gratitude, could not have been more different. The clown on the wall seemed to think that funny. At least in that moment, his smile appeared to be one meant to mock me, the change a tribute to Jill's ability to depict with subtlety.

"I have nothing but glowing memories about you," I said. "Please don't think you did me harm." I knew something of the effects of pedophilia and sexual abuse on preteens and adolescents. I'd suffered that long before I'd met her. "If anything, you helped me. At the time, I was seriously confused about sex. I thought I should be bi-sexual. So many of my friends were enjoying that, yet I experienced only frustration trying to get there. My experience with you informed me about my sexuality. I ceased to be troubled about it. Men aren't the right shape for me. They don't smell right, either. I don't love them any less, but I'm heterosexual, no two ways about it."

"I was so much older," she said, still unable to let go of her pain. "I was the responsible adult, and I can't know that I didn't manipu-late—"

"Marlene," I said cutting her off again, "perhaps it was wrong, but let me assure you that I don't remember being manipulated. You were loving and good to me. You gave me what I wanted. Nothing that you wanted from me was in any way difficult for me to give you. In no way did you coerce. I remember that time as making all the sense in the world in the midst of a troubled adolescence."

"I hope that's true. I have hoped that was true." Marlene sounded less upset.

She asked me about my life, and I told her the truth. I asked her about hers. As our talk continued, I had the sense that she felt better.

The clown's smile seemed to have softened, become less threatening.

Wrapping up our conversation and saying goodbye, I had the impression that she'd never feel entirely good about what happened. A shame that I didn't have the words to help relieve her of the burden.

Frederick would never understand such things. He took my lack of overt response to his insults as a form of weakness.

I figured he could go fuck himself.

We walked past workshops of some sort, arrived at a tenement in West Street, and knocked on one of several ground-level doors. The lane of granite paving stones dead-ended not far away, I saw an old fire plug of a type I'd seen in pictures online of the middle Victorian period in London. That got me slightly closer to pinpointing the time period.

A nervous, middle-aged woman, missing most of her teeth and gray hair, answered the door.

"Mr. Bledsoe," she cried, her voice cracking with emotion, "you said no leeches!"

Her bizarre reaction surprised me.

She's a lunatic, *Frederick thought, addressing me.* Perhaps you, too, are a lunatic.

His tactic of dismissing me entirely with trite insults spoke of desperation, and a continued questioning of his own sanity. I took small comfort from that.

The woman had extremely unpleasant breath, more like that of a dog. I thought of the title of a Frank Zappa song I'd always liked, "Dog Breath in the Year of the Plague."

"Yes, Miss Lillian," Frederick said. "I have the scarificator and cup you requested."

She stood aside and allowed us to enter. The single room stank of boiled cabbage and human waste. Gray hair, her hair I presumed, littered the floor. I imagined her sitting alone much of the day and fretting, pulling her hair out. Maybe she suffered some sort of anxiety disorder.

A tiny unmade bed sat against one wall, a dirty chamber pot peeking out from beneath it. An old beaten up armoire stood in a corner. A pot of steaming water, with a small, undefinable hunk of flesh in it, rested on a small iron stove that had a pipe running out through a broken window pane. Rags stuffed between the remaining shards of glass and the pipe helped keep out the weather.

"May I place the cup in your mutton tea?" Frederick asked.

He'd identified the flesh in the hot water.

"Yes," Miss Lillian said.

Frederick pulled a small, thick-walled glass cup from his case and placed the vessel in the hot water.

Miss Lillian pulled a stool toward her bed and gestured for Frederick to sit. She lay on her stomach on the straw mattress, and, with trembling hands, reached behind her to pull her chemise open, exposing her lower back and the cleft of her shriveled, spotty buttocks.

"My unease has become an unbearable pique," she said, the stiffened bedclothes muffling her shrieking voice somewhat. "You must draw it all off. You mustn't leave a single bad drop."

Frederick, having taken a seat on the stool, removed a small, rectangular device made of brass from his case; the scarificator to which he'd referred. The thing had a knob and a trigger. Frederick adjusted the knob and pulled the trigger. Eight small blades popped out.

"Try to relax, Miss Lillian, he said, as he placed the contraption on the skin over her left kidney.

She grunted her assent and lay quietly, her quaking so pronounced that the bed knocked rhythmically against the deteriorating wall, knocking loose small bits of plaster. The quaking largely subsided when Frederick placed a hand on her warm back.

He held the scarificator with one hand and pulled its trigger with the other. Miss Lillian flinched and made a shrill cry into the mattress. Leaving the device in place, Frederick moved to the stove and pulled the cup out of the water. He bounced the vessel from hand to hand to keep it from burning his fingers as he carried the hot thing back to the woman. Blood rose from eight tiny cuts, revealed when he removed the scarificator. Frederick quickly placed the cup over the wounds. Miss Lillian flinched again, then lay still as blood welled up out of the cuts in her lower back and collected under the cup.

While we waited for sufficient blood to pool, Frederick's left leg began to quiver. The room tilted suddenly and pulsed with light. I had a hope I might be going home....

~ ~ ~

Frederick and I seemed to awaken simultaneously as Miss Lillian crouched over us. We lay on the floor, the upset stool beside us. I don't know how long we had been unconscious. The cup lay unbroken on the floor, a pool of blood beside it. Blood stained the edge of the mattress and Miss Lillian's chemise.

"Please take some of my mutton tea," she said. The woman no longer trembled and quaked. "You'll feel much better."

My heart sank as I thought about the seizure opening onto mere darkness.

"No, thank you, Miss Lillian. You're very kind. However, I must go." Frederick picked up the cup and the scarificator and placed them in his case.

I faced the idea that I might truly be stuck with Frederick.

"Your cure has worked wonders for me, Mr. Bledsoe. Here is your reward."

Indeed, she seemed quite calm as she smiled, and pressed a coin into Frederick's hand.

He didn't believe in bleeding, yet had happily performed the procedure for the shilling offered.

We attended several other people in the neighborhood, mostly those of the working class and lower middle class. Although I knew quite a bit about how people of the time lived, all my knowledge had come from things I'd read, much of the material from the period. That did not entirely prepare me to accept the level of poverty I encountered. Melody and I were far from rich. Still, we had so much compared to these people. I'm not merely talking about the size and quality of their homes, but also the possessions evident. The tiny rooms I entered remained spacious without the clutter of numerous belongings. Beds, normally one of the largest pieces of furniture, were few and shared by several family members. What possessions a family did have most often appeared worn out, the function of the items more hopeful or sentimental than practical. We visited a family of eight, living in one room. They had two beds, a table with a top three foot square, one chair, a little cabinet too small to hold more than a few pieces of clothing, a small fire place with a cooking pot on the hearth, a wash tub, basin, ewer, and chamber pot. Lines stretched across the room to hold clothes and linens, already dry, and a few utensils.

All the homes smelled of decay and neglect. The occupants, though dirty, sallow, and thin, had a light of hope in their eyes. I liked most of them immediately.

I hate them all.

At a small, brick house in Duke Street, An old man, with a giant mustache and a ring of wild white hair around the top of his head, answered our knock.

"Come in, Mr. Bledsoe. May I take your hat and coat?"

"Yes sir, Mr. Fennet." Frederick handed his garments over.

As with several of the other homes we'd visited, the place had elements of a bedroom, parlor, and kitchen all in one large room. Unlike some of them, this home was well-kept. The warm, trapped air had an old man smell, not too unpleasant. Some pieces of furniture suggested that at one time, the gentleman had earned real money. A tintype of a British Army officer, standing over a dead Asian fellow, sat on a shelf. The dead man stood out sharp and clear in the picture. Although the officer's features had a slight motion-blur I recognized a younger version of Mr. Fennet, and became curious about his history. Of course, I couldn't ask him anything.

The gentleman had heated water on a small stove that exhausted up the chimney flue. He'd set a chair beside a window to sit in while Frederick shaved him. As Mr. Fennet poured the steaming water into a basin atop a small table beside the chair, I saw that he had a pronounced tremor and understood why he hired Frederick to shave him. I got the impression the old man had a pride that wouldn't allow him to go unshaven for long. Mr. Fennet spread a towel out over the top of his shirt and sat.

Frederick withdrew from his case a shaving brush, a mug with a bit of soap adhered to the bottom, and a straight razor. He dipped the brush into the hot water in the basin, worked it into the soapy mug, and spread lather onto the old man's face.

As Frederick went to work with the razor, I wondered if Mr. Fennet still had the stuff for a fight he'd obviously had in his army days. Watching the razor move along the stubbly pink cheek, I thought about trying to exert control. If I could nick the man sufficiently, perhaps he'd get upset and turn on Frederick. Ridiculous, I know, but I was desperate. I tried to think about how driving Frederick's body had felt.

For fun, he nicked the man. Mr. Fennet didn't flinch.

"Please forgive me, sir. I've drawn a bit of blood."

"Think nothing of it."

Frederick knew my desperation, and the thoughts that went along with them. Apparently, that meant he'd learned about my control of his body last night.

You've caused enough mischief. I know how to deal with lushingtons.

He would get me drunk!

I feared that. As a recovering alcoholic, I did no mood-altering drugs because any high might take me back to my old ways. Particularly, I *feared that first drink. When a drunk, once I'd had the first one, I had an irrational desire for more. I never wanted to go back to that.*

You don't have a choice. *He seemed pleased with himself.*

I had been anesthetized for a couple of small surgical procedures in recent years. If the drugs served a good purpose, I didn't seem to crave more after they'd left my system. Hoping he might not notice the memories, I held them loosely and kept them soft on the edges.

I reminded myself that the drinking would be done with Frederick's body, not my own. That got me thinking about the location of my body, and I realized that it did not exist yet. Of all the revelations of the last day and night, somehow the thought that I had no body to retreat to was the most troubling.

A desire to reject that idea, spawned an even worse one: If my body did exist somewhere in space and time and I could return to it, did that mean that Frederick could get into my body just as I had his? If so, he could be a danger to Melody and Lysta!

The thoughts came so fast, I could not stop them. I could only hope that, from the glimpses he got of what went on inside me, Frederick couldn't piece together that ultimate fear.

He chuckled at my distress, but the humor didn't seem to be of a particularly knowing type.

I tried to relax.

"A good joke to share?" Mr. Fennet asked, sounding hopeful.

"No, sir," Frederick said, "just the foolish voice in my head. Please forgive me."

"Not at all. We all need a good laugh each day."

When he'd had his shave and a hair trim, Mr. Fennet paid Frederick and we left the little brick house. Daylight failed as we returned the way we'd come. Perhaps the beautiful pure red of the sunset came from the dust of Krakatoa still circling the Earth far up in the atmosphere.

Nearing the storehouse, Frederick detoured into The Crown. A busy pub, the place had people waiting to be served, tables with drunks holding court, some patrons sitting together singing, a few angry words here and there, and a good deal of laughter. The floor was strewn with sawdust. The air reeked of smoke from poor-quality tobacco.

Finding an opening, Frederick approached the publican, who stood at the taps, a man he knew as Mr. Haines.

"A quart of gin and a glass, sir," Frederick said.

As Mr. Haines drew the gin into a bottle from a large cask, Frederick's mouth watered—my reaction.

You're weakness is not mine.

Frederick poured himself a drink from the bottle and downed half of the liquid in a way meant to help him avoid its taste. The drink disgusted him, a reaction that told me he'd rarely ever had any alcohol.

Ah… then I knew why—his father had been a drunk, and had beaten Frederick and his mother when intoxicated. He'd stayed out on the street quite a lot, even when he'd had a home.

Frederick tried to submerge the memories even as I tried to reel them in. As they bobbed back up a couple times before going under, his irritation with me came clear.

Mum had taken numerous blows meant for Frederick. By that sacrifice, she'd won the only true love Frederick ever gave anyone.

His sister, Abigail, had always been their dad's pride and joy. He struck her only once and afterward cried and begged her forgiveness.

Then the memories of Frederick's family became hidden again, obscured in the black depths of his heart. That was all I'd get.

Frederick polished off the gin in his glass. The alcohol did *taste like shit. Weaker than I'd expected—maybe watered down—and oily, the liquid felt a bit like I'd imagined kerosene did going down. Still, I felt that warm spot that spreads out so comfortably from the gut. I remembered fondly that feeling from back when I drank. The warmth came on best if my stomach was empty or if I'd not had a drink for a while.*

I liked it way too much.

Frederick took the bottle and glass with him up the stairs to a table beside the railing that overlooked the first floor and the taps. The table had a number of empty glasses. One had tipped over, spilling its contents on the table. Someone had used a broadsheet to absorb some of the mess. An image of a man hanging in the air from a ballooning sack caught Frederick's eye and my attention simultaneously.

Professor Baldwin, the parachutist! Perhaps my desire to try to help the man had determined when in time I'd arrived. His parachute feat, if that had not occurred yet, would probably happen soon. That would put me in August or early September of 1888.

Pick up the broadsheet, *I thought.*

My reaction made Frederick want to ignore the notice, but apparently his interest was piqued. He lifted the ad, shook it out, and read:

The Greatest Scientific Sensation of the Age! The daring Professor Thomas Baldwin will rise in a balloon to a height of two miles above the Alexandra Palace Grounds, then leap free and fall, returning safely to the ground by means of his invention, the parachute. The spectacle will take place at precisely three o'clock on Friday afternoon, September 14. Come one, come all. Don't be late!

With the reading of the date for the event, Frederick's mind inadvertently made a comparison, and coughed up my location in time: September 7, 1888.

Annie Chapman would die that night! The Ripper would murder her in the early hours of the morning. No—I wasn't there for the parachutist—if I had been drawn to that time and place to help someone, that someone would be Annie Chapman.

I immediately imagined going to find 29 Hanbury Street. I pictured myself crouching late at night in the shadows of the stairway to the cellar of the building, and waiting for Chapman and the Ripper to arrive. Once I heard them enter the yard, I'd reveal myself, yelling and screaming to frighten the killer away. But then in my imagination, the murderer turned on me with his knife. Horrified, I tried to let the fantasy go. I did not truly believe I had the courage to do that, even if I were free from Frederick. Still, the fantasy hung on. I had a need to rectify past failures—particularly the one with Warner—with some grand good deed.

My reactions to knowing the date confused Frederick. I think he'd seen my whole fantasy scenario about the Ripper unfold within my mind. Thinking he should know he wasn't the only game in town, I showed him more. I gave him a quick tour of what I knew of Ripperology.

Do you know the man who murdered? *Again, he thought asking the question made him seem weak.*

I realized I'd had a fear of addressing Frederick with my thoughts. If he felt he could freely communicate with me, I worried that he might overwhelm my mind with his thoughts and feelings; that I could lose my sense of identity and begin to take up his predilections, his beliefs, his desires. Noting his confusion, I lost some of that fear.

Nobody knows who the killer is, *I thought. I let Frederick know something of my time and the excitement that still existed for the crimes of the Ripper.*

He finally understood that I'd come from a future time.

He has an audience, even then?

Yes, *I thought,* so horrible were his crimes, he has an audience of millions one hundred and twenty-seven years later.

Frederick became uncomfortable as he thought about having an audience of one, as he realized that I was his only witness.

I steered clear of all thoughts of the torso mysteries. I truly did not know if Frederick had committed the specific murders known variously as the "Thames Mysteries" or "Embankment Murders," yet I intended to withhold that information.

He saw competition in an arena he hadn't known existed. Jealousy welled up in his heart. He deserved an audience!

You are not the only one who lashes out, *I thought.* Your efforts are tame by comparison. I gave him a memory of the photos of Mary Jane Kelly.

Angry, Frederick filled his glass with gin and downed the liquid as quickly as possible. He coughed and choked. Women, occupied with men at a table in the corner, looked up at the noise and laughed.

"Take it slow, Nickey," one of the women said. "you keep trying, you'll get a taste for the lush."

I was delighted with his reaction too.

Frederick wanted to cut the woman's throat, but knew better than to do it so close to home. Instead, he poured another glass full, and drank it down.

The previous drink had brought a warm fuzziness to my mind. I'd missed that, though not enough to throw away a good life and suffer the consequences of returning to my addiction. His body, I reminded myself again.

Swaying slightly, Frederick got up, descended the stairs, and exited the pub. He returned to the storehouse and walked around behind the building. Pushing aside a mass of vines, he uncovered his barrow, and pushed it over close to the coal chute in preparation for hauling the dead woman to the river later on. Climbing the rungs into the cellar, he fell partway down the chute. We lay sprawled on the dirt floor for a moment. His coordination suffered from all the gin, and I didn't help him much.

If he'd broken his neck and died, so much the better, I thought. Despite that, my instinct was to avoid being harmed.

Much? *Yes—I hadn't helped him* much!

In that moment, I realized I'd been exerting some control over his body ever since we'd left the pub, trying to keep him upright and pre-

vent his stumbling stagger from causing us real harm. I'd thrown out his hands, elbows, and knees to help arrest his fall down the chute. He wasn't asleep, and yet I had some control over his body.

I don't think Frederick noticed. He also had not responded to my thoughts and feelings for a while. Alcohol, the drug that almost killed me, had come to my aid, creating a buffer between me and the asshole.

That got me thinking about what I'd be willing to do to stop him. I reflected on my regrets about Warner. I could not go back and save my friend, but I might find the opportunity to change the bit of history in which I was presently trapped. That would make me feel a whole lot better about myself, I decided.

To do so, I would probably have to kill Frederick, and I would die too. Facing the choice of making the ultimate sacrifice seriously pissed me off. I knew then that I'd lost most of my fear of him.

You won't be remembered, *I thought, addressing Frederick.* You're just an angry man who had a hard life. You can't accept pity, so you have to get even. Nobody pays any attention to you now, nor will they in the future.

Frederick did not like my thoughts one bit, yet there was nothing he could think to do about it except take another drink. He'd had half the quart. Enough to knock a person unused to drinking down.

He didn't know how to be drunk, but I *did. Horribly, I'd driven drunk many times and always got home safely without hitting anyone. I'd negotiated all kinds of social situations while drunk—shit-faced, in fact. Although many years had passed since I'd done anything of the sort, like riding a bicycle, it all came back to me.*

Sleep.

He wanted sleep, and I was glad for him to have a nap. Frederick crawled toward his pallet and lay down, planning to awaken later to haul the butchered body of the young woman to the river. I figured he'd be asleep for a long time. That gave me an opportunity and inspired a half-baked plan.

Aiden/Frederick: 5

In my drunken state, my plan, though truly frightening, seemed like a good one. Even so, I racked my brains looking for an alternative. I wanted more than anything to go home to my good life; my wife and child, the dogs, my house, and my work. I'd thought that another seizure might do the trick, yet the one we'd had at Miss Lillian's place had served up only blackness.

The idea was to show up at the murder scene of Annie Chapman and scare the Ripper off, just as I'd fantasized. Then I'd chase the murderer so he'd be forced to turn on me and kill Frederick. No way did I want to face an end like that, but I'd come to the conclusion that living in Frederick's head and watching him periodically mutilate women wasn't a life I wanted to live.

If I could not get home—and I still saw no way to do that unless another seizure opened a route—then I had to stop him. Having one killer murder another seemed as good a way as any. I figured that thwarting the murder of Chapman would go a long way toward quieting my regrets about Warner, even if I didn't have long to think about it.

With all that, though I was drunk, traumatized, and not thinking straight, I had a secondary plan. I would take the head and torso of the woman in the barrow with me so that if I saw a constable along the way, I could chicken out on the larger plan and merely hand myself over to the authorities. With the remains as evidence, I'd be charged with murder. I'd hang. I wasn't certain which death would be worse.

When nearby church bells rang the 11:00PM hour, I got Frederick's body moving. I hauled the oilcloth sack that held the young woman's head and torso up the chute. Although the opening to the large bag was cinched with the rope, as I loaded the thing into the barrow, the sack periodically exhaled a stench of decay and raw sewage that made me cough and choke. Once I got the sack situated, I lifted one side and tucked the opening underneath the weight of the torso within. When I let go, the thing exhaled again. I turned away and vomited.

Frederick awoke!

To the Thames.

I felt no alarm in his thought.

Yes, *I assured him, even as I choked, coughed, and tossed up more kerosene-gin,* I'll take her to the river.

His consciousness seemed to slip back into the dreamless sleep from which it emerged.

I gripped the handles of the barrow and steered the thing through the weeds and around to the front of the storehouse, the task all the more difficult because I was shit-faced drunk.

Alfie approached as I tried to wrestle the barrow onto the paved area in front of the building. "Are you leaving?" he asked, sounding worried. I assumed his concern lay in getting his daily dose.

He helped me lift the left wheel of the barrow up out of a rut at the edge of the road. Then he stepped back and looked at me. The question remained in his expression.

I opened Frederick's mouth and tried to speak. The bark that came out startled the big man.

I tried again to reassure him, but I couldn't form the words.

"Have you been harmed?"

I shook Frederick's head.

"Been drinking?"

I nodded, pointed at Frederick's throat and shook his head again.

Looking troubled, Alfie nodded and backed off.

With other things to worry about, I merely turned away. I would have to travel between four and five miles to get to 29 Hanbury Street and reach Annie Chapman. I lifted the handles of the barrow and moved forward, heading west. The vehicle being too wide for the sidewalks, or footways as the Brits called them, I steered along the left edge of the road. Unable to see what lay ahead of me, I stepped in a horse pie. I wondered how many times that would happen before I got to my destination.

I'd rented cars in Caribbean countries where people drove on the left. I ran into trouble at intersections. Making turns, I had a tendency to automatically seek the right side of the road. At that late hour, I saw less traffic than earlier. Still, London at night remained an active environment with plenty of foot traffic as well as the horseback and horse-drawn varieties. Traffic moved a lot slower, though—a good thing since my reaction time sucked.

I figured I'd have to eventually ask for directions, so I practiced the use of Frederick's voice as I went, singing quietly Zappa's "Dog Breath in the Year of the Plague."

Trying to concentrate on putting road behind me despite the drunkenness, I kept up a pace with the barrow that allowed the grind of its iron wheels on cobblestones to provide a weird, decent rhythm for the song. Although I suspected I hastened toward my own death, I tried to push that aside and keep moving.

Even if the stench diminished with air moving around me, I knew the barrow dragged with it a hideous atmosphere. Flies abandoned fresh dung piles in the road to swarm over the oilcloth sack. One buzzed my face and landed in my open, panting mouth. I cursed and spit, then thought aloud, "Frederick's body, not mine. I should have swallowed the damned thing." But I knew I'd be experiencing the crunch and the flavor and he wasn't even conscious.

Pedestrians who came too close to me shied away quickly with a sour expression. Nobody complained aloud. They were used to bad smells.

On the corner of a building at an intersection, I saw a road sign that read "Orchard Street." I'd follow the road as long as the way headed west toward Whitechapel.

The buildings on my left ended. I heard the deep groan of straining rope cables, and the sounds of men working in the distance. I saw ships unloading at the docks, and wanted to have a closer look at them. My quest wouldn't allow the detour.

The road bent northward, then ended at an intersection. I turned west, almost crossed a narrow gauge rail line that ran down the middle of the street, then remembered to keep to the left. Terraced houses created a wall to the North. A sign informed me that I traveled along East India Docks Road. More beautiful ships appeared to the South, as seen through gaps between warehouses. The silhouettes of their masts, spars, and rigging created beautiful crisscrossing lines against the dim haze.

Why did I have to see all this while caught up in such horror? If only I could have paused the terrible circumstances and done a bit of sightseeing!

Feeling sorry for myself would do no good. I bent to the task, increasing my pace through residential neighborhoods, anxiety snapping at my heels.

By the time I got tired of singing "Dog Breath…," I'd barely cracked understandability. I moved on to Zappa's "My Guitar Wants to Kill Your Mama" with increasing success. Strange to hear my city-southern drawl slowly emerge from Frederick's voice. He'd had a nice British accent, even

215

though I hated hearing him speak.

I'd gone about a mile when I saw a police station on the right, and suddenly, I had an important decision to make. Tempted to end the nightmare and turn myself in, I thought through the scenario that would no doubt follow. I thought of the stress I'd undergo in the legal system waiting to be hanged. In seeking mercy, I could imagine breaking down and admitting that I wasn't Frederick. Assuming the authorities listened to me at all, I'd be seen as insane, and they'd stick me in some dingy hospital like Bethlem, or Bedlam as the place was known to the locals. Hanging would be better than rotting away slowly like that. I regained some of my courage and kept moving.

I tried to relax as I passed by the constables talking out front of the station. Having difficulty feeling Frederick's facial expression, I didn't know how I looked. I reached up to trace his features, making the action look as if I scratched an itch. That gave me a weird déjà vu. I still couldn't tell how I looked, but apparently my appearance didn't raise an alarm. Being on the opposite side of the road, the policemen had perhaps not smelled the worst of what I carried.

Flies were not all that followed me. I'd gone two and a half, maybe three miles when I saw a couple of dogs of mixed breed loping along, sniffing the air in my wake. They didn't look particularly dangerous. I'd seen a loose board—something like an oak two-by-four—resting in the barrow that might serve as a weapon if needed.

East India Docks Road must have become Commercial Road while I wasn't looking. At an intersection, I saw public urinals on an island in the middle of the road half way up the block to my right. I hurried to them, left the barrow—nobody in their right mind would take the thing—and entered the facility. After the rotting, shit filled corpse I could barely smell the interior of the urinal. The bells for midnight sounded as I relieved Frederick's bladder. I hoped the mutts had lost interest in me. Of course, I wasn't the source of their fascination. Upon exiting the urinal, I found them sniffing around the barrow, one with its paws up, considering a leap to get to the contents of the oilcloth sack. Seeing me, the mongrels took off running. They didn't go far before turning back and watching me. Another dog joined them. As I continued, all three followed.

Again, I picked up the pace, hoping the dogs would lose interest. Despite the exertion, Frederick's body performed well. He had the muscles and the stamina needed for me to keep the barrow moving. Breathing and heart rate were up, but remained comfortable. I became concerned that I might metabolize too quickly the alcohol in Frederick's system and that he'd awaken.

I checked his pockets for money and found a few shillings and pence. If I began to feel sober, I'd step into one of the pubs that appeared amidst the buildings every few blocks.

As I neared Whitechapel, I saw more variety of races among the people on the streets, including blacks, Asians, and folks who looked to be from the Middle East. The clothing they wore was more varied as well, not all the garments western in design. One Asian fellow walked backwards in front of me for a time, tracing patterns in the air with a finger. He spat and seemed to cuss at me. I didn't recognize the language, and had no idea what he was doing.

By the time I got to Whitechapel High Street and turned left, I had at least six dogs following. When I made the turn, unfortunately I tried to cross over to the right side. A wagon loaded with crates of some sort had to turn suddenly to avoid me. "Glocky Bastard!" the driver shouted. He glared and shook a fist.

I quickly made my way back to the left side of the road.

Frederick emerged briefly from his dreamless repose, perhaps took what he experienced of me propelling his barrow down the street as a dream, and slipped back under.

I left the barrow at the corner of Middlesex Street and Whitechapel High Street and walked into the Blue Anchor pub. I stepped up to the barkeep and asked for a "Gluss of june."

"Sir?" he asked impatiently. Grimacing, he turned up his nose, and I decided I'd gotten some of the corpse stink on me.

"Quater ob gin," I said. He seemed to get that I meant a quartern of gin, and he fetch my order. I held out a shilling. He took the silver coin and made change. The drink had cost me four pence.

"Hurry and drink it and get out," he said. "You'll drive the customers away with your stink."

I turned the glass up, and felt the burn run down my throat. Yes—I still liked the feeling.

Stepping outside, I saw a constable poking around the oilcloth sack in the barrow. With my surprise and fear, Frederick's heart leapt and I feared he'd emerge again from sleep, yet I felt no stirring.

I was torn: wanting simultaneously to turn and get away before the constable noticed me, wanting to give Frederick and the corpse up to the policeman, and wanting to persuade the constable to let me go about my business so I could go to 29 Hanbury Street, and save Annie Chapman. Concerning the latter, even if I succeeded in scaring away the Ripper, I could not reasonably hope that the Whitechapel Murderer would attack Frederick unless I posed a big enough threat, and I didn't think I could control the body well enough for that. Frederick would no doubt survive the encounter.

Thinking about having to make a decision, my mind chose the option that best delayed making a choice, because none of them were any good. Everything sucked. I'd been trying to choose the lesser evil among a raft of bad choices and was truly too drunk to think through the possibilities and make a rational choice.

"Sir," I blurted.

The constable turned to me with a sour look on his face. "Your barrow?"

"Yes, sir," I said, trying to think fast on my feet. "Dogs, sir, trapped in the sewer an' drown."

"Have you had strong drink?"

"Yes, sir." My voice had gotten better, I hoped not too late. "I'm sorry sir. The smell were s' bad, I couldn' take it without drink. No one else 'ould go in there after 'em. Choke Damp claimed two brothers what tried."

I'd gotten into the role, now. I tried to remain calm as I approached him. "The surveyor fo' The Board of Works charged me with the task."

"You can't leave them here." The constable turned away, gagging.

"Stopped for a drink," I said, "on my way to have 'em burned. I'd be pleased for you to take them if you have a better way to dispose of 'em."

"No," he said coldly, "you're attracting feral dogs. Take your barrow and go."

Eight or ten mongrels paced at a distance, sniffing the air hopefully.

I wanted to ask for directions to Hanbury Street, yet he'd already turned away, and I believed that I still had a ways to go westward before heading north to my destination.

Hastily, I took up the handles of the barrow and moved west.

The dogs followed.

I heard the bell for 1:00AM and had the feeling I should hurry.

Having slept little the night before, I'd become weary, and found myself mechanically putting one foot in front of the other, moving in a stupor. I remember the road changing to Aldgate High Street, and thinking I should finally stop and ask for directions, but then not much more after that for a while. Although Frederick's body continued on with the barrow, both he and I seemed to be unconscious for a time.

When asked in substance abuse treatment if I'd had any blackouts, I'd been cute, and tried to joke with my counselor. "I don't remember having any blackouts," I'd said. The humor fell flat because of the context.

In truth, I had experienced blackouts. I knew the only way to know that one had occurred was to see it from the back end. I had on occasion awakened to unanticipated circumstances with no knowledge of how I got there.

That was exactly what happened to me on the streets of London.

Aiden/Frederick: 6

The first dog bite awoke me.

Startled and confused, Frederick awoke too.

The pain in his right ankle forced our combined cry of pain.

A rush of adrenalin brought sudden, perhaps temporary sobriety.

Frederick remained in an alcoholic daze. He wasn't completely aware of our situation. I think he believed he was in the midst of a nightmare, one of a recurring type he'd already had several times before. If not for that, he might have abandoned the barrow. He seemed not to notice me.

At least twenty dogs followed behind the barrow. Despite Frederick's limp, I increased the pace to a trot. He picked up the oak board, swung at the nearest dog, and missed.

Apparently already curious about the hungry pack, and hearing our scream, pedestrians gave us their attention, though they also backed out of our way. We still progressed along a road of granite pavers. The numbers of gas lamps had increased. Although I didn't know the time, I was surprised that so many pedestrians still moved about the streets. The clothing they wore was finer than much of what I'd seen earlier.

I saw up ahead the monument to Admiral Horatio Nelson, the great hero of the Royal Navy. Somehow we'd traveled more than a mile—maybe several—in an unconscious state, and at present neared Trafalgar Square while traveling along West Strand.

A couple of good-hearted fellows shouted and rushed the flank of the dog pack, trying to help disperse it and allow us to escape.

I wanted that help, but Frederick wanted to lose the attention of the pedestrians more. He took a left turn into an empty back lane. Not anticipating his move, I was unable to stop it. Still intoxicated, he did not have complete control of his body, yet neither did I.

The pedestrians did not follow.

Finally, fully awake, Frederick had an impulse to abandon the barrow, but I held on tight and kept moving forward.

You cause me no end of trouble!

I hope that's not the half of it, *I thought.*

You think this funny?

No.

He took—no, we took another swing at the nearest dog. The blow landed on the animal's neck and the creature fell. We stumbled, nearly losing our balance. Although the cart had been dropped onto its skids, the thing continued forward under its own momentum. I held on tightly to one handle with Frederick's left hand. Recovering from the stumble, I shoved the barrow forward, and we continued.

The fall of one dog hadn't seriously discouraged the pack.

The Head!

I saw the idea in Frederick's mind, and wanted nothing to do with it. All the same, I found myself acting out of desperation or perhaps in concert with his desire, like I'd done when swinging the board. In those moments, I could not easily distinguish my efforts from his. Even as we pressed forward, we tugged loose the opening to the oilcloth sack. Luckily, the rope cinch had loosened. We leaned far forward, briefly riding the skidding cart, to reach the head in the bag. The smell hit us and we vomited over the sack. I felt slimy hair in Frederick's fingers, then his digits closed on the locks and we drew the horrid object out. Struggling for balance, we got back into the rhythm of running while I again held onto the barrow tightly with one hand.

Luckily, the alley remained empty—no one saw the severed head.

Her head, *I thought, trying to remember the life it had belonged to, yet not wanting to picture its features in motion.*

We'd have to dump the grisly thing before emerging back onto the street. I didn't want to view that ruined face any longer than necessary. I swung it—we swung it—behind us, and tried to let go. She held on, tangles of her hair hooked on Frederick's fingers. We glanced back, and flailed the arm, trying to get free. A dog leapt for the head, the canine teeth connecting mostly with Frederick's wrist. Pain shot up the arm, we cried out again, and yanked back on the hand. The teeth of the dog must have snagged some of the hair too, because the head fell free and the hand returned empty but for a tangle of blood-clotted locks.

The dogs' argument over possession of the head retreated into the distance as we fled. About to emerge from the back lane, I saw a street sign on the side of a Turkish bathhouse that said "Northumberland Avenue."

Several dogs still followed. I hoped the most aggressive ones had stopped to fight for the spoils.

The bells for 2:00AM rang, and I knew I'd missed my chance to help

221

Annie Chapman.

I had nothing left but to turn Frederick in. I held on and pushed forward as he tried harder to let go and flee.

On a building up ahead, a sign read "Victoria Embankment." I knew that to be the road running along the north shore of the Thames in Westminster, the seat of British government. I also knew that Scotland Yard was on the Victoria Embankment, about a block north of the Westminster Bridge, not far away. Conveniently, we headed in that direction.

Pedestrians jumped out of our way as we rushed into the road. Following the curve of the lane around a cluster of buildings, a strong wind hit us, perhaps coming off the river. A block further on, I could see the river below buildings to the right.

The driver of a fancy, black carriage angled his vehicle off to the left to avoid us, as Frederick tried to ram him with the barrow. The horse drawing the carriage brayed in protest.

I wrenched the cart back on course. That took much greater effort than I anticipated, and I realized that Frederick's control slowly increased. I needed more alcohol!

Traffic scattered as we dashed down the middle of the road.

Frederick's right shoe had filled up with blood. A glance down revealed a split right trouser leg and a gash in the calf at least four inches long. We'd begun to stumble a bit with the slippery shoe and the pain. When need be, I allowed the barrow to fall to its skids and slide forward, as I struggled to maintain our footing.

Glances back revealed that the dogs had rallied for another attempt at the torso. They had made short work of the head. At least fifteen of the curs came up fast behind us. That sight got more cooperation out of Frederick's legs.

One dog fell under the wheels of a wagon that turned suddenly to avoid us. Almost immediately, the hooves of a draft horse struck down another one. The cry of the injured mongrels gave the other dogs pause. They avoided the center of the road and ran along the footway.

Police whistles sounded behind us at some distance, their shrill notes warped in the strong wind.

Frederick panicked and increased the pace. Again, he tried to abandon the barrow.

I managed to keep hold of its handles.

I wanted to halt and give him up to the police, but now Frederick *struggled to keep his legs moving. As long as he headed toward Scotland Yard, I figured, so much the better.*

I will have you out!

He knew I'd seriously screwed him.

With pain if need be!

Would he withstand pain better than I did? I seriously doubted that.

He saw something in the distance that got him excited. As we ran, I couldn't make out what he saw, perhaps because his eyes had become dry from squinting into the strong wind. What I got from his head didn't make sense: A thought of raw dirt.

We ran on, his hope, and mine, growing. He still headed straight for Scotland Yard!

Coming from the north and taking a right turn onto the road, a large wagon stacked too high with barrels pulled across the oncoming lane. Maybe the driver did not see us because of a tall van that had lumbered past. To avoid us, he quickly engaged his brake. His momentum was too great. Ropes around his cargo snapped, barrels tipped and fell, barely missing us. Ale—I could smell the brew—flew in all directions, liberally splashing us. Although the wagon tipped, it kept to its wheels as we dashed by. A glance back showed that most of the dogs had stopped to lick the drink from the road.

I saw Westminster Bridge not three-hundred yards away. Scotland Yard should be on the right up ahead, but I saw a gap where I expected the building to be. As we got closer, I saw the raw dirt Frederick had envisioned—an excavation for a foundation.

No—that couldn't be! I was merely tired out. I blinked Frederick's eyes to better focus them down the block. No building stood where Scotland Yard belonged; the structure that would house the police headquarters hadn't been built yet! Still, Frederick headed straight for the site. I couldn't make sense of it.

We heard more police whistles, closer this time, and Frederick's system flooded with adrenalin again. A glance back did not reveal the constables. They couldn't be far behind. We had caused all the mischief up and down the road. Surely, someone questioned would point the police in our direction.

I thought he'd pass the construction site by. Instead, he rammed the barrow into a berm at the edge of a retaining wall. That knocked my death-grip on the cart loose, and I was stunned as we banged into the hard back railing of the barrow. The oilcloth sack and the oak board went flying into the excavation. Frederick pulled himself together, and scrambled after them. The adrenalin seemed to all belong to him. He had possession of his limbs now, and I rode as only a passenger again.

A watchmen appeared as we moved forward.

"What's this?" he asked, approaching the oilcloth sack. The big bag billowed out in the wind. Perhaps he had not seen the torso, which had flown out of the sack and lay naked and pale beside a pile of stones.

Frederick got to the oak board while the watchman, inspecting the emptied bag, choked and gagged. The fellow looked up as Frederick brought the board down on his head.

Hopefully, the blow wasn't enough to kill the man.

I saw a bottle of whiskey that must have fallen out of his pocket. Reaching for the liquor, and for control of Frederick with all I had, I got the bottle to his mouth, chewed away the cork, and got some of the stuff to burn its way down his throat.

He wrenched the bottle away and poured the rest onto the unconscious watchman. Frederick was not done. He gathered the torso into his arms and headed for a stone structure within the excavation.

Then, I understood how he knew about the place—he'd buried a leg inside the small structure less than a month earlier. I knew what he planned and had to stop him.

As I struggled to regain control, the fetor of the filth that oozed from a shoulder stump and ran down into Frederick's shirt front, staggered me. Vomit—my reaction—flew out of his mouth and down his chest.

Meanwhile, Frederick had kept moving. The chamber had a small door with a padlock, its shackle not driven into the case. He got the door open and rushed inside, tripped in a small ditch in the dark, and inadvertently released the torso. Flying a few feet, the ghastly thing disappeared into darkness.

Frederick found his feet, spun around, and exited. He turned to shut the door and snap the padlock closed through the hasp on the door. Although clumsy from my efforts to stop him, he succeeded.

Fuck! Now, if the police caught up, they would not immediately find the torso. All my plans were screwed.

We both got up and ran, but in opposite directions. Frederick's body fell in the dirt. The new dose of alcohol or the burning off of the adrenalin weakened his control.

The oilcloth sack snapped open, filled with wind, lifted, and sailed away northward.

Dogs appeared at the edge of the excavation.

Immediately working in concert, Frederick and I got up and ran away from the growling curs. We climbed out of the excavation and made for the Westminster Bridge.

Once on the footway beside the road, we moved better, yet Frederick's right leg and foot had become swollen, the shoe too tight and causing a lot of pain. We kicked it off and continued.

Glancing back, we saw the dogs flowing around the excavation to get to us. Their blood was up. I saw the hunger in their eyes. As much as I loved dogs, I feared that pack. A sharp knife, the Ripper's blade, was one thing, but I would avoid a ripping pain from canine teeth if I could.

Thinking about it, I did want Frederick to suffer that fate, and had the smallest desire to hold my ground and wait for them to catch up. No—death by dogs would be unbearable!

I allowed him to carry us out onto the bridge. The pedestrians we encountered looked upon us with shocked expressions as we blundered past.

The dogs had quickly closed the distance. Another good Samaritan tried to disperse the pack with shouts and waving hands. Most others drew back in terror.

The lead dog leapt forward and tore at Frederick's bleeding right leg.

"Get it, Jasper," I heard Melody say. "Break its neck!" I remembered her saying that when one of our pups violently shook a toy animal, and Littlebean as a child, giggling.

No way had that truly been Melody. But sure enough, the dog shook the leg, tearing loose the Achilles tendon.

The pain—straight from his leg into my mind, a surge of jagged lightning.

Then a brief buffer between me and the agony. Had I again reached the limit of physical pain, or been blessed by an angel of mercy? I couldn't tell.

Frederick remained in agony. I might have laughed, if I'd had more control of the body. He would never walk properly again. Small victory!

Instead of exerting my will, I gave up and let go entirely. No more control. The dogs could have him. To be rid of the monster, I would endure whatever came.

Another dog leapt for Frederick's throat. The animal missed, con-

necting instead with his cheek, and tearing away a chunk. Again, the pain, like an electric charge into my mind, yet endurable. The hole ventilated his mouth and flooded it with the hot iron taste of blood.

Another dog got hold of his right arm.

Frederick wrenched and tore the limb free of the ravening maw, even as more dogs seized his lower limbs. Ratcheting fear and desperation gave him strength. He made for the edge of the bridge, dragging the dogs with him. I gave him no help.

"Get it, Jasper. Don't let it get away!"

Delirious from the pain and fatigue, I heard the voice I most wanted to hear at the end.

"You would be rid of me?" I asked Frederick aloud, using his voice and laughing. "You'd do it with pain?"

I tried to hold him still, to make certain the dogs ate his cruel, fucking ass.

Frederick was stronger. His anger and frustration helped drive him forward. He got to the edge of the bridge.

A man in some sort of uniform hurried toward us, began striking the dogs with a cane. They turned on him, snarling and snapping. He backed away, still swinging.

That gave Frederick the opportunity to claw his way onto the parapet. Though I tried to slow him, he had the will to survive. I fought a losing battle until I smelled the strange odor that accompanied my temporal lobe hallucinations.

A seizure!

In that moment I stopped fighting and allowed Frederick to carry us forward. I did not want to die the moment before I might gain passage back home.

Frederick also recognized the smell.

You think you've won, but your body will get me close to Melody and… Little…*Bean.*

He'd made sense of my earlier fears. Again, I tried to stop him, to give his body back to the dogs. I had to kill him before he got to my family!

His left leg began to shake as he rose up and leapt from the bridge. The light around us flickered.

We fell for only a moment, and hit the water hard. Frederick was stunned.

Suddenly in my element—I'd been comfortable in the water ever since surviving the deep end as a child—I took control. If the seizure had mere blackness at the other end, I would make sure Frederick found that at the bottom of the Thames. Whatever the case, to protect my family, I had to drown the motherfucker before the seizure ended. I swam downward into the cold and murky, gray-brown depths. Frederick's ears ached as the gas in them compressed, but I made no effort to clear them. Disoriented, he fought weakly. Blowing out all of Frederick's air, I dove further until I felt the slime at the bottom.

I lost my sense of direction, as the muck seemed to surround me. Frederick would suffocate in the dark goo, his oxygen run out.

My death, as a drowning, seemed appropriate in that moment.

I pictured Melody and Lysta as if to say goodbye, and the water pulled away...

Alan: 1

…To reveal air, light, and my studio.

"Break its neck, Jasper," Melody said again. She sat in her computer chair watching two of our dogs play with a braided rope toy.

I saw them in my peripheral vision. Jasper shook the thing, as if breaking its spine.

"Look at him," she said, turning to me. "He's so *damned* cute."

I couldn't. Fearful that Frederick had followed, I probed my mind. I sensed no other presence, though. Had there been a time when he wasn't aware of me? No—I remembered that he addressed me as if out of the blue, shortly after I arrived in his head. I told myself that he could not truly hide as I'd tried to do.

"Are you okay?" Melody asked.

"Uh-huh," I barely managed.

My eyes were focused right across the room at the closet doors. I couldn't turn to look straight at Melody for fear that, as mere illusion, she'd disappear. Wiping my face with my hand to hide my emotional state, I looked down. The edition of *The Star* still lay open on my drafting table as if no time had passed since last I saw it.

"I'm sorry," she said, "I interrupted you while you were concentrating. You've been standing there quietly ever since I got home."

"How long," I croaked, not wanting to move, not willing to use much energy for fear of being flung back to London and a watery grave.

"Maybe ten minutes. You were reading when I came up here, but you looked so absorbed, I was quiet so I wouldn't disturb you."

"Thanks."

"Are you going to watch the eclipse with me later?"

I remembered that the astronomical event would take place Sunday, September 27, starting about 6:00PM. How could it still be Sunday? Had the entire two day episode with Frederick been an elaborate, extended hallucination that occurred within the span of one seizure? No—that didn't seem possible.

"It's the *super blood moon total eclipse*," Melody said brightly, as if selling a product in a radio spot.

I recalled the descriptive phrase. The words sounded in my head like another amputation. Did the eclipse have something to do with what had happened to me? I didn't think so, since it hadn't occurred yet.

"Are you okay?" Melody asked again.

"Long day," I said. "Glad you're home."

I took deep breaths and suppressed tears that welled up. I'd become somewhat confident that I, alone, occupied my head.

Jasper grabbed the rope toy with his teeth, and ran down the stairs, Conway following.

"What's for dinner?" Melody asked.

Having been gone for two days, I couldn't remember what I'd planned. "Leftovers," I said, not trusting myself to say more.

"Mmm, chicken enchiladas, then."

I nodded and moved to the stairs without making eye contact with Melody. She got up and followed me down the stairs.

The living room had been transformed into a dining room.

"Did you do this?" I asked.

She didn't answer for a moment.

"What?"

"Change the room? Where did you put all the furniture, the television?"

Again, she didn't answer, and I still couldn't look at her squarely.

I looked around, unable to relax and *be* home because things weren't quite right. Something else "felt" different about the room. I couldn't put my finger on why for a moment. I saw a figure of a horse that looked like a junk sculpture I'd created, but one I didn't remember. The piece of art stood on the ledge between the kitchen and the living room. The sculpture did have my signature on one of the back legs.

The kitchen looked different too. I didn't see the credit card reader for the hot water faucet. The walls were yellow and orange. I realized that color was the change in the living room as well, and spun around. Yes—besides the transformation to a dining room, its walls had become off-white instead of blue.

How long had I been gone?

"Alan?" Melody said.

I swung around to face her. She had the expression she got when she thought I teased her.

"What did you say?" I asked.

Her expression immediately turned to one of worry. She took my hand.

"I-I'm con…fused." I said.

She felt my neck to see if I had a fever. "Come lie down. We can eat later."

I allowed her to pull me down the hall, although I had a feeling Frederick might jump out at me from behind a door along the way. Halfway through the hall, I saw a painting on the wall that looked like one of mine, but that I knew I'd never painted. I stopped to look at the artwork. Based on a Leonardo da Vinci medical sketch, the painting depicted a baby in the womb. Aside from the evil eyes, the face of the infant looked like Lysta had as a baby.

Melody gently pulled me away. Once past the closed door to Lysta's room, I moved toward the door to the left, while she pulled toward the one on the right. "Okay," she said, stopping and opening the left-hand door, "we'll sit in the living room."

Our bedroom was gone, replaced with a bathroom and a short hall that led into a room that didn't belong on our house.

As I'd feared, I hadn't come home! Not the home I remembered, anyway.

I began to quake.

Melody pulled me close and hugged me. "Are you all right?"

"No!"

She felt so good against me—a perfect warmth, the same as she always had—and instantly I knew I'd been mistaken. I *was* home.

At the same time, I realized that my actions in the past had altered history. The idea was common to many time travel stories I'd read. I decided that subtle changes had echoed forward to the present.

"What's wrong?" she asked as she led me to a sofa I'd never seen, and sat me down.

I couldn't begin to tell her. She would think I'd lost my mind, and I didn't want to frighten her.

Clearly, most of my world had remained the same. I needed to relax, and look to those aspects that would not have changed.

"Did you talk to Littlebean today? Is she planning to come home next weekend?"

"Little what?"

An instant chill and gooseflesh swarmed over me. "No!" I cried, scrambling to my feet and reaching into my pocket for my cell phone. I didn't find it. "Your cell phone," I demanded, holding out my hand.

Her mouth gaping and eyes narrowed, Melody looked at me silently for a moment.

"Now!" I said.

I followed her back to the new dining room. She got her cell phone out of her purse and handed it to me with an angry expression.

I went into her contacts. Lysta's number wasn't there!

Had Frederick gotten here before me and done something to Lysta?

I hurried down the hall, and opened the door to Littlebean's room. Nothing inside spoke of my girl!

Had so much time passed since Littlebean's death at the hands of the murderer?

Melody appeared beside me, her angry expression turning to one of fear.

I asked as calmly as I could, "Did you move her stuff?"

The confused, frightened look in Melody's eyes suggested a totally different answer from what I expected.

I made a frantic search of our home in the dimming dusk, horror welling up, even as I tried to deny the possibility of what I was thinking. I turned on all the lights in each room as I went. Every nook and cranny of the house confirmed my worst fear. Melody followed, but could only stand and wonder, her eyes wide and mouth gaping. I could tell she'd thought I'd gone mad, as I went through all the drawers in the bedrooms and kitchen, tore apart the closets, dumped boxes out in the garage. Finally, I ran out back into the night, lit eerily by the thinning orange crescent of the eclipse. I wasn't interested in the broader universe, just one beautiful, small piece of it. I had to find the garden stepping stones that had impressions of my girl's feet and hands.

They were gone. All evidence of my sweet Littlebean's existence had been wiped out.

I turned to Melody, tears streaming down my cheeks, still unable to pose the *one* question worth asking in the entire *fucking* world!

Frederick had not killed Lysta Littlebean.

I had!

Alan: 2

Exhaustion and a desire to escape the world as I'd found it, allowed me to sleep. My last thought before slumber: *Eclipses are transient.*

I don't know how long I slept. I awoke to Jasper nuzzling me for attention. All three dogs lay in the bed. I scratched each behind the ears and said their names.

I lay there for a time trying not to think and failing. Over the years, I'd toyed with a notion inspired by a play on words, using the expression "will have not been" run together as a compound contraction to become "will'ven't been." In my mind, I'd always replaced the word "been" with "bin" to create a sense of a cosmic trash receptacle where things were tossed that had never and would never work out, and so should not exist. That had been a humorous notion. While I feared that I'd somehow managed to throw Lysta Littlebean in the will'ven't bin, I still wasn't without hope of being wrong. If anything *should* exist, that would be my daughter. I cursed my imagination for having conceived of the device.

Despite soreness from lying down too long and a need to go to the bathroom, I didn't get up until a nagging question occurred to me. The painting in the hall of the infant in the womb—why did it have Lysta's likeness?

After visiting the bathroom, I went to look at the artwork. Although formatted as a book cover, the painting told me little else. I liked the image, yet still did not remember creating it. Upstairs, I looked for the cover art among the shelves of books I kept in the studio; volumes to which I'd contributed artwork and copies of novels I'd written.

The books were arranged differently. Some volumes appeared to be missing, while others I had not seen before. The largest, fanciest limited editions were by a writer I'd never heard of named Stephen King.

I found the book with the infant-in-the-womb-image on the cover: Brian Keene's *The Rising: Selected Scenes from the End of the World.* In another reality, that edition had a cover that Lysta and I had done together.

My heart collapsed further, crushed under the weight of my loss. I exhaled and kept myself from taking another breath. My heart would starve for oxygen and fail.

Stupid, I know, but I persisted until little white flashes pinged around in my field of vision.

Then I heard Melody coming in downstairs, and I gulped a breath without thinking. Slowly, I pulled my eyes up from the image of the book cover, and I looked across the room to read 5:36 on the wall clock. With the light level outside the windows, I assumed that Melody was returning home from work in the evening. I knew she'd look through the rest of the house, not find me, and come up to the studio.

She'd left me alone when I'd been reading the edition of *The Star* on my drafting table, so I went and stood there with the hope that she'd do that again.

Glancing down, I began to read the article about the parachutist, Professor Baldwin.

"Now, the object is to get as flat a surface exposed to the wind as possible, so that when the parachute oscillates the air on the side that is tilted up may readily escape, and the equilibrium be restored. But my parachute, non-rigid as it is, must to some extent be dome-shaped when inflated. In the top, however, there is a hole; through this the compressed air rushes, and in this way my parachute rights itself."

Had the newspaper changed too? Had his words always included reference to the hole in the top of the chute?

No! The frustrating irony of having the knowledge to help the man yet no opportunity, contrasted with my regrets about having had the opportunity to help Warner but insufficient knowledge and ability to do so, had helped bring on the seizure that took me into Frederick's head. The power of my desire to help either Professor Baldwin or Annie Chapman had perhaps taken me to that point in time. But then I didn't have enough control over Frederick's body to complete either quest.

I knew now that my desire to do some good, to change history for the better, had been motivated by pride. Stupidly, I'd wanted to offset with good deeds my regrets, as if they sat on a scale that could be balanced. That's why I decided I'd been the one to kill Lysta. If I'd endured the hideous ride in Frederick's head and done nothing, I might have been returned through a seizure to this time with history in the shape I'd left it, and my sweet Littlebean still a matter of fact.

"Alan?" Melody called out as she came up the stairs.

I remembered her calling me that right after I got home. I knew then that even my name had changed. Standing one step from the top of the stairs, she smiled, even with deep concern evident in her expression.

"I know you don't like going to see the doctor, but I'm really worried about you."

I'd wanted so badly to return from London to Melody. I wanted to hold her now, yet I remained afraid.

"No, I'm feeling better today."

She pressed her lips together tightly, maybe to keep from saying more.

I'd been shit since I got home. Melody didn't deserve that. She existed here, even if Lysta did not. I loved Melody, and needed her more than ever.

She approached cautiously. I embraced and kissed her and she kissed me back with an insistence she hadn't had in a long time.

The temptation to ask about Lysta became powerful. Even so, I resisted. Despite my growing comprehension of the world I'd found, I knew that once asked and answered, that reality would be set. I wasn't willing to give up the tiny sliver of hope I still had that, like the shadow of the earth that kept the sun's light from reaching the moon in the eclipse, separation from my child would be temporary.

"I brought home sandwiches so you wouldn't have to cook," Melody said.

"Thank you."

Life had changed. I'd become Alan. He was well-loved—I could see the affection in her eyes.

If I didn't want his life, I'd better decide soon.

The buckeye in my pocket found its way into my hand. The smooth surface told me there would always be opportunity.

Looking at Melody, I decided that with her help, I could get used to being Alan.

Epilogue

Finally, my fear was indelibly confirmed. I spent some time looking for evidence of my daughter. I called Oregon State University, the DMV, I looked online for her Facebook page, tried and failed to remember her cell phone number.

Nothing. My separation from her was not a transient eclipse. No mere shadow kept me from her.

Several days after I'd returned, while still racking my brains for a way to hit the "Undo" option on reality, I thought of the book, *Redshift Rendezvous*, by John Stith that I'd been reading in the hospital twenty-six years earlier when I'd had my second and third temporal lobe seizures. I wondered what would happen if I read the book again. I had the title on a shelf among my contributor copies. Would that same sequence of words trigger another hallucinatory seizure? If so, and if Frederick had somehow survived, I might go back.

Then what? Help him figure out a way to get around on one leg? Help him finish off his list of murder accomplishments? I tried to look them up, but didn't know how to determine what was his. Information about the Torso murders wasn't much help. The Pinchin Street Mystery still existed, the one in which the torso had been found under the railway viaduct. With a small amount of research, I discovered that the victim was not the daughter of the Midland Railway General Manager, George Noble. No doubt, the torso had never belonged to her, and I'd been mistaken in thinking she would be Frederick's next victim. At least one torso mystery seemed to be missing. A new one had taken its place. The torso Frederick and I had left within a vault at the construction site of what would become New Scotland Yard was referred to as the Whitehall Mystery, and it remained an unsolved murder according to history.

If I could have tracked down his victims from the reality I destroyed, would I have helped Frederick kill them to get my daughter back? I still wonder what the honest answer to that question might be. I cannot say for certain since the opportunity doesn't really exist.

That truth was driven home by my discovery that Professor Baldwin had indeed survived his parachute feat. If my being in that time had set something in motion that helped him reach a decision to put a hole in the top of his parachute, I'm glad for that. At the same time, I had to realized that the fact that I hadn't come in contact with the man and yet his history had also changed meant there was no way to track down all the influences I'd had on reality during the two days I spent in 1888. Therefore, I would find no clear path to revive Lysta's existence.

Still trying to bargain my way out of the current reality, I considered persuading Melody to have another child with me, but though I knew her mind might become willing, her fifty-three-year-old body was incapable of reproducing.

A month after I'd returned home from London, I told Melody the whole tale of my time-travel experience. Even if I'd stopped lying to her years earlier, I continued to prey upon her gullible nature for good humor. As I began the tale, she got a skeptical glint in her eyes. She quickly became engaged in the story as the telling went on and on with details that spoke of the fullness of true experience, even the parts about Frederick Bledsoe's life.

I never said anything about Lysta.

"You just made all that up in the last few days?"

I choked back the truth and lied. "Yep, my life becomes a pretty good horror story, huh?"

"Yes. You should make it your next novel."

And so I did.

She'll continue to think the story is fiction, even as she proofreads this line.

I discovered that my sister, Carol, had a son in his early twenties. She'd divorced her first husband—the only one I'd known—and married a man named Keith Evans. Their son, Ethan Evans, has the weird gene that Grandaddy, Daddy, and I have—the one Lysta had as well. I've spent some time getting to know him. He loves the bizarre and he's a good writer and artist. We've collaborated together on some paintings.

I found several paintings that I'd done over the years—ones I didn't recognize—that had Lysta's likeness, some that seemed to represent her when young, others that depicted her as an adult. I removed those from my online store. They will never be for sale.

Much later, I discovered that Melody's father had died in a car accident when she was four years old. Something about the experience of growing up without him had left her with no desire to bring a child into the world. I knew my actions in the past had set into motion the chain of events that sent her father to an early grave. I cannot feel any worse about that.

I've arrived at perhaps the darkest, loneliest deep end of my life. Until I began to tell the tale, I'd thought it might well be bottomless. Now, I feel a floor beneath me. I will keep kicking off that bottom and rising to the surface. I *will* reach the edge and pull myself out.

If there is a moral to this story, it is that regrets are for shit. Those that lead to a desire to change the past are hubris of the highest order. We don't have the chance to test-drive such desires and see the results. Considering our regrets a healthy moral response, we reflect upon them wistfully, sadly, or even obsessively, sometimes for a lifetime. But life is of a piece, the good, the bad, and the indifferent. One learns from mistakes or not. There is no more to be had from those circumstances. With imagination, we can project ourselves into all sorts of perfect scenarios, past, present, and future, yet the only power we have over reality, and ultimately history, is that of influence, a flawed potential that requires working with what we have.

If I'd been more grateful for what I had, for what I'd become, for all the lessons life had given me, the good and the bad, my life might still be whole.

With the loss of Lysta, I feel as though I've lost a limb.

Yes—that would give Frederick a lot of satisfaction.

Like an amputee, occasionally I feel a stirring, as if the limb continues to exist; as if she still lives.

Sometimes, I allow her to make decisions in my artwork, and that gives me a sense that she's there, collaborating with me.

Lysta Littlebean, I hold you in my memory. I love you still.

About the Author

Alan M. Clark, fine arts painter, illustrator, and author hails from Tennessee, where he grew up in a house full of human bones and old medical books. At present, he lives in Eugene, Oregon with his wife, Melody. In his 31 year freelance career, he has created illustrations for hundreds of books, including works of fiction of various genres, nonfiction, textbooks, young adult fiction, and children's books. He is the author of fifteen books, including nine novels, a lavishly illustrated novella, four collections of fiction, and a nonfiction full-color book of his artwork. The World Fantasy Award and four Chesley Awards are among the honors he's received for his work. Mr. Clark's company, IFD Publishing, has released thirty books, including hardcovers, paperbacks, ebooks, and audio books. IFD Publishing's authors include F. Paul Wilson, Elizabeth Engstrom, and Jeremy Robert Johnson.

www.alanmclark.com

Connect with the Author Online.
You can email the author or find out more about him through the following websites:
http://www.ifdpublishing.com
http://www.smashwords.com/profile/view/IFDPublishing

Books from IFD Publishing

Paperbacks

Novels:
Death is a Star by Christina Lay
Baggage Check by Elizabeth Engstrom

Nonfiction:
How to Write a Sizzling Sex Scene by Elizabeth Engstrom
The Surgeon's Mate: A Dismemoir by Alan M. Clark

EBooks

(You can find the following titles at most distribution points for all ereading platforms.)

Novels:
York's Moon, by Elizabeth Engstrom
Beyond the Serpent's Heart, by Eric Witchey
Lizzie Borden, by Elizabeth Engstrom
A Parliament of Crows by Alan M. Clark
Lizard Wine, by Elizabeth Engstrom
Northwoods Chronicles: A Novel in Short Stories, by Elizabeth Engstrom
Siren Promised, by Alan M. Clark and Jeremy Robert Johnson
To Kill a Common Loon, by Mitch Luckett
The Man in the Loon, by Mitch Luckett
Jack the Ripper Victim Series: Of Thimble and Threat by Alan M. Clark
Jack the Ripper Victim Series: The Double Event (includes two novels from the series: *Of Thimble and Threat* and *Say Anything But Your Prayers*) by Alan M. Clark
Candyland, by Elizabeth Engstrom
The Blood of Father Time: Book 1, The New Cut, by Alan M. Clark, Stephen C. Merritt & Lorelei Shannon
The Blood of Father Time: Book 2, The Mystic Clan's Grand Plot, by Alan M. Clark, Stephen C. Merritt & Lorelei Shannon
How I Met My Alien Bitch Lover: Book 1 from the Sunny World Inquisition Daily Letter
Archives, by Eric Witchey

Baggage Check, by Elizabeth Engstrom
Death is a Star, by Christina Lay
D. D. Murphry, Secret Policeman, by Alan M. Clark and Elizabeth Massie
Black Leather, by Elizabeth Engstrom

Novelettes:
The Tao of Flynn, by Eric Witchey
To Build a Boat, Listen to Trees, by Eric Witchey

Children's Illustrated:
The Christmas Thingy, by F. Paul Wilson. Illustrated by Alan M. Clark

Collections:
Suspicions, by Elizabeth Engstrom

Short Fiction:
"Brittle Bones and Old Rope," by Alan M. Clark
"Crosley," by Elizabeth Engstrom
"The Apple Sniper," by Eric Witchey

Nonfiction:
How to Write a Sizzling Sex Scene by Elizabeth Engstrom

Audio Books from Amazon and Audible.com

Novels:
The Door That Faced West by Alan M. Clark, read by Charles Hinckley
Jack the Ripper Victim Series: Of Thimble and Threat by Alan M. Clark, read by Alicia Rose
Jack the Ripper Victim Series: Say Anything But Your Prayers by Alan M. Clark, read by Alicia Rose
Jack the Ripper Victim Series: The Double Event by Alan M. Clark, read by Alicia Rose

www.ingramcontent.com/pod-product-compliance
Lightning Source LLC
Chambersburg PA
CBHW051239250626
47155CB00009B/3094